DEATH UNTOLD

THE WITCH'S REBELS BOOK FIVE

GET CONNECTED!

I love connecting with readers! There are a few different ways you can keep in touch:

Email: sarah@sarahpiperbooks.com

TikTok: @sarahpiperbooks

Facebook group: Sarah Piper's Sassy Witches

Twitter: @sarahpiperbooks

Newsletter: Never miss a new release or a sale! Sign up for the VIP Readers Club: sarahpiperbooks.com/readers-club

ONE

LIAM

Nothing was certain, they said on the material plane, but Death and taxes.

Yet the longer I lingered among them, the more deeply I came to understand that despite the frequency with which such platitudes were offered, Death and taxes were merely constructs in their eyes, words to encapsulate complex systems and ideas too vast for the human mind to grasp.

The only *true* certainty in their world—a world to which I so desperately ached to belong—was love.

It broke all the rules. It decimated once-immutable truths. It kicked down walls and spilled blood and burned so fiercely its heat possessed the power to bond that which, by all the laws of the cosmos, should have been severed.

Indeed, even as the fae's silver blade had severed Emilio Alvarez's spine, Gray's fierce love for him kept him tethered to her essence, against all odds.

His soul vibrated inside my raven form, guiding me on

fierce winds high above the burning warehouse, far beyond the small town of Raven's Cape, through time and space and back again. When I finally felt called to stop, I found myself soaring through the deep indigo skies of Gray's magical realm.

It was as if she'd guided us both here, though she couldn't have known I'd already claimed him. I saw her now in my limitless vision, leading the witches from the warehouse, her incubus and vampire steadfast at her side.

All of her companions were fighters, just like Gray.

Just like Emilio.

Sighting the glow of her stone altar in the meadow below, I swooped down and dropped soundlessly to the earth, shifting into my human form just as Emilio Alvarez's broken body materialized on the ground before me—part man, part wolf, ruined and very near an end he didn't want to accept.

I suppose I hadn't wanted to accept it, either. If I had, I would have retrieved his soul, leaving the body for his loved ones to mourn and bury, as was their custom.

Instead, I'd brought him with me.

His blood soaked through the dark green meadow grass, and once again, his soul writhed and spun inside me, a frenzied dance that quickened beneath the shadow of the rune gate and the Shadowrealm beyond. Further down the path, its stone archway loomed, beckoning me to carry him through.

It was, after all, my sacred duty. My purpose.

Yet I was immobilized.

Whether it was his unfathomable strength in resisting Death's call, or my weakness in performing my task in the face of the pain I'd already caused, I could not bear the thought of escorting the soul of Gray's wolf to his eternal resting place.

Not until she had the chance to say her farewell.

One more day, one more hour, one more moment to hold a loved one close and whisper all the right words… Every human who'd ever suffered the loss of someone dear to them had wished for the same thing. Begged for it. They believed that the gift of time, however brief, would be a balm for their shattered hearts.

It was the least I could give the woman who'd captured mine.

As if he understood my intentions, Emilio's soul heated from within, making my skin glow silver. Human or raven or some other creature altogether, none of my vessels were strong enough to contain him long term. His energy was too bright, too strong, even in death.

The pentacle carved into Gray's altar pulsed a violet-blue, and ahead of us on the path, two of my strongest and most loyal ferriers appeared—a great horned owl and a white raven. They perched in the lower branches of a barren, oil-black tree, awaiting my orders.

But those orders would not come. Not yet.

"Tonight," I said, "in the realm where all things are still possible, we shall endeavor to stop time for them." I had no idea how long it would take Gray to arrive—only that she *would* arrive. Ronan would tell her of Emilio's passing, and she would find us. Find him.

I knelt in the grass beside his broken body and reached for his hand, his human fingers curled in agonizing pain against the forepaw of his wolf form, his entire body caught mid-shift. His death had been agonizing, but he felt no pain now. The blade had done its work carving through flesh and bone; the silver poison had done the rest.

I brought his hand to my chest, held it close. The blood of the wolf soaked my human clothing through to the skin, and an inexplicable wetness leaked from my eyes.

He deserved better.

Such was the way of all brave men.

"She is coming," I promised him in a voice so despondent, I hardly recognized it. "Gray will be here."

TWO

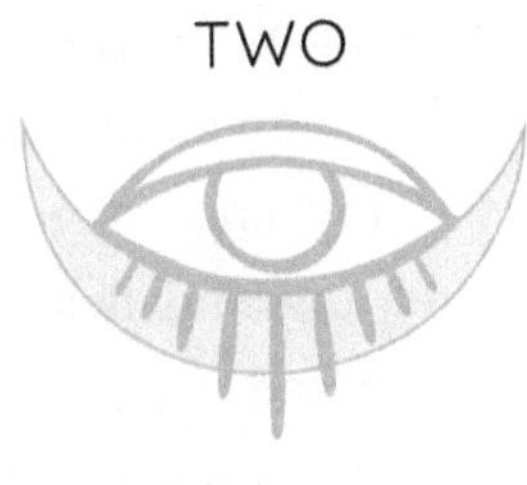

ASHER

Busting out of the smoke-filled warehouse and into the chilly night, I sucked in a deep breath. I almost didn't recognize the smell.

Air. Fresh, free, glorious air and a cloudless sky full of stars that not even the fire behind us could dim.

But as much as I wanted to drop to the ground and roll around in the grass like a puppy, there was no time. We had to get everyone to shelter, and pronto. The witches needed food and medical attention, all of us needed showers, and someone—hopefully not me—would need to come up with a plan.

Orendiel was still out there. Fucking coward. And I was pretty sure none of us would sleep until Emilio was well again, and we'd given that sick fae fuck the brutal farewell he so deserved.

"This way," one of the shifter cops shouted, and in a blur, our group raced down a side street, fueled by nothing but adrenaline and freedom, and fear that it could be snatched away again. We reached a row of unmarked vans and hurried inside—me, Darius, Gray, the witches, the cops, and the fae princeling who was now in the mix. Oh, and the hellhounds that had somehow, in my absence, attached themselves to Gray, and were now jumping on her lap in the back seat, yelping and licking her face like she was a piece of steak smothered in peanut butter.

Not much to look at, those two, but they were fiercely protective of her. Never thought I'd say it, but I was damn grateful they were on our side.

"Alright, we're rolling," one of the cops said into his comm device. Lansky, I thought Gray said his name was. After a quick head count and confirmation from the other two vans, we were off, Lansky phoning ahead for EMTs and food delivery, ordering his people to meet us at the rendezvous point.

The house belonged to Emilio's sister, I was told—another part of the story I was still trying to catch up on.

"It'll be tight," Gray said as we poured out of the vans and headed inside, the hounds halfway up her ass with excitement. Seemed they thought of this place as home, and they were glad to be back. "But it's warm and safe, and there aren't any electrified bars on the doors."

"Always a bonus," I said with a wink.

She was right—the house wasn't exactly set up for an influx of two-dozen witches. But for now, cramped as it was, we'd find a way to make it work. Whether they were from the Cape or the Bay or someplace else entirely, the witches couldn't go home yet. Not with the power balance so out of whack in all the surrounding communities. As far as we knew, Lansky had told me on the drive over, Blackmoon Bay had been the hardest hit, with supernatural crimes and violence mucking things up over there in a major way. But other cities would soon fall, and we needed time to regroup.

"It'll be awesome," I assured Gray as I took a look around the living room. It was open, with hardwood floors and bright orange walls. Seemed like a nice place. "Hot water, freedom of movement, food, drinks, safety? Hell, this place is a fucking palace." I gave her a smile, best one I had for the moment, and she blew out a relieved breath. I was about to pull her in for another hug when my eyes landed on a small lump at the center of the couch, snoring softly beneath a pile of blankets.

"Reva," she said, following my line of sight. "Safe and sound. Judging from that empty pizza box, probably suffering from food coma."

"Last time I saw this kid, she was slipping into the shadows of the caves like a pro spelunker." I knelt in front of the couch and ran my hand over her shorn head, careful not to wake her up. Even more careful not to let Gray see the tears of relief flooding my eyes.

Damn, is someone cutting onions in here?

"Brave girl," I whispered.

"Hey, help me get her out of here," Gray said. "I don't want her in the middle of all this tonight."

With a light touch, I scooped the kid up in my arms and

followed Gray to the master bedroom down the hall, depositing her into Elena's bed. Reva yawned and turned over on her side, falling into a deep sleep once again.

"She'll be good in here for the night," Gray said softly, kneeling down at the side of the bed and pulling the blankets up over Reva's shoulder. "We'll figure out more permanent sleeping arrangements when Emilio and Elena get back later. He'll probably need his own room for a while."

"Oh, *hell* yeah," I said, forcing a smile I absolutely didn't feel. "Big motherfucker like that? He definitely snores."

She let out a quiet snicker. "Oh my God, you have no idea."

"I... Wait. How do *you* know how Alvarez sounds when he sleeps?" I teased. Clearly, they'd gotten closer—another part of the plot I'd missed. "Hmm. Something tells me we're gonna need to invest in a bigger bed for you, Cupcake."

Gray opened her mouth to shoot something back, but then shut it, emotion suddenly overtaking her face. Her brows drew together, and she shook her head, fisting the blanket at Reva's shoulder. "If Ronan can't heal him, Asher, I—"

"Hey. Don't do that. Ain't *nobody* got time for doubt tonight. *El Lobo* is a tough sonofabitch. He'll be back before you know it, along with Ronan and everyone else. And guess what? Tomorrow morning, we're gonna have the best fucking reunion breakfast you can dream up."

"With bacon?" she asked, that smile finally coming back to her lips.

"*So* much bacon. And scrambles and pancakes and OJ mixed with whatever booze the she-wolf keeps in here, because after tonight, I think we *all* need a stiff one."

"You're telling me." She laughed again, and I took her hand and tugged her to her feet, drawing her close and nuzzling her neck and pretending I couldn't smell Emilio's blood congealing in her hair.

THREE

ASHER

The main living area was a hotbed of activity, and Gray and I dove right in, helping Darius, Lansky, and anyone else who had the strength to move furniture and set up the living room for triage. The two EMTs—panther shifters—had beaten us here, and those guys were already hard at work, checking vitals and administering IVs, patching up wounds, wrapping sprains, passing around clean T-shirts and sweatpants and blankets. No one wanted to risk exposure at the hospital—there was too much at stake now, too many questions with answers that humans wouldn't understand.

And here, at least, we could keep an eye on everyone, pool our resources, and figure out some kind of plan.

While Gray and I helped out the medics, Jael and a few of the more experienced witches who'd already been treated headed outside to set up more wards around the perimeter. Lansky called in a few men from a neighboring pack to help patrol the woods that backed up to the property. In the dining room, someone had set up a buffet of sandwiches and pizzas and Chinese takeout, and the witches who'd already been cleared by the medics were seated around the table picking at the food, the shock from their ordeal slowly receding.

Not one to stand on ceremony, I helped myself to a slice of pepperoni-and-mushroom pizza and grabbed a chair between Haley and the smoky-voiced witch with the yellow eyes.

"Your friends came through for us," Yellow Eyes said approvingly. Then, reaching for an apple from a bowl of fruit hidden among the pizza boxes, "I damn near forgot what real food looked like."

"You came through, too, Ash," Haley said, rubbing the chill from her arms. "In a big way. Who knows what would've happened to us if you hadn't shown up."

"Come on, Hay. You guys would've figured things out." I licked the pizza grease from my fingers and shot her a cocky grin. "It just would've been a little less interesting."

"A little less bloody," she said, "that's for sure."

"Hey. He had it coming to him."

"Which one?" she asked, but then she just shook her head and laughed. "Dude. I still can't believe you took out Benson's eyeball."

I shrugged, swallowing a bite of pizza. "It was all part of my bigger… *vision.*"

"Did you… did you really just say that right now?" Haley asked, cracking a smile.

"Look, Hay, I'm sorry we don't *see eye to eye* on this," I said, "but Benson was a little *short-sighted*."

"*Really, Ash? Really?*"

I grinned at her. "Girl, I could do this all night."

"Please don't," Yellow Eyes said, but she was laughing so hard she had to blot her eyes with a napkin.

When we all finally stopped busting a gut over poor Benson, I blew out a breath, the seriousness of the situation sending a chill down my spine. "The truth is... As far as I'm concerned? When it comes to men who think they can take away a woman's power, every damn one of them deserves to bleed. Matter of fact, soon as we find the rest of those hunters, I'm gonna take out more than just eyeballs, and that's a promise."

I wolfed down the rest of my pizza and grabbed another slice, along with a carton of something Chinese that smelled like spicy chicken and peanuts. I offered it to Haley first, but she shook her head, her brow creased like she was trying to figure something out.

The chopsticks were halfway to my mouth when I felt her eyes boring into me again.

"Darius told us that Gray sacrificed herself to trap Jonathan's soul in the Shadow Realm," she said. Her tone held a mix of confusion and awe, even a shade of disbelief. "For *us*."

I nodded, and even though I hated remembering the moment Gray had ripped out Jonathan's soul and vanished before my eyes, I couldn't help but be proud of her for doing it.

"She thought it was the best way to take him out and give the rest of us a chance to escape," I said. "Hell, maybe it was. Wished she didn't have to go there, though. We damn near lost her, from what I understand."

"How is she even alive?" Haley asked.

"No idea, but I'm looking forward to the story." I still wasn't sure what had gone down in the Shadowrealm—Gray and I hadn't gotten a chance to talk about any of it yet—but she'd beaten the odds and come back. That was the main thing.

"Fucking badass," Yellow Eyes said, taking a bite of her apple.

"That she is." I finished off the chicken and rose from my chair, overwhelmed with the sudden need to be close to Gray. To hold her, to take in her scent, to taste the sweetness of her kiss. "Speaking of which, I should probably go check on her. And *you* badasses need to eat. No more nibbling like mice, unless you want the EMTs to put you on an IV drip."

"Hard pass," Haley said, reaching for a plate and a slice of veggie pizza. Her skin was a couple of shades warmer than it had been a few minutes ago, and it looked like the fiery spark had finally returned to her eyes.

Progress. The best kind.

FOUR

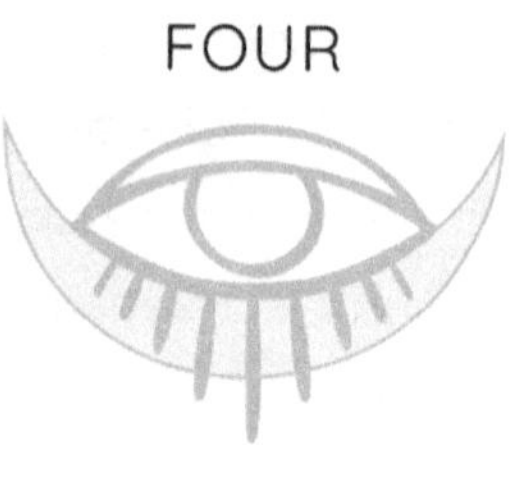

ASHER

At an agonizingly slow pace, I made my way through the press of bodies crammed into the house, everyone talking at once—cops asking the witches questions about our captors, EMTs admonishing them to back off, the witches trying to reach their loved ones on the few phones being passed around. It took some maneuvering and far more patience than I typically had, but I finally found my way to the back of the house. To Gray.

She was sitting in the bathtub in her pants and a bra, knees drawn to her chest, arms curled protectively around herself as the shower water beat down incessantly. She hadn't even bothered to close the door all the way.

The hellhounds—Sparkle and Sunshine, I'd been told—stood guard outside, but lucky for me, they gave me a quick sniff and let me pass.

Promising them I'd take good care of her, I stepped inside the bathroom and shut the door tight behind me.

Through clouds of steam, Gray sat motionless, bra hanging half off her shoulder like she'd started to take it off but gave up halfway through. The hot, pounding water was turning the skin on her arms and chest bright red.

"Gray?" I asked softly.

She glanced up briefly and nodded, barely acknowledging my presence. When I didn't say anything else, she looked down again, staring blankly at her knees.

Pain emanated from every inch of her skin. Her limp, blood-caked hair hung in matted locks around her face.

"Are the witches okay?" she finally mumbled.

"Damn straight. They're a strong fucking bunch, those witches."

Half of her mouth curved into a smile, but it fell just as quickly. "Any word from—"

"They'll be here, Gray," I said, knowing she meant Ronan and Emilio. "Give them time."

She pressed her forehead to her knee, her shoulders trembling. I could tell she was working overtime to keep her voice steady. "It feels like Emilio and I just found each other, and now…" She trailed off, her words like an anchor around my heart.

Not because I was jealous. Because I didn't know how to make it better for her.

There were a million things I *wanted* to say, and a million more I probably *should've*, but all of them felt big and dumb in my mouth. So instead of forcing it, I went for the diversion, kneeling down beside the tub and tugging on one of her matted curls.

"I realize I'm way out of practice at the moment," I said, "as I'm sure you can tell by my just-sprung-from-prison, don't-remember-what-soap-looks-like scent. But I'm *pretty* sure you're doing this whole shower thing wrong."

My attempt at humor fell flat. Gray lifted a shoulder in a gesture that barely qualified as a shrug, her bra strap sliding the rest of the way down. "I couldn't figure out the shower head. I wanted to change the pressure, but it wouldn't turn, and I just... I just kind of climbed in here and sat down. I don't even know how long I've been in here."

I got to my feet. "Okay if I join you?"

"Be my guest. I'm betting we smell the same right now, anyway."

"Ahh, you'd lose that bet, Cupcake." Her scent had always driven me wild. Not even the stench of dirt and sweat and smoke and blood could change that. "I hope you don't mind if I disrobe for this one. I know how much you love a man in camo."

This—finally—got a smile.

Returning it, I stepped into the tub, trying not to wince. Mother*fucker*, that water was hotter than Sebastian's balls—at least, what I imagined the Prince of Hell's ball temperature to be, which I'd admittedly never done before that moment and would hopefully never do again.

Shielding Gray from the lava-water, I helped her to her feet, then fucked around with the ancient shower head until I got things to a more tolerable pressure and temperature.

"Better?" I asked, maneuvering her beneath the spray,

"Mmm." She tilted her head back to rinse her hair, exposing the pale expanse of her neck and throat. I reached up and stroked her, my thumb tracing her jaw, her neck, her collarbone, slowly working over to her shoulder. Her bra finally gave up and dropped away, and holy *fuck*, I wanted to kiss her. To bite her. To suck on every inch of her until she melted with pleasure and forgot every last one of her worries, just for a little while.

It wasn't long before she finally ditched her remaining clothes. She tossed them unceremoniously into the corner of the tub, then stood on her toes and looped her arms around my neck.

Her full body pressed against mine, skin on skin, warm and slick, making me instantly hard. I felt the pulse of her magic, calling to me, strengthening me, just like it had in the prison. The incubus part of me wanted nothing more than to bury myself between her thighs, but the man in me just wanted to feel her. To hold her close.

For now, the man was winning out.

Barely.

Ignoring the ache in my balls, I wrapped my arms around her and held tight, my chin resting on the top of her head as the water ran down our bare bodies and washed away the evidence of tonight's battle. The water swirled black and red down the drain, tinged with blood.

Wolf's blood, I reminded myself, and my gut clenched, my mind flooding with nightmarish images of Emilio lying on that concrete floor, torn up and broken and writhing in pain, one faint heartbeat away from death's door…

No. I couldn't go down that road. Going down that road meant falling apart, and right now, I had to keep it together. For Gray. For Ronan and Darius. For Haley and Reva. For the other witches out there—strong, amazing women who'd just jumped out of the frying pan only to find out they'd still have to walk through fire, still have to face the Darkwinter and the hunters and whatever other crazy shit was waiting for all of us around the next corner.

"My hair feels like yarn." Too soon, Gray pulled out of my embrace and reached up to wring out her hair. "And not the soft kind."

Honestly, I was grateful for the distraction. Clearing the tightness from my throat, I pushed away the lingering thoughts of Emilio and grabbed the shampoo.

"Ever had your hair washed by a demon?" I teased, forcing myself to keep it light. Simple. Un-fucking-complicated in the face of the epically tangled, supremely fucked-up maze we were all stuck inside.

"No," she said. Despite the exhaustion in her eyes, her mouth curved into a playful smile. "Only by a vampire."

"Wait. What? You let *Beaumont* wash your hair? Seriously?"

She nodded, new mischief glinting in her eyes.

Keep talking. Keep distracting her from the blood still swirling at our feet...

"You're fucking kidding me," I said. "Well, screw that bloodsucker. I'm *way* better at this. Turn around."

With a small laugh, she did as I asked, and I eased her

head back, squeezing shampoo into my palms and gently massaging it into her scalp.

She sighed, the sound of it more like pleasure than relief. I was taking that as a good sign.

"Told you," I said. "*Way* better than Beaumont."

"Not better. Just different."

"Oh, I beg to differ, Cupcake." I pressed my thumbs into the base of her skull and massaged upward, working my fingers across her scalp, unleashing the scent of mint and lavender—some expensive-ass spa shit that probably belonged to Emilio's sister. A soft moan escaped Gray's lips, and she shivered, despite the heat of the shower.

"Um, okay," she breathed. "Where did you learn how to do this, exactly?"

"First admit I'm better at washing hair than the blood-sucker, then I'll tell you."

"You each have different... strengths and... and skills," she said, the pleasure taking hold of her, making her gasp. "Okay. You... you're better at this. You're fucking amazing at this."

"Cosmetology school," I blurted out.

At this, she let loose a full-on laugh, turning around to meet my eyes. "Seriously, Ash? Cosmetology school?"

I nodded.

"You're kidding me."

"Hey. I wouldn't joke about something like good hair, Gray. Close your eyes and rinse." I guided her head back under the water, careful to block the soap from her eyes. "Natural talent can only get you so far. Crafting beautiful hair artistry takes training, practice, and experience, and you can't just—"

"You are the *most* full-of-shit demon I've ever met." She laughed and tipped her head up, blinking the water from her eyes and looping her arms around my neck again. *Fucking bliss.* "Asher, the friendly neighborhood demonic hairstylist? Please. You were just trying to pick up girls."

"Demonic hair *designer*." I lifted a shoulder. "Besides, maybe *they* were trying to pick *me* up. Ever think of that? Not that I could blame them."

"Of course not," she said, dragging a finger down my chest, tracing a spiral pattern on my abs that had my cock stirring again. "Who could resist this? Big, bad incubus on the outside. Sensitive, artistic hairstylist—sorry, hair *designer*—on the inside…"

"That does sound like a winning combo, doesn't it?" I grabbed her hand and brought it to my mouth, pressing a kiss to her fingers. It's not that I minded her touch—the opposite, actually. I just didn't know how much longer I could resist the siren call of her body, her smooth skin, her luscious lips, the tug of her magic… The last thing I wanted to do was scare her off with my insatiable appetite.

No matter what I felt about her, we'd only been together the one time, and that was just to save my ass from the devil's trap Jonathan had injected into my bloodstream. Now, despite the fact that we were both standing here naked, I still wasn't a hundred percent clear on her feelings for me. This thing between us—whatever it was now, whatever it was destined to become—it was all her call. It had to be.

Because the last woman I'd claimed as my own, the last one I'd claimed on my terms… she ended up dead.

So I held Gray's hand and smiled and waited for her to make another joke, some crack about me picking up girls or becoming a beauty school dropout, but the jokes didn't come. Her eyes had turned serious once again. She pulled her hand from my grip and slid her palm against my cheek, her thumb brushing my lips.

"I love you," she whispered.

My throat tightened with a lump the size of Texas. Damn near felt like it, anyway. Had she really just said that?

"I don't know what I would've done if you weren't there tonight," she went on. "If anything had happened to you, I… I don't…"

"Shhh." I took her face in my hands, my gaze drifting down to her mouth, then back up to her eyes, cataloging the curves and lines of her face, the blue of her eyes, the arch of her brows. Her words echoed in my mind, filling me up with something that felt a lot like magic.

I love you…

"Gray, I—"

"Asher," she whispered, her eyes fluttering closed, and suddenly I forgot how to fucking talk and just lowered my mouth to hers, brushing a soft kiss over her lips.

Threading her hands into my hair, she returned the kiss, deepening it before pulling back with a sharp gasp.

"Sorry," she said, pressing her lips together, then offering an apologetic smile. "Still stings a little."

I traced the edge of her mouth with my fingertip, finally noticing the redness. "What happened?"

"Ronan… I kissed him at the warehouse, and…" She shook her head and lowered her eyes, clearly flustered. "We can't… Whenever we touch now, it burns. Sometimes worse than this."

"It *burns*? What the fuck kind of fairytale curse bullshit is that?"

"Not a curse. A deal. When I was stuck in the Shadowrealm, he and Darius staged a rescue. They came through the hell portal."

"So this is Sebastian's doing." *Of course.* My blood began to boil, my hands clenching into fists. Why was that motherfucker so wrapped up in our lives? He had no claim on Gray. Not until her death.

Gray nodded. "It was the only way he'd let them use the portal."

I took a deep breath, trying to calm down. Fucking hell, so much had happened while I'd been stuck in that rotting hole of a prison cell. Where did I even *start* to put this story together?

Ronan… Shit. He must be gutted.

"Half of me wants to beat his ass for making another deal with that greasy soul-pimp," I said.

"Well, a full three-quarters of *me* wants to beat his ass, and that's when I'm feeling generous."

"I get it. But the thing is, Gray… I'd do the same damn

thing a hundred times over if it meant getting you back safely. I can't blame him, and neither should you. You're here. Alive."

She nodded mutely, but she didn't look convinced. She just looked devastated.

"He loves you more than anything else in the world," I said. "He's been in love with you for basically ever, but he gave that up for you. He'd fucking *die* for you. You know that, right? From the moment you came into his life, that was never a question, and it never will be."

It was a long time before she moved again, and when she did, she looked up at me with the saddest eyes I'd ever seen.

"Newsflash, Asher." She blew out a breath, her shoulder lifting in a weak shrug. "I don't want him to die for me. I just want him to kiss me again without bursting into flames."

"Okay. Let me tell you something about our boy, Ronan." I grabbed her hands, squeezed tight. "He plays his cards close to the vest, and half the time you've got no idea what that motherfucker's up to, right? But we both know he's *always* up to something. He *will* find a way out of that deal—hell, he's probably already started renegotiating with Sebastian behind the scenes. And when this is over—when all this shit is back to normal and the witches have gone home and the fae fucks are in the ground with the hunters and our crew is back together, strong and fucking solid, we're gonna have a big party. A feast. Fucking massive. Cage dancers, live band, those guys who paint butterflies on faces. And the main course? Barbecued Sebastian nuts. What do you think of *that*?"

She tried to hold on to her sadness, her anger, but she couldn't—not completely. The laugh broke through, lighting up her face once again.

"I think I'll pass on the nuts," she said. "But I do appreciate your enthusiasm. Not to mention your brutally on-point sense of vengeance."

"Hey. Anything for you, Cupcake." I stroked my hand down the side of her ribcage and squeezed her hip, the moment turning serious again. "Absolutely anything."

"I know."

She closed my eyes, and beneath my touch, her body trembled. It was slight at first, a tremor that began in her shoulders and rolled straight on down.

I reached up over her head and adjusted the water so she'd get more of the warmth.

"You were right earlier," she said, her eyes still closed, the skin between them creased as if she were trying her damnedest to keep the images at bay. "When I found you in that cell, you asked me if I'd missed you. I missed you so much... so fucking much. I thought about you every day we were apart, and the picture of this moment right here..." She put her hand flat against my chest and shook her head. "It got me through some of the scariest shit I've ever faced."

"Hey. You got your*self* through that shit, because you're strong as hell, Gray. You fought some epic shit, and you still came out swinging. Every time. That's all you."

"All I wanted was for all of us to be together again," she

went on. "Now you're here. We got you out of that prison. We saved the witches. But we can't exactly celebrate, because Ronan is bound by Sebastian's deal. I'm bound by my own deal with him. I found out my birthmother tried to kill me. Darius doesn't remember anything, and—"

"Wait. What? Gray, slow down. Breathe. I don't understand what you're saying."

She shook her head, but I couldn't tell if she'd even heard me.

"Emilio's hurt," she continued. "Really hurt. And Ronan and Elena were just… They looked like they'd already lost hope. How can he come back from that?"

She opened her eyes and looked to me as if I had the answers, but nothing I could say would make this right. Make it hurt less. I shook my head and reached for her face again, wishing I could kiss away the pain.

"I'm sorry. I'm so, so sorry."

"I know." She lowered her eyes, water droplets collecting along her dark lashes. "I'm sorry, too."

"You have nothing to be sorry for," I said. But before I could take another breath, she was stretching up on her toes again, pulling me close.

Her mouth covered mine in another kiss, this one so intense it rivaled the heat of the water.

"Your lips," I mumbled. "I don't want to hurt your—"

"I don't care," she breathed. "I just… I want you. Us. Right now, Ash. I need to feel you inside me. *Please.*"

Fucking hell, this woman was going to wring me right out.

"Gray, you're freaked out and upset and I get it. But..."

I trailed off, not sure where to take it. She felt so volatile right now—and who could blame her? But what the hell was I supposed to say? *No, Gray. I don't want you to use me as a painkiller. No, Gray. I want you to need me, not just because my touch feels good, but because it brings you happiness. Because you really do love me, just like you said...*

"Asher," she said, curling her hands into my hair, desperation seeping into her voice, "I can't... I can't think about this shit anymore tonight. I feel like my head is going to explode. Right now, I just need you. That's all."

That's all...

Despite her earlier declarations, the doubts crept in again. And there, in the darkest part of my tattered soul, pain flickered.

I forced a smile and pulled her close. "Whatever you need, Cupcake. You know that."

Didn't matter what I felt in that moment. I'd meant what I said—I'd give her anything she asked for, without question. I knew what it felt like standing on the edge of the cliff, staring down over the yawning chasm of grief, the fear of death nipping at your heels. Times like that, all you wanted was to feel alive. I fucking got it.

But it still stung.

I held her gaze, and her eyes softened, a sad smile just barely touching her lips.

"It's not like that, Ash," she whispered, as if she could read my thoughts. Hell, maybe she could. I could sarcasm my way out of just about anything, but I'd never been great at hiding my feelings—especially from her.

"I don't need sex," she said. "I don't need a distraction. I need *you*. I… there's so much more to say, so much I want to tell you about. But right now, everything feels so… so fragile. A lot of bad shit happened, and even though I made it out, I feel… off. Like, there's this thing inside me, this magic, and it keeps getting stronger, but I'm not sure what to do with that. There's this whole legacy thing we found out about, and I'm supposed to lead the witches… I don't even know what it all means. All I know is that sometimes, when I close my eyes, all I see is a big, black pit. And all I want to do is jump." She shivered again, her voice dropping to a whisper. "I don't even know what's real."

"You don't have to figure it out tonight." I cupped her face, tilting her up to meet my gaze again. "And you don't have to figure it out by yourself."

"I know. But for a little while, I thought I lost you." A tear slid down her cheek.

Brushing it away with my thumb, I said, "You haven't."

"I need to feel you inside me," she said again. "Not just to feel good and forget everything else, but to know that you're really here. That you're whole. That you're not going to disappear on me the minute I close my eyes again."

"That's not gonna happen," I said. "I'm never leaving your side again. *That* is a damn promise." I leaned in close, kissing her swollen lips, her chin, her collarbone, sweeping lower with each pass. Her skin was hot and slippery, and when I got to her breasts, she arched her back, pressing herself against my mouth as I sucked one of her nipples between my teeth, my fingers finding the other one and tugging, rolling, teasing her just right.

"Yes," she breathed, threading her hands into my hair.

Back in the cave prison, there'd been no time for teasing or slow, lingering kisses. I hadn't even laid eyes on her bare breasts before tonight—only her thighs, a quick blur of pale skin as she'd wriggled out of her pants and climbed into my lap, desperate to give me the strength to fight off the devil's trap poison coursing through my blood.

Well, it'd worked. She'd strengthened me in more ways than she'd even realized, and ever since that moment, I'd dreamed of *this* one—the chance to truly taste her, to inhale her scent, to make her gasp with pleasure at the hot slide of my tongue between her thighs.

I almost came just thinking about it, but I forced myself to hold out. Right now, it was all about her. All about bringing her to the edge of bliss and back again.

I licked and sucked, kissing every inch of her silky skin as I worked my way across the lower curves of her breasts and down her ribcage, dragging my tongue over her hipbone, across her belly, and across the tops of her legs.

When I was finally down on my knees, I gripped the backs of her thighs and looked up at her through a spray of hot water.

"You'd better find something to hold on to, Cupcake. Because I'm about to go all in on this gorgeous pussy of yours, and I'm not coming up for air until you damn well forget how to stand."

FIVE

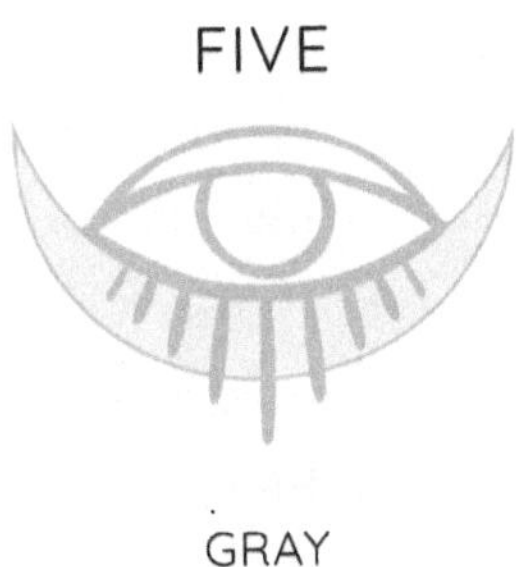

GRAY

Without warning, Asher slid his tongue between my thighs, his mouth hot and demanding and insatiable and oh my *God* I was already trembling. I braced one hand against the tile wall and fisted his hair with the other, but there was no way I'd be able to hold out much longer.

With a surge of hot water sluicing down my back and clouds of steam smudging Asher from my view, I melted beneath invisible kisses, my body going wild for the teasing, fluttering strokes of his tongue and his soft moans of pleasure, each one vibrating through my core and making my knees weak.

"You're… amazing," I managed, wanting him to know how much I was enjoying this. How much he was unraveling me, one delicious kiss at a time. "Don't… stop."

Holy hell.

It was no surprise that an incubus knew how to please a woman. But before tonight, we'd only been intimate together once—for about ten minutes in the cave prison, if that—yet somehow Asher was reading the unique needs of my body as if he'd studied it for years, sensing my shifting desires before I'd even consciously registered them myself. Everything he did—every kiss, every hot breath, every nibble—felt like it'd been custom designed just for me.

I would've come five times over by now, but it turned out Asher wasn't just a master of my body's desires.

He was also a master of the epic tease.

I ached for release, but each time I felt those initial tingles building in my core, he'd pull back, easing the perfect pressure of his tongue, blowing a hot breath across my clit until the elusive orgasm slipped away once again.

And then he'd come back, his mouth whipping my body into a new frenzy.

I was going insane.

After everything I'd come through, every demon and battle I'd fought, *this* was going to be my end. Tonight, I would die in the shower by this man's mouth.

And I was pretty sure I'd be smiling when I did.

Asher shifted before me again, dragging his tongue along my clit, then dropping lower to leave a trail of light, fluttery kisses on my inner thigh, all the way down to my knee.

"This is torture," I groaned. I tightened my grip on his hair, tugging him back up toward my center, but that only seemed to encourage his incessant teasing.

"Torture?" He glanced up at me, his eyes fiery, his

mouth wet with the evidence of my desire. "I can *taste* how much you love it, Gray."

He was right, of course, and he left me no choice but to give up the last bit of my control, putting my pleasure in the hands—and mouth—of the incubus who'd been driving me crazy since our very first meeting.

The incubus I'd somehow fallen in love with.

"You're beautiful," he murmured, then leaned forward again, his tongue flicking and teasing, his hands sliding up to cup my ass and pull me close. My hips arched to give him more access, and he slid his tongue inside me, stroking and sucking as his lips buzzed my clit.

"Ash," I breathed, tugging his hair, my body rocking against his face, desperately chasing the release he was holding just out of my reach. I felt the pressure building inside again, more intense this time, my core throbbing, and I bit my lip to stifle a groan of pure frustration.

He was going to stop again, and I was going to ache. To burn. If I didn't come soon, I'd explode.

"Please," I begged, my head lolling back as he plunged in deep, then pulled back, grazing my clit with his teeth before sucking it between his lips. His hair was silky on my palm, and I fisted it tight once more, desperate to hold him close.

"Don't stop," I whispered now, near tears from the slow build, the sheer intensity pushing me to the absolute edge of my limits. "Please don't tease me."

A sound that might've been laughter escaped his lips, and he slid a hand between my thighs, his fingertips grazing my entrance. Then, without warning, he thrust two fingers inside me, curling to hit the perfect spot with each thrust as he licked and sucked, faster now, deeper, more intense, almost there, and I…

"Asher! Don't stop! Don't… oh my God… That's…" I was out of my mind, babbling and gasping for breath as the heat rushed up my thighs and finally, blissfully, thank-the-fucking-universe-I-thought-I-was-going-to-die-fully exploded in a white-hot starburst of pure, unadulterated pleasure.

A tremor rolled through my body, starting in my thighs and working up my core, my chest, my spine, across my scalp, and down my arms. Whatever Asher was doing to me, I could feel it in my fingertips, my toes, everything warm and tingling, pleasure breaking over my body like waves against the shore.

And still, he didn't relent.

He kissed and sucked until I thought I'd burn up from the intensity, pushing past the sensitivity, the too-much, too-hot, too-good, too-*everything* rush of sensations until I suddenly felt the pressure building again, my muscles convulsing into another wave of bliss as a second orgasm burst inside, chasing the aftershocks that still lingered from the first, combining to ignite my heart, to steal the very breath from my lungs.

My knees finally buckled and Asher laughed, catching me in his arms as he rose to his feet.

"Told you I wasn't stopping till you couldn't stand up anymore," he teased, holding me against his chest.

I nodded, leaning into his embrace. It was all I had left. Couldn't stand up? I couldn't even speak anymore. If it wasn't for the embarrassingly loud panting coming from my mouth, I would've thought I'd forgotten how to breathe, too.

Without another word, Asher lifted me up, guiding my legs around his hips. I had just enough strength left to wrap my arms around his neck and hold on for dear life as he spun us around and pressed my back against the tiles. Water streamed down his face from his hair, and with a fiery gleam in his eyes, he shifted his hips, giving me a taste of just how turned on he was.

"Yes," I whispered, answering the unspoken question with a bubbly laugh. "God, yes."

The press of his steel-hard cock against my entrance stirred me back to life, and I welcomed his touch once again, feeling every perfect inch as he slid inside me, filling me up.

The moment we connected, I felt the tug of his incubus hunger, an invisible force that unleashed an answering call in my own magic. I realized then how much he'd been holding back.

"Take it," I urged him, knowing he wouldn't unless I offered, despite everything we'd already shared. Everything he'd already given me.

He nuzzled my neck, kissing his way up to my ear. "You sure?"

I shivered in his arms, his voice and the proximity of his

hot, wet mouth threatening to unravel me once again. Everything he did with his lips drove me wild.

"It's yours, Ash. *I'm* yours. Don't you know that by now?"

"Mmm. I'm starting to get the idea." Asher claimed my mouth in a bruising kiss I gladly returned, my burned, swollen lips all but forgotten. Beneath the saltiness of my desire still lingering on his tongue, I tasted his unique fire, like cinnamon and hot peppers. It made my mouth water for more.

Unlike our time in the prison, tonight there was no resistance on his part, no worries about what consequences awaited us on the other side. We were in love—the real deal. Only Sebastian meted out punishment for something so pure, so beautiful. The universe worked in mysterious, mind-bending ways I'd probably never figure out, but one thing was absolutely sure: when it came to real love, there were no consequences.

Pinning me against the wall again, Asher rolled his hips, sliding deep inside me. I felt my magic flowing into him, connecting with his own power, melding, strengthening. He grew harder with each thrust, his eyes full of love and lust and beauty as he held my gaze, our breath mingling, water running in rivulets over our curves and dips, both of us sliding closer and closer to the edge.

I clung to him, my heart beating strong and steady despite the terrors this night had brought. In Asher's arms, I was safe. Tonight, in this raging storm of grief and pain and confusion and fear, he was my anchor.

And for all his toughness, I suspected that I was his, too.

"Harder," I breathed, biting down on his shoulder to keep from crying out as he obeyed my wishes, plunging deep inside me, my back sliding against the tiles. I kissed his neck, his jaw, his beautiful mouth. I gave him everything I had. And I took everything he offered.

There was power in telling a man what you wanted. Power in claiming your desires. Power in recognizing his, and giving in to those as well.

Like me, he wanted it hard tonight, too. Hard and deep and soul-shattering.

"Harder," I said again, and I kissed him fiercely, feeling my body clench around him, and that was all it took. The now-familiar rush of pleasure snuck up on me fast, shattering me as Asher moaned into my mouth, coming hot and hard inside me, shuddering against me as tears spilled from my eyes.

He didn't ask me what was wrong. Didn't offer pity or sympathy or platitudes. In that instant, I knew he was feeling what I'd felt, and he just continued to hold me, to remain deep inside me, his gaze locked on mine as he waited for me to finally catch my breath.

Something strange and thrilling had just passed between us—something that went beyond the magic and his incubus energy and the raw desire. Time seemed to stop. And there, in the ocean-blue depths of his gaze, I'd seen the ferocity of his love for me, his passion. I saw his loyalty to Ronan and the brotherhood he felt for the others. I sensed their presence, too—all of them. It was as if my connection with Asher was calling out to Ronan, Darius, and Liam as well.

And of course, Emilio. My wolf. *Our* wolf. His essence was fainter than the others', but he was still there, still with us.

Still alive.

Tears continued to spill, and Asher kissed them away, one by one.

"He's okay," I whispered, knowing Ash would understand. "He's still with us. I can feel him."

"Yeah. Me too," he said. "When we… finished… Something about it brought them all in. I even thought of Liam's spooky ass." Asher laughed. "Does that sound fucking crazy or what?"

"It's our bond," I said. "Being together like this brings us all closer. I think it's only going to get stronger now. Not just with you and me, but with all of us. Did you really feel Emilio, too?"

"Not as clear as the other guys, but yeah." He finally set me down, still holding me as I regained my footing on the slippery tub. The jeans I'd cast off earlier were balled up in a wet heap in the corner, still bloody. I'd be throwing those out the first chance I got.

"I know it was bad," I continued, toeing the filthy jeans. A stream of red water ran out beneath them. "But if Emilio…" I swallowed hard, unable to say the d-word out loud. *Died.* "I would feel it if he did."

I *would* feel it. I knew that for a fact. Believed it with such unshakeable faith that even when Darius knocked on the door fifteen minutes later to tell us a car had just pulled in, even when I opened the front door and saw Elena's shocked, vacant eyes, even when Ronan met my gaze and shook his head, wordless, his whole body covered in wolf's blood, I still believed Emilio was okay. That any minute he'd walk in behind Ronan and Elena, naked, grinning his wolf's grin, cracking some joke about how he'd lost all his clothes during the shift that'd miraculously healed his body.

As we stood in the entryway, the door wide open, Asher's arm came around my waist, holding me up. Our bodies were still warm from the shower, hair dripping into our eyes, and even when I felt his own gasp of shock at Ronan and Elena's obvious despair, I kept looking past them, looking out into the darkness, searching for my wolf.

When was he coming back? Had he driven separately? Had he decided to stop for supplies? Did he have to file a report at the station?

My mind served up all kinds of logistical questions, because despite the painfully obvious evidence laid out before me, some part of me *still* believed that my thoughts, my intentions, my imagination, my heart, my bond with him, my hope, my faith, my magic… that all of those things were stronger than Death.

Stupid girl.

"We couldn't save him," Ronan finally said, his voice cracking, his face as pale as the moon. "Emilio is dead."

SIX

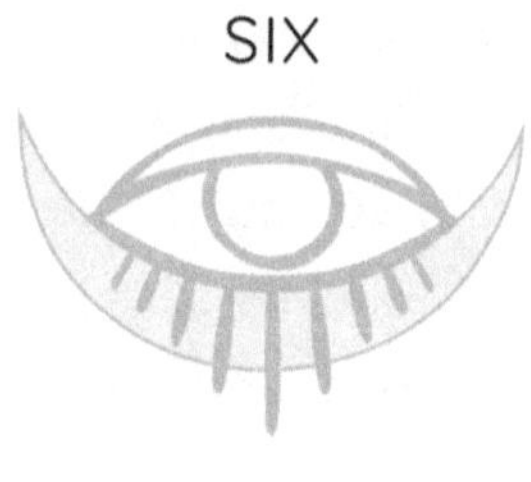

GRAY

"He isn't," I insisted. It was that simple. Emilio wasn't dead.

Which meant that Ronan and Elena had left him in that warehouse somewhere, bleeding and probably unconscious.

I was wearing only a thin robe I'd found hanging on the back of the bathroom door, but I didn't care. Ignoring Ronan's desolate stare, I pulled open the hall closet and grabbed the first jacket I saw, already shoving my bare feet into a pair of old boots.

"Let's go. We need to find him and bring him back here. He needs medical attention."

No one made a move.

"Why are you guys standing around? Let's go!" Now it was my voice that was breaking, a tiny crack on the first word that'd turned into a fissure by the last, huge enough for all the doubts and fears to seep in.

My knees buckled, and I felt a pair of strong arms come around my waist from behind, catching me before I hit the floor.

"He's gone, baby. He's gone." Asher's voice, which only moments ago had been a source of pure pleasure, was like rusty nails on a china plate now. I wrenched free of his hold, still refusing to accept that Emilio—strong, powerful, beautiful Emilio—was dead.

I could still feel his presence. His essence. Why were they all looking at me like I'd lost my mind?

I stepped toward Ronan, leaning in as close as I dared. My skin and hair were still damp from the shower, and here in Ronan's forbidden presence, steam rose from my body in iridescent swirls.

I searched his eyes, seeking the lie. The loophole that would let our wolf be okay.

But Ronan was a shell. His eyes were empty. It felt like his whole body was about to turn into dust and blow away.

I looked to Elena instead. She hadn't uttered a word since they'd walked in—just stood beside Ronan, her mouth opening and closing as if she couldn't suck in enough air, her hands coated in dark, dried blood.

"You'd *never* leave his body behind," I said to both of them. "So, if he's really dead, where's his body?"

No response.

"*Where?*" I demanded, feeling the eyes of the witches and the rest of our houseguests burning through my back. They'd all gathered in the living room behind me, keeping a respectful distance, but still. They were watching.

I wouldn't let myself fall apart in front of them. Not like this.

Stepping back from Ronan and taking a deep breath, I tried again, keeping my voice neutral. Even. Pushing out all the doubts and sealing up all those cracks and fissures behind them.

"Where is the body?" I asked again, calm. Collected. Logical. Behind me, I felt the presence of my hellhounds. They stood guard beside Asher and Darius, all of them apparently waiting for me to break.

I wouldn't, though. Not now.

"We searched the entire warehouse," Ronan said, his voice weakening with every word. "What was left of it, anyway. Inside and out. The raven came, and he's... he's gone, Gray. Just gone."

The words cut to the bone, but their bite quickly faded as my brain processed their meaning.

"Raven? Wait, you mean Liam?"

Ronan nodded. "He took him."

"His soul?"

"Everything."

"So he's not dead, then." I let out a shaky breath. Then, more firmly, I repeated it. "He's not dead. Not without a body. If Liam took everything, there has to be another reason. Something we haven't thought of."

"Gray, there's nowhere... We searched the entire area." Elena's voice was no more than a whisper, her eyes blank, her face gray. "There's nowhere he could be. I'm sorry. I didn't want to have to tell you this. He's just... *mi hermano…*" She blinked back tears, struggling to rein in her emotions in front of a house full of witches and shifters and strangers. "He's passed on. We have to accept it and mourn him and move on."

Move on?

I wanted to scream at her. To grab her by the shoulders and shake some sense into her. But the pain in her eyes snapped me from my anger, and instead, I drew her in and held her close. She was shaking.

Through the knotted tangle of her blood-drenched hair, I stared over her shoulder at Ronan, waiting for him to realize his obvious mistake. To finally connect the dots. To tell Elena they'd missed something and spring into action.

But he didn't. He just stood there, silently holding my gaze with a look I could read like an old book.

Pity.

It sparked a rage inside me that I couldn't contain. Without a moment to spare, I pushed Elena away and spun toward the now-empty dining room, a burst of magic erupting from my palms and slamming into the china cabinet, full force, totally out of my control.

The wood splintered. The glass panes on the front and the dishes inside shattered, exploding outward in a million razor-sharp projectiles before turning—instantly and inexplicably—to water.

Deirdre.

I hadn't seen her come in, but somehow she stood behind me with her hands raised, neutralizing my magic with a spell of her own. The shards fell like a harmless rain, soaking the leftover food spread across the dining table.

Her hands landed softly on my shoulders, gently squeezing. Heat emanated from her palms and warmed my damp skin.

"Breathe, Gray," she said softly, and I felt the gentlest push of unfamiliar magic against my own—probably a calming spell. The scents of lavender and honey and baby powder filled the air, and her soothing words felt like grand-motherly hugs. "Breathe in, exhale out. Release the anger. Call back the magic. Fill yourself with pure, white light."

I took a deep breath, exhaled it like she instructed, but... no. I didn't want this. Didn't want some magical numbing agent. I had important work to do. I was going to... do... something.

Wasn't I?

"That's it, Gray," the soothing voice murmured. "Nice and easy. Come back to yourself."

Mmm. That sounds nice. Maybe I should come back...

Haze clouded my thoughts, smudging everything around the edges.

Wait... What was I just doing? Aren't I supposed to be some-where? Meeting someone? But I thought...

I glanced around the room, dozens of eyes on me. Why were they all so sad?

Ronan, Darius, Asher... I looked over each one in turn.

"That's it, Gray," the soft voice said. "Follow my voice and come back."

Ronan, Darius, Asher…

Ronan, Darius… Emilio. Wait, where is Emilio?

I blinked rapidly, scanning the sea of faces—most of them unfamiliar—for the wolf.

"Where is…" I began, then shook my head, clearing away the haze. He wasn't here. He was… they were saying he was gone.

Everything came rushing back, breaking through the spell and hitting me again like a bucket of ice water to the face.

"What are you *doing* to me?" I shouted, whirling around toward the source of the placating words. Deirdre was still whispering her soothing mantras, still bathing me in her magic, but I was done with that. I broke her magical hold, welcoming the rush of fury that boiled up inside, once again set loose. I *needed* this madness, this dark energy, this wild magic, no matter how ugly it got. No matter how uncomfortable it made everyone else feel.

My skin was crackling with magical energy, the hairs on my neck and arms standing on end. It reminded me of that day on the beach in the Shadowrealm when Liam and I had kissed—those intense sparks, the moment just before lightning struck the sand.

"Emilio is still with us," I said, my voice trembling with anger. "Maybe not in this realm, but he's not gone."

At this, Ronan reached out, his palm facing up. There in the center was a black feather sticky with blood. "This was the only thing left behind."

"That's… good," I said, the barest blush of a plan formulating in my mind. "No, that's actually *really* good."

I turned around and searched the wide-eyed faces of the witches gathered in the living room for my sister.

"Haley?" I said, and she got to her feet, smoothing a hand over her near-bald head. "You're with me."

Haley nodded without hesitation, crossing the room to join me. If I'd scared her with my outburst, she didn't show it, her eyes flashing with renewed determination that made me glad to have her on my side.

"Darius," I continued, "I need you to go into the kitchen and find me a clear glass bowl, some bottled water, matches, candles, salt, and the sharpest knife you can find. Ash? Your job is to keep an eye on the hounds and keep everyone away from us. *No* one disturbs us—and I mean *no* one—unless we come under attack or the house is literally burning down around us." Then, to Deirdre and the rest of the witches, "Are you guys up for a little protection magic? We need to keep this place on lockdown as long as we can."

They nodded in unison—even Deirdre, who was watching me with a mix of frustration and pride that almost made me smile.

"Where are you *going*, Gray?" Ronan asked, his voice barely recognizable now. He still hadn't moved from his position in front of the door. It was as if the weight of Emilio's near-death had fallen on his shoulders, cementing him in place.

All he had to do was believe me. To have faith. But I knew from the look in his eyes that he didn't.

"Where am I *going*?" I snapped. "Where am I going?! Let me tell you something, Ronan Vacarro." I shoved a finger into his chest, welcoming the brief burn. "This crew... Since all this shit started, we have fought demons together, hunters, rogue vamps, hell's curses, fae traitors, illusions, and every single sharp, pointy, flaming, cursed obstacle the universe has thrown at us. And you know what? I'm tired. I'm tired and I'm pissed off and I am *done* playing games. We deserve a break."

"Gray. You can't just—"

"Watch me." I snatched the bloody feather from his hand and turned around to find Darius with his arms full of the supplies I'd asked him to get from the kitchen. Haley and I took everything, and then I met Ronan's eyes one last time. "I'm going to find Emilio and Liam, and then I'm going to bring them *both* back here. Because I don't care what hell beasts are waiting for us tomorrow or which contracts and rules I have to break now. This crew—no, screw that. This *family*—we've just been fucked with for the *last* goddamn time."

SEVEN

GRAY

"Nice speech, Aragorn." Haley closed the guest room door behind us, then turned to face me, her arms full of supplies. "I assume you have an actual plan?"

The shaved head made the fire in her eyes burn even more brightly, and despite the dark circles beneath them, she looked energized and ready to rock.

"It's percolating," I said, shedding the robe and grabbing a T-shirt and an old pair of leggings from the closet. "But here's the short version: you're going to help me do some blood magic to track them down."

"Gray, are you sure you—"

"Look, Hay. I don't have a lot of time for a debate." I quickly pulled on the clothes, then wrapped my hair in a bun. "Either you're in on this, or you're in my way."

I held her gaze, my heart hammering behind my ribcage. I needed her help—wanted her by my side through this—but if she wanted to bail, I'd find another way. There would be no talking me out of this—not even from the woman who shared my blood.

Haley rolled her eyes. "Of course I'm *in* on this, you crazy bitch. God." She set the supplies on the bed and plucked the feather from my hand. "I just wish we had more to go on. And better supplies. And maybe some of Nona's lasagna."

"Help me figure this out and I'll bake you a month's worth of lasagna."

"Do you even know how?"

I leaned in and kissed her cheek. "For you? I'll learn."

After that, I was a whirlwind, scouring the room for anything else we could use while Haley sorted through the stuff Darius had scavenged. The Tarot cards Emilio had given me were on the dresser, so I gathered them up into a neat stack and placed them with the other supplies, hoping we could harness the power of the cards as well as their connection to Emilio.

Stuffed in draws or shoved out of sight on the closet shelves, I found a lighter, which I slid into my T-shirt pocket, and a couple more half-melted candles. Then I unearthed a terra-cotta bowl, a half-spent tube of bright red lipstick, and—a more recent addition to the space—one of Emilio's T-shirts. I brought it to my face and inhaled, his woodsy-vanilla scent bringing tears to my eyes.

This was the room we'd shared together. The room where we'd spent one amazing night in each other's arms. The room where we'd shared our first time... and our last...

I closed my eyes, barely stifling the tears.

Focus, Gray. Get him back.

Shaking off the melancholy, I opened my eyes and tossed the shirt to Haley. She found a pair of scissors and got to work cutting it into seven strips.

"We need a circle," she said, toeing the dark green throw rug that covered the floor beside the bed. "Help me with this."

We rolled it up and shoved it out of the way, revealing the bare wood planks beneath. Dropping to my knees, I drew a pentacle on the floor with the old lipstick, then set the candles at each of the points.

As Haley lit each one, I poured a line of salt over the threshold before the door and along each of the windowsills. Haley poured the bottled water into the glass bowl and blessed it, and then we sprinkled that around the circle, too.

Between our actions in here, the witches' collective protection magic, and the perimeter Jael had set up, we'd be safe for a little while—hopefully long enough for me to track down my guys and bring them back. There were dark fae to hunt, threats to eliminate, people to save, order to restore... and I needed them by my side. We all did.

Certain we'd prepared the makeshift space as best we could, Haley and I knelt down at the center of the circle, the terra cotta bowl resting on the floor between us, the blade in her lap. Following her lead, I helped tie each of the T-shirt strips into seven knots, then placed all of them into the bowl.

From the deck of cards, I selected the two that most

reminded me of the guys. For Emilio, I chose the King of Cups, honorable and compassionate, sensitive, full of love and strength and wisdom. For Liam, the Death card.

My eyes lingered on the words carved in stone before the black-robed angel of Death.

Vita mutatur, non tollitur. Life is changed, not taken away.

The last time I'd drawn this card, it'd brought me to Liam. I hoped now it would do the same. That the message would hold true.

I placed the cards on each side of the bowl.

Haley set the blood-drenched feather on top of the knotted fabric strips, then nodded at me.

It was time.

"Okay, blood priestess," I said. "Let's conjure up something good."

"Blood priestess. I like that." With a wicked gleam in her eye, Haley reached for my hands, clasping them tight over the bowl. At her touch, my magic sparked, and she let out a little gasp of surprise, then laughed. "Okay, we need to work on your grounding skills after this."

"We will," I told her. "We'll work on everything." *Including the part about us being sisters,* I thought. I still wasn't quite sure how to tell her—there were so many implications, so many unanswered questions. But that was a conversation for later. Right now, we had a job to do.

My magic settled, allowing me to feel the pulse of hers, our bond growing stronger the longer we held tight. Her touch was warm and solid, a reassuring connection in a night that had threatened to blow us all away.

My eyes misted again, but not because of Emilio or the struggles that still lay ahead. In that instant, I thought of Sophie, and a smile touched my lips. She'd brought Haley into my life, despite my resistance. She'd brought my sister and me together. I felt her presence now, her friendship. Her support.

I sensed Haley did, too. I saw my own emotion reflected in her eyes, and a silent understanding passed between us. She might not yet know about the nature of our relationship, but even if we *weren't* biological sisters, Haley and I were sisters in all the ways that counted.

And it'd all started with our connection to Sophie.

"She's here," I whispered, and Haley nodded, knowing exactly who I was talking about.

"She's always with us, Gray. She always will be." Haley returned my smile, a tear glittering on her cheek. Then, taking a deep breath and squaring her shoulders, she said, "It's time. Close your eyes, center yourself, and try to call up the ones you seek—images, feelings, emotions, sensations, words, anything that will bring them closer to you."

I obeyed, letting my thoughts drift to Emilio and Liam. It wasn't hard; they were always on my mind, always in my heart.

I saw Emilio's deep, soulful eyes. His warm smile. I tasted the rich, chocolatey brownies we'd shared. I felt the warmth of his kisses, his touch, his love for me. My palms tingled as I remembered stroking his coarse fur the first time I'd seen him shift into wolf form. My shoulders dipped as I recalled the time the wolf had pinned me to the ground at the safe house during our training, and the time he'd pinned me to the bed as a man. I heard the music of his laugh in my ears, and I held him close until his image was as firm and real as if he were standing right beside me.

Liam came to me just as easily, though not as comfortably. With Liam, there was no escaping the bitter taste of betrayal, the pang of something precious lost. But I wouldn't push it away. Acknowledging and confronting that pain was the only way I'd ever be able to forgive him fully, and I wanted to. More than anything. So I welcomed even that, the hollow ache in my heart, the twist in my gut that accompanied the rush of butterflies and the electric sparks of our first kiss. Goosebumps rose along my arms when I remembered our first meeting the night Sophie had died and he'd come to take her soul. My fingers tingled at the spider-webby touch of his robes, and a shy heat crept to my cheeks as I pictured the first time he'd taken his human form, just to make me more comfortable.

He was with me now, too. Both of them were—side by side in my mind's eye. Side by side in my heart.

I let out a deep, slow breath, and I felt Haley's energy shifting before me. In a soft, meditative tone, she reminded me to hold on to whatever images I'd called forth.

She was still holding my hands, and now she gently turned them so that my palms were facing up. I knew what was coming next, but I barely felt the bite of the blade as she sliced it across my hand. Instinctively, I curled my fingers into a fist, squeezing my blood into the bowl.

Haley released me, and seconds later I heard the sound of a match being struck. The scent of sulfur filled my nose, and the contents of the blow flared to life in a blaze of light and heat that radiated across my face.

Haley began to chant, and I joined in, speaking the words like a mantra until I'd slipped into a deeply meditative state.

"Earth, air, water, fire. Earth, air, water, fire. Earth, air, water fire…" The words became automatic, and though Haley hadn't instructed me to do so, I continued the repetition dozens of times, not stopping even as she altered her own chanting to speak the spell:

> *Your connection runs deep*
> *As blood in the vein*
> *Let it guide you this night*
> *Through distance, through pain*
> *May your souls become one*
> *Across time and space*
> *And bring you together*
> *In his resting place*

The blaze of the bowl dimmed, and silence descended. My lips still uttered the chant, but I could no longer hear the sound of my own voice.

A gentle breeze stirred my hair, and I breathed in the

scent of lavender and lilac. When the moment felt right, I opened my eyes.

Haley was gone. I was no longer sitting on the floor of Elena's guest room.

I was, unsurprisingly, back in my own magical realm, the now-familiar black trees glittering with silver threads. Slowly, I got to my feet, trying to get my bearings. The spell had brought me here, which meant that Liam and Emilio were somewhere in my realm, probably near the gate to the Shadowrealm.

The crunch of leaves and branches sounded at my back, and I spun around expecting Liam, my lips already curving into a smile.

But the gaze that greeted me was not the peaceful, ancient blue of Liam Colebrook's gaze.

The half-human, half-beast creature before me didn't even have eyes. Just two black pits oozing with foul blood, carved into a bashed-in skull that was covered in a patchwork of tattered flesh and bloody, matted fur. A long, crooked muzzle extended out beneath the pits like a door loose on its hinges.

He snapped his jaw, revealing a series of rotten, infected holes where his pseudo-vampire fangs should've been. And though he couldn't speak, the haunting words of the past slithered into my memory, filling my mouth with the taste of bile.

Leaving the shadows already, Sunshine?

It seemed the twisted monster who'd been hunting me for a decade had caught up with me once again.

EIGHT

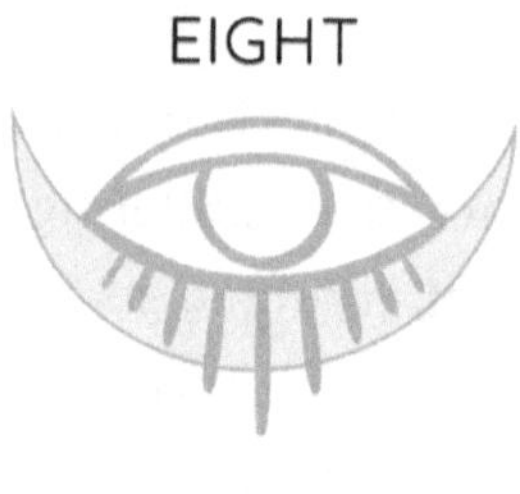

GRAY

My brain checked out, leaving my instincts in charge. I lunged, slamming Jonathan's deformed hybrid body to the ground and straddling him. My hands wrapped around his neck, fingers breaking through the loose skin and sinking into the flesh, right down to the brittle bones beneath. I swallowed back a gag as his putrid blood spilled over my hands, but still, he writhed and bucked beneath me, some unnatural force giving him superior strength.

In a blur, he shoved me off and rolled on top of me, pinning my arms at my sides with hands that were part human, part monstrous paw, tipped with razor-sharp claws that pierced my skin. Blood from his neck wounds dripped onto my face, and I closed my mouth and turned my head, trying to look for something in the grass—anything—to hit him with.

No rocks, no sticks. I had no weapons but the dinky

lighter in my pocket, which I couldn't get to… and my magic.

Jonathan lowered his head and nosed my cheek, my jaw, my neck, inhaling my scent. The smell seemed to make him tremble, and something in his lower body—I didn't even want to imagine *that* deformed thing—hardened against my thigh.

I bit back another gag.

Oh, hell *no. This is* definitely *not happening.*

He shoved his cracked, bleeding muzzle into the curve where my shoulder met my neck and licked me, his tongue like sandpaper, his hot, sick breath coming more frantically. His jaw opened, and he bit down hard.

I braced for the pain that never came.

He had no teeth. No bite. Nothing but festering, stinking gums that smelled as rotten as the rest of him.

I took a deep breath through my mouth and closed my eyes, willing my heart rate to slow. I was in my own realm, surrounded by my own magic. Everything here was connected to me, including the Shadowrealm on the other side of the forest. This beastly *thing* might've had strength left in his body—hell, he might've been immortal, for all I knew—but he couldn't hurt me here. Not really.

In that moment, the truth blazed inside me like its own sun.

Jonathan was evil and repulsive. His appearance alone was enough to give me nightmares for the rest of my life, never mind the stench.

But I was no longer afraid of him.

He had no power over me.

A sense of utter calm descended on me like a heavy blanket, and I stopped struggling against his hold. Instead, I redirected my energy and sent a gentle call to my sacred place, pulsing my magic into the earth, sending it deep beneath the surface. I felt it trickle down through the grass like water after a rainstorm, slowly seeping into the dirt, through tangled roots and loose rocks, past earthworms and beetles and the decaying bodies of creatures long since buried. There were layers of bedrock, each colored band marking the passage of an eon, and the skeletons of creatures that no longer existed. It was a mirror of the earthly plane, one of many dimensions that touched and overlapped and called us home.

I wasn't sure how much time passed, but I felt it the moment my magic reached the source. The energies connected instantly, warming me, and the deep, ancient magic of this place twined with mine, inviting me to draw it upward, inward.

We are part of you, blood of Silversbane, came the whisper in my mind. *As you are part of us.*

My skin began to glow. The magic simmered inside me, heating my blood.

It was time.

There was no force, no explosion of sparks and violence, no out-of-control burst that shattered glass and splintered wood. Only a gentle nudge, and Jonathan was flat on his back, the air rushing back into my lungs in the absence of his crushing weight on my chest.

Unhurried, I slowly got to my feet, wiped my face on the bottom edge of my T-shirt, and searched the area for a piece of wood or a stick. I finally settled on a thick, foot-long chunk of tree bark near the forest's edge, wrapped in dried moss that seemed perfect for kindling. Certain it hadn't been there a few minutes earlier, I glanced up into the shimmering tree branches and smiled, sending the woods a silent thank-you.

A muffled grunt behind me alerted me to Jonathan's presence again, and I turned to face him, scrutinizing the sockets where his eyes used to be. "Why won't you just die?"

He shook his head in response, but I couldn't translate his answer. Maybe he didn't want to die, and haunting my realm would be his final stand. Maybe he *did* want to die, and just didn't know how. I couldn't imagine anyone—even a piece-of-shit hunter like Jonathan—would *want* to remain trapped in that form.

It wasn't a life.

It was a mistake.

Well, I certainly didn't owe him any favors, but if death was what he wanted, I'd be more than happy to put him out of his misery.

I fished the lighter out of my shirt pocket and lit the mossy end of the bark, blowing the red-hot embers to a flame.

"I'd cut off your head, half-vamp, but I didn't bring a blade. So, fire it is." I held up my makeshift torch, my own magic surging inside, warming me as much as the fire. "Fair warning… This might sting a little."

I lunged for him again, but he spun away out of my reach and dashed into the forest.

Using the torch to light my path, I chased him. He'd haunted me for far too long. This needed to end. With light, sure steps, I charged into the forest, hopping over tangled roots and fallen limbs, dodging sharp branches, ignoring the pounding of my heart as I hunted the hunter.

When I finally broke free of the thick, tangled trees, I found myself in a peaceful meadow. Jonathan was gone. I'd lost him.

But what I found instead more than made up for it.

Tears sprung to my eyes, and I extinguished and dropped my torch, blinking rapidly in the darkness until my vision adjusted, bringing them back into view.

"Emilio," I whispered. "Liam."

In the meadow before my white stone altar, Liam was on his knees beside my wolf. He looked as if he'd been there for hours, and now he stretched out a hand toward me, beckoning me forward.

"Hurry, Gray," he said, the urgency in his voice turning my blood cold. "There isn't much time."

"Time?" I crept closer, my muscles suddenly stiff with fear. Why wasn't Emilio moving? Was that… was that fresh blood on the ground? He still appeared to be trapped between his human and wolf forms, just like he had been at the warehouse. Why hadn't he shifted fully?

Why hadn't he healed?

Wordlessly I knelt down beside Liam and reached for Emilio's hand. He looked just like he had earlier tonight—gravely injured, caught between forms, carved up and poisoned by Orendiel's silver blade. But the face that had writhed in pain before had long since gone slack, and his skin was cold and clammy. His eyes were open, but they were glassy and vacant, holding no sign of the man I loved. No spark of life.

"Time for what?" I pressed, though I was pretty sure I knew the answer. My stomach was already twisting at the possibility, heart thudding in my throat.

Liam turned to me, human but for the glowing blue eyes and a faint pulse of silver-blue light emanating from his skin.

A soul, I realized. He was holding Emilio's soul.

Tears filled Liam's otherworldly eyes, and he reached for my face, touching it so sweetly and gently, it almost shattered my heart. He shook his head and closed his eyes, and the words came out slow and strangled. "It's... time to say goodbye, little witch. I'm so sorry."

NINE

DARIUS

Ronan had nearly worn a groove in the living room floor with his incessant pacing, and if there weren't so many warm bodies in the way, I might've joined him. It'd been hours since Gray and Haley had sequestered themselves in the guest room, and other than a muffled conversation early on, we'd heard nothing. Saw nothing. No news. No updates. No sign of success or trouble but the iridescent glow of magic leaking out beneath the gap at the bottom of the door.

A trickle of worry crept down my spine, but I refused to let it take hold. Refused to show even a fraction of outward concern. The others wouldn't understand; in the wake of my memory loss, their claim on her heart felt much more legitimate than mine. But while my mind was unable to remember her presence in my life, some deeper part of me *did* remember. I felt it more and more the longer I spent in her presence.

And right now, that part of me wanted nothing more than to break down the bedroom door.

I glanced at the closed door down the hall, but the sentinel posted outside of it shook his head. Asher had taken Gray's demands seriously; he and the hounds would maim anyone who attempted to disturb her.

"Perhaps she's traveled to her realm," I reasoned aloud. "It's the most logical explanation, is it not?"

Ronan grunted something that might have been an agreement, though I couldn't be certain. "That thought doesn't bring me any peace," he said. "The freakshow hunter who's tried to kill her at least a dozen times already is supposedly running wild out there. She may as well have a target painted on her back."

"Liam will protect her."

Another grunt. "I don't like it. We should be there with her."

"Hmm." I rubbed my fingers over the stubble on my jaw. "My recollection is a bit hazy, but it's my understanding that the last time we tracked her to another realm, things went a bit sideways on us."

He stopped pacing long enough to glare at me, clearly not appreciating my attempt at humor.

"Regardless," I said. "We all know that when Gray sets her mind to something—"

Ronan's grunt turned into a growl, his eyes blackening as he stormed past me on his hundredth trek across the hardwood floor. "Don't tell me what I know, vampire. You can't even tell me what *you* know."

"I'm not sure I appreciate your tone, demon."

"No? Then why don't you take your smug face and your perfect little accent and go… I don't know. Go shove a scone up your arse."

"Ronan. Darius." Deirdre emerged from the kitchen, her presence stopping me from putting Ronan into a wall. "Why don't you redirect some of that toxic male aggression and help me with the coffee?" She made her way around the room with a tray of steaming mugs, handing out coffee to the witches, some of whom had curled up together on the couch and chairs, others in smaller huddles on the floor. As exhausted as they must've been, no one had dared nod off. Not while Gray was unaccounted for and Emilio's fate was still unknown.

"And if you can't make yourselves useful," the old woman continued, "at least make yourselves quiet. The last thing Gray needs is to come back and referee a pissing contest between—"

"You're something else, you know that?" Ronan shook his head, a look of utter disgust twisting his features.

"Ronan," she said, her eyes imploring him, "we will discuss our personal differences another time."

"Differences?" he snarled. "*Differences?*"

I felt the spike in his aggression mere seconds before his eyes turned demon black.

"So," he continued, "do you want to tell them about these *differences,* or should I?"

Deirdre visibly stiffened, but her eyes blazed with a new warning. "Now is *not* the time."

"You're right, witch. Twenty years ago was the time, but you failed. You made a bad call then, and every day you keep your secrets, you're making it a hell of a lot worse. For Gray, for yourself, and for everyone else."

"I had my reasons," she said. "As did you."

"Yeah? Why don't you come over here and remind me of them?"

"Careful, demon. I'm not as old and docile as I look."

"Oh, for fuck's sake," I said, moving to stand between them. As much as I would've loved to see a brawl between a powerful old witch and a crossroads demon with an ax to grind, Deirdre was right. Now was *not* the time.

Fortunately, I was spared from having to intercede further by the opening of the front door and the sudden and rather grim entrance of the fae prince. His face was red with cold, his eyes full of something that looked a lot like fear. Real fear.

"I've finally made contact with my sister," he announced.

"Kallayna?" One of the witches on the couch asked. "Is everything okay?"

"It's… a long story," Jael said. "But the short version is that she's infiltrated the Darkwinter contingent in Blackmoon Bay under guise of a romantic relationship with one of their knights, and has been transmitting intelligence through a secured fae channel ever since. I hadn't heard from her in some time, but she finally managed to get a message out tonight, and the news isn't good."

Deirdre handed him a mug of coffee, which he accepted

with a small bow. After taking a few sips, he pulled one of the dining chairs into the living room and took a seat.

"After the surprise attack and ensuing defeat in Raven's Cape tonight," he said, "Orendiel and the remaining Dark-winter Knights, along with the hunters still loyal to the cause, retreated to Blackmoon Bay to regroup."

"We figured that might happen," Ronan said, the argument with Deirdre seemingly forgotten in the presence of a far greater foe. "As far as we know, the Bay is still under their control."

"Yes," Jael confirmed. "But I fear the situation back home has taken a turn for the worse."

"How can that be?" I asked. "They've just suffered massive casualties and the loss of their most valuable prisoners. They retreated, presumably to lick their wounds."

Jael shook his head. "Apparently, they've called in reinforcements. According to what Kallayna was able to uncover, two hundred additional knights have been dispatched to the Bay, and that's not counting the hundred or so already in place."

"Another two hundred?" Ronan let loose a heavy sigh. "We saw what they could do with less than half that number at the warehouse. It took all of us working together, with powerful magic and the element of complete surprise, just to survive the night. And not all—"

He cut off abruptly, but I knew what he'd been thinking.

And not all of us had *survived.*

I glanced down the hallway, hoping for a sign from

Gray, but there was only Asher and the hounds, as still as marble statues. Asher's eyes were alert as he listened to our conversation out here, but he wasn't moving from his post for anything.

"There's more," Jael said, his face going a shade paler. "The Bay has been locked in a brutal winter storm for several days. White-out conditions, heavy accumulation, frigid temperatures."

"What?" Ronan asked. "But we never get weather like that. I can't even remember the last time it snowed there."

"Precisely," Jael said. "Kallayna believes the weather was conjured by Darkwinter. She hasn't found proof, but the timing and nature of the storm is too suspicious to be anything natural."

"To what end?" I asked.

Jael closed his eyes and sipped his coffee, lingering over every drop. He seemed to be avoiding the question, but just before I could press him again, he finally lowered his mug and met my gaze. "According to the official news reports, which are of course controlled by Darkwinter now, the storm has resulted in the closure of the two main bridges into and out of the Bay and all ferry service to and from Seattle and the surrounding areas. Without access to the city, vendors cannot deliver necessities like food, bottled water, medical supplies, and gasoline. Prior to announcing the road and waterway closures, Darkwinter Knights—with the backing of the law enforcement community that's also under their influence—seized control of the city's grocery stores and gas stations and began rationing out food and supplies."

"Holy shit," one of the witches—McKenna, I'd heard someone call her—said. "It's like martial law."

"Yes," Jael said. "Under guise of protection from the dangerous conditions of the storm, they've instituted a mandatory travel ban and curfew."

"And no one in the Bay has questioned this? Not even the humans?"

"Everything has been designed to look like a genuine emergency, including the extreme response," Jael said. "For the first few days, people were calm and orderly, trusting that the storm would pass, that the city officials would deal with any issues. But my sister tells me that panic has started to set in. Because of the curfew and restricted travel, many people—humans and supernatural alike—have not been able to go to work or open their businesses, and there have been reports of widespread looting and property damage. The Knights could easily quell this, but we believe it's all part of their plan to destabilize the city. Children are being kept from school. People can't get medical care. Sanitation services have been suspended, so garbage is piling up, and the water supply is now at risk. Boats have been frozen in the marinas, bringing the local fishing industry to a grinding halt. There are intermittent power outages, many of the older Victorian homes and original buildings do not have modern heating systems, and now the people are almost out of food. Rations or not, that is a terrifying proposition."

"It's a powder keg," I said, the implications hitting me full on. "All the pieces are in place."

"All that's left to do now is light the match." This from Elena, who'd just emerged from her bedroom. She'd excused herself to check on Reva soon after Gray and Haley had locked themselves in the guest room, and we'd all given her some space.

Her face was gaunt, with deep lines around her mouth and eyes. She'd showered, but she still smelled of wolf's blood.

My stomach twisted. The worse part? If I could detect it, she could, too.

I met her gaze, but then realized I had nothing to offer her. No compassionate smile, no words of encouragement, nothing that would truly help. For all intents and purposes, I was as much a stranger to her brother as most of the other guests in this house.

She nodded at me anyway, a gentle smile touching her lips.

Then, crossing to the center of the living room and addressing the group, she said, "The problem, of course, is that we don't know what that match looks like or when they plan to strike it."

"Sounds like we've got some things to sort out," I said, moving to stand at Ronan's side. I put a hand on his shoulder to let him know that for my part, all was forgiven. I had no interest in fighting with my brothers, even if I didn't remember them as such, and I wanted him to know that.

"Darius is right," he finally said, making no move to shake off my hand. "We need to make a solid plan."

"I'll put on more coffee," Deirdre said. "Something tells me this endless night is about to get a lot longer."

TEN

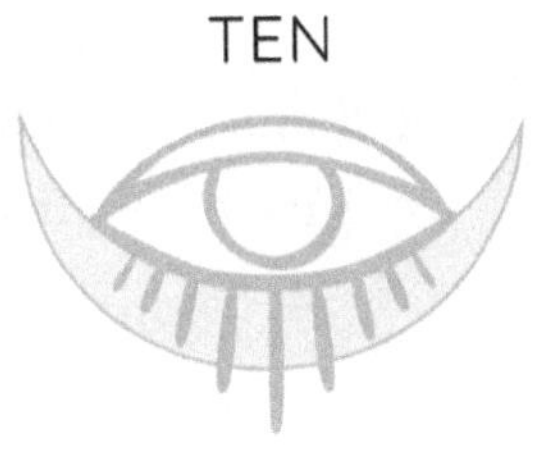

RONAN

It was damn near impossible to concentrate, but I was grateful for the challenge. It kept my mind off Gray and Emilio and Deirdre and all the other fucked-up shit swirling around inside, and right now, that was the best I could hope for. Distraction.

"So Darkwinter is amassing an army in the Bay," I said, still pacing, "where they've subdued most of the population and seized control of the city's resources. Meanwhile, we've liberated the witches, but not the hybrids the hunters created, or the other supernaturals they were experimenting on in the cave prisons."

"We're assuming they're being held elsewhere," Lansky said. "Possibly another warehouse in town, or—depending on how fast they bailed out last night—possibly in the Bay."

"You're assuming they're even *alive*," McKenna said. "From what we saw in there, none of them looked healthy.

The hunters treated those guys even worse than they treated us."

"How do you mean?" I asked, though I suspected I already knew.

"Beat the shit out of them," McKenna said. "Tortured them. Basically, they were trying to trigger their predator response."

She wasn't telling me anything I didn't know, but fucking hell, those hunters were some sick bastards.

"If we're going to be prepared for all possible scenarios," Elena said, "we need to consider the *worst*-case scenario here. So yes, we're assuming they're alive, strong, and ready to attack on Darkwinter orders."

"You think the experiments worked?" I asked her.

"I think it's possible, and therefore I want to be prepared for that possibility." Despite the dark circles under her eyes, she glanced at her notes with extreme focus, tapping the notebook with her pen, totally absorbed in the task at hand.

Seemed I wasn't the only one who thrived on distraction.

"Before the warehouse mission," she continued, "Gray and Liam confirmed that Jonathan was still alive, albeit trapped in her magical realm. As Gray described it, he'd essentially transformed himself into some sort of human-shifter-vampire hybrid. If that's true, then there's a chance similar experiments were conducted on other beings, and possibly worked in the same way."

"But she also said Jonathan was falling apart," McKenna said. "Like, literally rotting away."

"True," Elena said, "but that doesn't mean he or the others like him can't do a lot of damage before they hit their expiration date."

Detective Hobb—a shifter cop I was pretty sure was banging Elena—spoke up next.

"So if we follow the logic here," he said, shouldering his way to the center of the packed room, "let's assume they've relocated these hybrids to the Bay—or they've created new ones at that location—and that they're at least somewhat operational as an attack force. Now we've got a city that's been isolated from the rest of the country, militarized by an invading fae army, stripped of most of its necessities, banned from traveling freely, and unable to communicate with the outside world—the only exception being Kallayna."

"Exactly," Jael said. "And we don't know how often she can reliably transmit information. She's already put herself at great personal risk."

"Fair point." Elena blew out a breath. "Okay, so if you're Orendiel, and you've got an entire city on lockdown and an army to back you up, and you want to cause the most damage in the shortest amount of time, what's your play?"

"Tell you what I'd do," I said. "Assuming I was a grade-A psychopath, which I'm not."

"Debatable," Beaumont said.

I shot him a death glare, but I let him get away with that one, mostly because I still felt guilty about the scone-up-the-arse comment. *Shit.* The sooner he got his memories back, the sooner he'd remember that insults and veiled threats were how we showed affection around here, and the better off we'd all be.

"I'd strategically unleash the hybrids," I went on. "Let them cause some ruckus at the local businesses, break into houses in the different supernatural neighborhoods, tear shit up, take a few people down in the process. Make the others believe they're being attacked from within—shifters burning down law-abiding vamp houses, vamps draining fae kids, fae manipulating shifter women, demons preying on witches, that sort of fucked-up shit. Then I'd sit back and watch the whole place turn on each other. Once that happens, they'll tear each other apart—we've never been totally at peace over there, anyway. Not even among our *own* kinds, let alone across species. And they'll have nowhere to go, no one coming in to help, because the 'benevolent' Knights of Darkwinter aren't going to break up that fight for anything. It's exactly what they want."

"*Madre María*," Elena said. "You're absolutely right— Emilio and I talked about this very thing after he'd found out about Talia's betrayal. Orendiel's going to light that fire, throw some gasoline on it, and watch the whole city burn to ashes."

"No," Beaumont said. "He won't let it burn to ashes. He'll be sure the humans get involved first. Think of it—it's the perfect scapegoat with a perfect message: Monsters have been living among you, and look what they've done to each other. They'll be coming for you next." He shoved a hand through his hair, losing some of the cool elegance he was known for. "He'll use that as leverage to get them to turn over even more of their freedoms. It starts in the Bay, and it spreads outward, especially when Darkwinter are controlling the messaging and communications."

"And that, my friends," Lansky said, "is how you stage a coup."

"We're talking about mass exposure of the supernatural community," Elena said, and a collective chill went around the room. "The Bay falls, then the neighboring cities, the state, the whole west coast…"

"This may already be happening in other places," McKenna said. "Haley and Reva were telling us that Norah had heard from some of the other covens in America and even a few overseas that weird shit was going down. Witch murders, disappearances, things like that. Norah didn't want to get involved—not even when they asked for her help directly."

"Gray told us about that, too," I said. "Haley and Sophie had apparently dug up some emails or something, and tried to confront Norah. She wanted nothing to do with it."

"Because she's in league with the hunters," the older witch with the yellow eyes said. "She sold out her own kind, and as far as we know, she's still on the loose."

"That's right," Elena confirmed. "We've got an APB out on her, but other than one credit card charge, we haven't heard a peep."

"She's the least of our problems," I said. "My gut tells me her part in this is over, and now she's on the run, trying to get ahead of the very nightmare she helped unleash. Right now I'm more concerned about Orendiel's plans in the Bay and the bigger implications for the country."

The room fell silent once again, hopelessness settling in like a death shroud.

"Let's not," Beaumont said, stepping out of the shadows to stand at the center of the room. "This is all very doom-and-gloom, and it's serious—no doubt about that. But we've faced down greater odds before, haven't we?" He flashed a grin. "Well, *allegedly*. I don't remember the specifics, on account of my—"

"The point, vampire," I said, rolling my eyes. "Get to it."

"The point, dear demon," he continued, "is that we need a plan of attack, and we can't afford to get sidetracked with fear and speculation. While we know that witches have been kidnapped or murdered in other locations, we also know that the Bay, in particular, is under total siege. We have no such confirmation from any other cities or countries, so I humbly propose that we focus on the Bay first. We can assess each new situation as we receive more information, but that one has to be paramount. It's my belief that Blackmoon Bay is ground zero for this entire operation."

"Agreed," Elena said.

"Thank you," Beaumont said. "Now, as I was saying. Yes, the situation is a powder keg over there. But the match has yet to be struck. And just like the warehouse siege, we have the element of surprise. They don't know that Kallayna is a spy, nor that she is still in contact with her brother."

"That is our hope, yes," Jael said. "But even so, we

cannot physically reach them. They've isolated the city completely—not just with the storm and route closures, but with magic. Anyone who attempts to enter without Darkwinter's knowledge and express permission will be turned around before they even get close. There is literally no way to breach city limits—not on foot, not with cars, not with planes, not even with tanks. Such is the deceptive nature of their magic."

"Fair point," Beaumont said, "But..." His lips curved into another grin, his eyes glinting with a look I'd come to know well.

Hunger.

"I believe I speak for all the predators in the room when I say this: If we can't get to them, we'll just have to lure them out to us."

ELEVEN

LIAM

Gray's twilight blue eyes clouded with ice, her whole body going rigid. From her energy, I felt nothing but cool detachment, even as Emilio's soul stirred into a hot frenzy inside me, recognizing her presence.

"I'm not here to say goodbye, Liam."

All the fear and concern and horror at Emilio's outward appearance vanished. She'd said the words simply, with a calm certainty I hadn't expected, as if there could be no other outcome.

I should've expected as much. Gray had always been determined, and she was fiercely protective of those she loved.

"You must," I said, though even I remained unconvinced. Still, it was my sacred duty to say these words, to inform her of his passing and offer her the option of escorting his soul to the Shadowrealm—or accompanying me, if she so chose. "It is your last chance before we—"

"There are *no* last chances here," she said, as resolute as I'd ever seen her. "I'm a necromancer, Liam. In the truest sense of the word. I have the capacity to give life, to save it, or to destroy it."

At that, I couldn't help but allow the faintest ghost of a smile to touch my lips. She was reciting my old words back to me—from the first time I'd told her about her nature. That was the night she'd lost Sophie, and she'd come so much farther since then.

"Clever girl," I said. "But did I not also tell you that all such beings are bound to me?"

She cocked her head, glaring at me with a power that would've frightened the strongest mortal. "It's a little late for that, Liam."

"Yes, I was afraid you might see it that way."

I had failed as her mentor. I had failed as her friend. And most of all, I had failed as a man who'd claimed to love her. There was nothing I could say now, no warning or long, metaphysical explanation, no truths or lies or anything in between that would alter her present course.

Gray placed a hand on Emilio's chest, her eyes softening for him and him alone. Then, turning back to me, she drew in a deep breath and said, "I am Shadowborn. I am the heir of Silversbane. And this man has my heart. If you think for one *second* I'm going to stand by and watch him vanish into eternity while I have the power to do something about it, you haven't learned a thing about me."

I offered a solemn nod, conceding her point. In truth, however, I'd learned more than she realized. For this moment, too, was a possibility I had seen. One I had hoped for, if I were being honest.

And here, at perhaps the most important meeting she and I would ever hold, honesty was my only choice.

"I know he hasn't yet passed on to the Shadowrealm," she said. "I can *feel* him. You have his soul."

"Indeed." I held up my hands, my skin glowing silver-bright in response. "Though I'm afraid I cannot hold him much longer. If I don't release him from my vessel, he will release himself, cursed to endlessly wander the realms without a guide."

She touched his face, her eyes softening once again. "So we'll put him back where he belongs."

"It's not that simple, I'm afraid. Even for a necromancer. His body is broken, Gray. His blood poisoned. His soul sensed the death of his physical form and departed of its own volition. To return it to his body now would simply trap him in pain and torment for all eternity."

"Not if we heal him first." She got to her feet and walked a circle around his body, her brow furrowed in concentration, her hands hovering before her as if she were trying to sense the last bit of his essence. "There must be something we can do. A spell."

"Perhaps," I said, standing to meet her eyes once again. "But there is no time. Not if we want to prevent his soul from wandering."

"Think, Liam. Think." Gray pressed her fingers to her temples and closed her eyes. "There's something we're not seeing here. Some way to heal him quickly or… something."

I watched her, in awe at her courage. Her calm. She'd come through so much in such a short time, and yet she still wasn't ready to concede defeat. With Gray, there was always another way.

"Well?" She opened her eyes, the moonlight reflecting on her hair, turning it silver in its pale light, and—

"Moonlight," I said, the answer coming to me now, sharp and clear.

And, like so many things I'd experienced since Gray had come into my life, completely forbidden.

But if it meant helping her restore the life of someone she loved, I wouldn't have it any other way.

"Moonlight what?" she asked, her hands on her hips. "Liam, we don't have time for your poetic riddles tonight. What are you—"

"Quiet, Gray. I must concentrate." Lifting my hands to the sky, I called upon the magic of the ancient fae, using it to channel light from the moon. I gathered it into my hands, so pure and beautiful it nearly hurt to look at. Then, with a spell as old as time, outlawed since the first Elemental Wars, I whispered the incantations and carefully spun in into a gossamer sphere no larger than a grapefruit.

Gray gasped beside me, but she remained still and silent, allowing me to do my precious work.

With a slow exhale, I released Emilio's soul, guiding the silver-white light into the moonglass. After a final incantation, the sphere sealed itself, encasing his essence in an unbroken bubble of protective moonlight.

"Moonglass," I said, holding the feather-light globe between us. "It will contain his soul until we are ready to release it."

My owl and raven ferriers, who'd been perched silently on the black branches overhead during our entire exchange, finally took flight. Despite the mesmerizing beauty of the sphere, they knew what its making had just called forth.

Gray and I had perhaps an hour by earthly reckoning to complete our task. Perhaps an hour before I'd be called to atone for my actions, sentenced to some punishment I could only imagine.

But that was a concern for another moment. Right now, Gray and I had more important matters to consider.

"What… what is it?" she breathed, still in awe. "How does it work?"

"It's a fae spell," I explained. "Almost as old as I am. It is the only known magic that can hold a soul indefinitely without damaging it."

"I've never heard of this before."

"Moonglass has been banished for more than four thousand years. While our purpose is to return life, the original intention was not so benevolent."

Her eyes widened as she peered into the glass. Its pearly sheen changed colors, shifting from silver to white to an iridescent pink, reacting to the soul inside.

"How do you mean?" she asked.

"The first fae tricked the moon into lending them her

light, and they used it to create a device that would imprison the souls of their enemies. During times of war, they would call the light onto the battlefield, performing the spell and luring the souls of recently deceased enemy soldiers inside. Once captured, the souls could later be released into the most hostile fae realms, condemning them to an eternity of torment so much worse than anything they'd ever faced as soldiers."

She was silent for several moments, mesmerized by the beautiful, undulating sphere, and undoubtedly horrified by the tale of its origins.

"Magic like this… It doesn't come without a cost," she finally said. "I know that better than anyone."

"No, it doesn't."

She swallowed hard, then met my gaze, the opalescent swirls of the moonglass reflected in her eyes. "What will this cost?"

"It matters not. The price will be paid."

Her eyelids fluttered closed, and she sighed deeply. "Liam, despite everything that happened between us, I don't want you to… I don't want something bad to—"

"I will not lie to you again, Gray," I interrupted. "I do not know what is to come of this—only that I will be called to atone for it. That is the truth. The moment I created the moonglass, I sealed my fate. I will take whatever punishment is meted out."

"But—"

"It is done. I've no regrets about that decision now, nor will I have them later. For there is no price I wouldn't pay to bring you even a moment's peace." I gazed into her eyes, needing her to understand the depths of my feelings for her, the boundlessness of my sadness that I'd caused her any harm at all. "You must know that, Gray."

My voice had softened to a whisper, and Gray nodded, a single tear slipping from her eye. She held my gaze a moment longer, but her thoughts were veiled to me. If she thought to say something more, she decided against it, quickly swiping away the renegade tear and nodding, once again resolute.

"What *you* must decide," I explained, "is whether you're willing to accept the risks and consequences for this decision and any that may come after as we endeavor to bring him back. If you're not, you may say your goodbyes now and leave this realm, as you should have already done, and I will face those consequences alone."

At this, she let out a hollow laugh and rolled her pretty eyes. "Come on, Liam. I thought you knew me at least a little better than that. I would never bail on you."

Nor I you, little witch. Not ever again.

"We're in this together," she went on. "Even if it wasn't Emilio's soul, and you'd asked for *my* help instead of the other way around, I'd still be here for you."

"That... that means more to me than you can imagine."

"I need you to know something. Everything that happened in the past—all the things you kept from me... It changes nothing. This means more to me than all of it. *You* mean more to me."

Emotion tightened my throat, but there were no

adequate words to express my gratitude, my feelings for her. So instead, I lowered my eyes to the sphere and said, "This is the last important thing we will ever do together, Gray. Fitting that it will be the *most* important."

Without further ado, I handed her the moonglass. She took the sphere into her hands, delicately and reverently, fully aware of the importance of its contents.

"Guard it with your last breath," I warned anyway. "For if it breaks before the ritual is complete, his soul will have no vessel."

"And he'll wander forever. I understand, Liam. I won't let that happen."

"Emilio is lucky to have you as a friend. As am I." It was all I'd dare to confess. I held her unwavering gaze for the span of one more breath, and then I turned back toward her wolf. "And now we begin."

TWELVE

GRAY

The moonglass felt as delicate as a soap bubble, and I held it close to my chest, my skin warming at the contact.

Liam had said this was the most important thing we would ever do together, and I couldn't deny that. But the last thing? No. Neither of us knew what the future held, what the price of our actions tonight would be. But I had to believe this wasn't the end. Not for any of us.

Because I had to believe this would work—that we'd succeed in saving Emilio. And if we could do that, what *couldn't* we do? What challenges couldn't we overcome? What price couldn't we pay? What rules couldn't we break and re-write?

Love made all of that possible. And I *did* love Liam, I realized now. We had a lot to work through together, a lot of trust to rebuild, a lot of pain to heal. But that didn't change how I felt.

"Are you ready?" he asked, kneeling down beside Emilio's body.

I nodded, kneeling on the other side, careful to keep the moonglass safe.

"I will drain the poison from his body and attempt to heal his physical wounds," Liam said. "But you must do the rest. You have a bond with him—one that goes far beyond the physical. Your souls are connected as flames lit from a single candle."

"We are," I whispered, feeling a tug low in my belly, a warmth that stretched outward toward the sphere, longing to feel Emilio's touch.

"Gaze into the moonglass," Liam continued, his hands already moving over Emilio's wounds, assessing the damage. "Call on your love for him, your connection, and reach out to his soul. You must be as a beacon for him, Gray, for even with our guidance, if he loses his way back to his physical form, we won't be able to revive him. Do you understand?"

"Yes," I said firmly.

"Once he's found you, you must guide the soul precisely back into his body. That is done with intense focus, precise visualization, and your magic. You must imagine his soul as a river of light, and your magic as the gentle but immutable force of gravity that guides it along its path. It will require more magic than you have ever expended, more concentration than you have ever commanded, and above all, unshakable faith that you can complete this task. There is *no* room for error on this, Gray. Not unless you want to turn him into something… else."

"Bean," I breathed, and a memory flickered behind my eyes—a young girl in a unicorn hoodie, blood pooling on the pavement, her life force leaving as I held her in my arms. It was before I'd learned about my powers, about being Shadowborn, about any of it, and I'd brought her back from the dead with no clue what that would mean for her.

I'd turned her into something terrible, an undead monster, cursed.

Swallowing the lump in my throat, I nodded again. That would *not* happen. Not again. Never again.

"I can do this, Liam. I know I can." I cleared my throat, then tried again. "I will do this. I'll guide his soul, bring him home. There are no other options."

Liam stopped his ministrations and smiled, catching my gaze. "I have complete faith in you, little witch, or we would not even attempt it."

His smile was brief, but his confidence bolstered me further.

"I have complete faith in you, too," I said plainly, because that was the truth. Just as I wouldn't create another cursed soul, Liam would never disappoint me again. I knew that like I knew the taste of Emilio's brownies, the scent of his skin, the feel of his wolf's fur on my hands.

"His body is almost mended," Liam said. "There will likely be scarring, but that is better than the alternative."

"Agreed."

"Call upon your magic, Gray. It is almost time."

Letting my eyes drift closed, I sought the magic within me, urging the gentle warmth to a flame, pushing it outward through my limbs. In my mind's eye, I saw the black streaks cover my hands, slowly igniting into the blue flames I'd come to associate with my Death magic. It was hard to remember a time that I'd feared this power, that I'd recoiled from it in shame. It came so easy now, as natural a part of my being as any other.

"Good," Liam said. "You're doing great. Continue to follow my voice. I will guide you through the next steps." His voice was soothing and calm, easy to follow, like drifting down a warm and lazy river in the summer. "Use your power to tap into the source. Draw more magic into you."

I did as he asked, just like I'd done earlier when I'd been struggling with Jonathan. It took even less time now; the source seemed to be expecting my return, and eagerly connected with my magic, filling me to the absolute limits. My physical body began to vibrate, my heart racing, my teeth chattering, but I held steady.

"You're incredible, Gray," Liam said. "Now, you'll soon reach a point where you feel as if you'll absolutely burst if you take in even one more modicum of magic. Are you close?"

"I'm there," I said, my voice quavering. "I can't... hold... much longer..."

"You can, Gray. And you must," he said firmly, leaving no room for argument. "Actually, you must take even more.

Push past your perceived limitations, Gray. Emilio's life depends on it."

I obeyed without question, drawing more magic toward my center, pulling it up through my chest, pushing it into my heart and lungs, my veins, filling myself beyond capacity. Brightness surged before my eyes, and I didn't have to open them to know that the light was coming from my own skin, barely able to contain this much power. My heart was now beating so rapidly it sounded like a snare drum in my ears, but I kept my breathing steady. Calm. Balanced. Even as every inch of me wanted to explode—to scream, to tear, to burst apart at the seams and unleash this magic.

But still, I held on.

Still, I drew more. I drank it in deep, fraying my nerves, grating my bones, squeezing my cells.

"You are almost there, Gray. Hold on."

I nodded, too afraid that opening my mouth now would let loose some of the magic.

"Okay," he continued. "When I give you the signal, I want you to open your eyes, smash the moonglass, and channel all of that magic into sending Emilio's soul back to his earthly vessel—just like we talked about. Can you do that?"

I nodded again, despite the dizziness making my head swim. My entire body was simply humming with magic, buzzy like a live wire after a rainstorm.

"Now, Gray!" Liam shouted. "Now!"

My eyes flew open, and I smashed the moonglass on the ground beside me. Emilio's soul spiraled outward, the purest silver-white I'd ever seen, so beautiful and breath-taking it brought tears to my eyes.

"Reach out for him, Gray. You must let him know you're here."

I blinked rapidly, refocusing, corralling the wild magic inside me. Lifting my hands, I sent out a concentrated pulse, guiding it around the silvery mist of his soul, urging the two energetic forces to connect. At first, I felt nothing—saw nothing—and a flare of panic rose in my chest.

But I ushered it out, quickly re-centering myself. This magic was mine. I could bend it to my will, direct it to my ends, guide it to bring back the man I loved. I had faith in myself, just as Liam had in me.

I relaxed, slowly increasing the pulse of my magic. It was a struggle to control it, but I held on. Familiar blue flames engulfed my hands again, surging bright, and I extended those flames, guiding them around his soul. At first, the mist recoiled, but then it finally stilled.

"Emilio," I said, pushing past the tremor in my voice. "It's me. Gray. Your *brujita*. I love you so, so much. Please come back to me. Follow the sound of my voice and come back to yourself."

"Good," Liam said. "Keep talking."

"You have nothing to fear," I told Emilio. "I will guide you every step of the way. But you need to want this, *El Lobo*. You need to want to come to your family. Me, Ronan, Asher, Darius, and Liam, too. Elena and her partners. The witches we saved from the prison. All of us are waiting for you at home. Your sister is already preparing a big feast.

Empanadas, I'm told." I kept talking, reminding him of all the guys, of the things we'd done together, the things we'd yet to do, the jokes we'd shared. Only good things. The sweetest moments, the happiest times, the love and camaraderie we'd all been building together. The moments, both big and small, that had bonded us together and made us a found family in the truest sense.

"You and the others found *me*," I reminded him. "Twice —when I'd first arrived in Blackmoon Bay, scared and alone. And more recently, after I'd lost Sophie. You helped me put the pieces back together, Emilio. You've healed my heart in ways you can't even imagine. Well, now it's my turn to come out and find *you*. To bring you home to us where you belong. So please don't make my job harder, *El Lobo*. Or you're going to owe me twice as many brownies later."

I didn't stop, not even to take a breath. For what felt like hours, I spoke to my beloved wolf, weaving a story of love and hope and friendship, of family and laughter, of joy, each shared memory a breadcrumb for him to pick up and follow home.

I spoke until my body was numb from lack of movement. And then, finally, when my voice was cracking and my tongue thick, I felt the change.

The magic inside me heated, and the air stirred, lifting the loose curls from my face and enveloping me in the familiar scents of trees and fresh-baked sweetness that could only belong to one man.

Tears spilled down my cheeks, and the words of my

stories turned into a spell, coming to me unbidden, but absolutely welcome.

> *I am your guide*
> *And you are my love*
> *In body and spirit*
> *Below and above*
> *Blood follows heart*
> *And heart follows soul*
> *What was once torn apart*
> *Shall now be made whole*

I repeated the spell a dozen times, visualizing Emilio's soul returning to his body, just like Liam had instructed. Even when my voice had finally given out and my throat was throbbing and raw, still I said the words, no more than whispers of breath now, finally fading out as the last of the magic and strength left my body.

On my final word, I collapsed, falling backward onto the ground, my eyes glazed, the glittery night sky a swirl of blue and white overhead.

I took deep, cool breaths of night air, waiting for my body to come back to itself. To stop its vicious trembling. To still.

I didn't even have the strength to turn my head or ask Liam whether we'd succeeded.

But then I felt the warmth of Liam's touch on my cheek. Slowly, his face came into focus, his all-knowing eyes looking down at me, shining with something that looked a lot like pride.

"Gray, you did it. You did it."

Before I could even return his smile, darkness descended, and thick, black smoke settled over us like a cloak. The ground beneath me rumbled, making my stomach pitch, my head spin. I tried to sit up, but couldn't —some force far greater than my own weakness was holding me down, sitting on my chest like an invisible monster, crushing the breath from my lungs.

I couldn't see. Couldn't hear. For the longest seconds of my life, there was only fear, rising inside me like a new fire, ready to consume everything in its path.

And then, in the wake of seemingly utter chaos, a spark of hope.

The darkness pulled back, revealing the stars once again, and all at once, the sounds came rushing back.

Another breeze, stirring me back to life.

A sharp intake of breath from the body beside me.

A rattling cough.

Another deep breath, this one more steady than the last.

And the faint sound of a familiar name, the most beautiful music I'd ever heard.

"*Querida?* Is that you?"

THIRTEEN

LIAM

The earthquake in Gray's realm was merely a warning. I had just enough time to send Gray and Emilio back to the material plane before the ground before me split wide open, trees toppling into the gash, the stone altar cracking in two. The pentacle-carved slab on top slid to the ground and shattered. The stars winked out, and darkness veiled the moon, turning the realm a murky gray.

And then *they* arrived.

From the newly formed chasm in the forest floor, a smoky essence emerged, dark and dense, its presence turning the air acrid, burning my eyes and my flesh, sending me to my knees.

It was nothing I hadn't expected. I just hadn't realized it would be so excruciating.

Known only as the Old One, the essence was nothing and many things all at once. Eternity. Power. Emptiness.

Completion. The void. The end, the beginning, and everything in between.

And, for all intents and purposes, my maker.

The Old One surrounded me, filled me, claimed my breath. Its formless voice was both singular and infinite, slicing through my mind and echoing in my skull, the raw, uncut power of it nearly shattering my vessel's bones.

"Lord of Shadows," the voices boomed. "It is long since we have last spoken. Longer still since we have been called to investigate the breaking of one of our most sacred laws."

It was an accusation, not a greeting, and though my instincts forced me to bow my head in deference to my superior, I wasted no time with return pleasantries.

"I could not let him pass into the Shadowrealm as such," I stated plainly, eyes downcast. "He is tied to her destiny in ways we cannot yet fathom, even with the gift of foresight."

"It matters not," came the emotionless reply. "He was to pass on. That was *his* destiny. The destiny of your witch is irrelevant."

"My witch, if you must call her so, is the Silversbane heir. She loves this man, and he loves her. I could not in good conscience allow that bond to be broken in such a way. Both of them deserve better."

"You are Death and Shadow, Lord of these lands and ferrier of souls between realms. Conscience does not concern you. Nor do the specifics of prophecies, Silversbane or otherwise, nor the emotional frailties of a witch who, for all the power inherent in her blood, is still scarcely more than a child."

At this, I got to my feet. The Old One had the power and right to scold me, to banish me, to torture me, as was their way in the face of abject disobedience. But I would *not* let them speak of Gray so dismissively. Not while I still had strength left in my vessel to defend her.

"The woman you call a child," I said, struggling to keep my tone respectful, "is destined to prevent the slaughter of thousands. *Millions*. Humans, vampires, shifters, fae, witches, countless others—your children. All of us would be wise to support her."

The smoke thickened around me, inside me, forcing a cough from my chest before it finally retreated, giving me a modicum of breathing room. Hovering over the ground before me, it roiled and twisted into the rough shape of a man, large and looming, with cavernous pits for eyes that glowed like lava. There was no mouth.

"Do not presume to speak to us of wisdom," the voice warned, and I stumbled a step backward from the splitting pain in my skull. "The witch is by all rights an abomination. She should have died long ago, many times over. Her life scroll has already been burned, has it not?"

It wasn't a question, merely another accusation. One I wouldn't deny.

"Yet she persists," I said. "Her strength, her fortitude, her compassion, her love for—"

"She survives by breaking our natural laws and

mocking the semblance of order we've abided by since the dawn of consciousness. She simply should not be."

"That doesn't change the fact that she *is*." I regained my footing and approached the smoky essence again, my feelings for Gray propelling me forward. She was with me always; by my nature I transcended the bounds of time, experiencing her every wondrous touch as if it were the first again, as if it were merely moments ago, as if she were standing right beside me.

The memory of our last kiss arched like fire across my lips.

"There is a spark in her," I said, "the likes of which I've not seen in others of her kind. I have learned a great deal during the time and space I've shared with her, and—"

"Learned a great deal?" The voice was mocking now. Cruel. "It seems you have *forgotten* a great deal, as well. Including your sacred oath."

I closed my eyes and lowered my head, the collective weight of the Old One's accusations piling high on my shoulders. I would carry the weight of my discretions for the rest of my existence, for it was true—I'd broken sacred oaths for her. I'd strayed from my path. I'd... I'd changed.

I was Death, the Great Change, the Ultimate Transformation. How many times had I told Gray just that, trotting out the appellations like badges granting me supreme authority?

A smile touched my lips. In the end, it wasn't the Shadowborn witch who'd been changed so drastically by our relationship.

It was me.

"Indeed, I have forgotten things," I conceded, my eyes meeting those glowing pits once again. "But I cannot regret the things I've received in exchange. Despite all that I've forgotten or discarded, there is one thing I know beyond the shadow of all doubts." I recalled the sight of the moon-glass, Emilio's soul swirling inside as Gray held him close. In that moment, I'd felt his thoughts, the ache of past regrets he'd feared he'd never have the opportunity to make right.

And I felt his love for Gray, burning brighter with every passing second.

"In the face of his sudden departure," I continued, "her spark would've been utterly extinguished. And the darkness of that loss would echo across the realms for eternity."

"For her, you have disobeyed your sacred duties at all turns. You say that her loss would've echoed across the realms, yet do you not believe that your own actions would have similar consequences?"

"It matters not," I admitted, "for I would do it all again, through time immemorial, if it meant sparing her even the briefest touch of heartbreak." Shame flared inside my chest for all the pain I'd already caused her, but I spoke the truth. "I will not bring the witch to harm again. *That* is my solemn oath now, and in obeying it, I must also serve those to whom her heart belongs. I must love and protect them as my kin."

"You've no obligation to her guardians."

"Obligation, no. But respect. Gratitude." And, dare I

hoped, should we survive what was to come, brotherhood. Family, just like Gray had said when she'd brought Emilio back to his body.

For that is what we'd become, Gray's men and I. Regardless of their feelings toward me, regardless of my form on this realm or another, regardless of my many mistakes and missteps, our love for her bound us as family.

I knelt down in the grass again, placing my hands on the impression Emilio's body had left behind, making my final decision. "I will not carry him through the gates to the Shadowrealm on this night or any that follow. Nor will I defend my decision further. This matter is closed."

"Very well. In creating moonglass and sharing it with the Silversbane witch, you have brought it forth from the mists of legend and into the realm of thought, idea, and possibility once again. Your primal oath has been broken, and even now, you remain defiant. As such, you shall inherit the consequences of this decision, to be determined by cosmic tribunal at such a time as we deem appropriate."

I bowed as low as I dared, respectful once again.

But not remorseful.

Not regretful.

And not ashamed.

"So it shall be," I said, expecting—and hoping for—its immediate retreat.

But the Old One lingered.

The glowing eyes dimmed, the smoke thinning, but still, it did not vanish.

Suddenly I felt it inside me again, filling my chest,

surrounding Liam Colebrook's heart. *My* heart. It beat frantically as a mouse caught by a predator, desperate for escape. My body flooded with fear. Adrenaline.

And beneath all of that, something else.

Hope.

"Your human heart shall be your downfall, Lord of Shadows," the voice echoed ominously. "And the downfall of those you've come to love as well."

Your human heart…

Hope surged, drowning out the fear. The Old One had touched upon something deeply personal within me; I'd never felt more human than I did in that moment, knowing I'd broken my sacred vows beyond all repair, knowing that I'd made my choices willingly, knowing that I'd sacrificed something precious so that others might have a chance at something even better.

"Perhaps," I countered, the beat of that almost-human heart as loud and steady as a drum in my ears, "it shall be our savior instead."

FOURTEEN

EMILIO

Snatches of memory flickered behind my eyes. The flash of magic... My wolf form lunging at a fae soldier... The metallic taste of his blood filling my mouth. The fierce clanging of swords reverberated off the walls. Ronan shouting, running toward me. Elena in the line of fire. Ronan's face, stricken and panicked.

And then came the burning. Poison. My body feeling like it was consuming itself just to escape.

Pain. So much pain, and everyone around me screaming, all at once. Shouting orders. Ronan bent over me. Elena, tears leaking from her eyes. And Gray, holding my hand...

Fire. Smoke. So hot, and still so much pain.

And then…. Nothing. I was floating, soaring like a bird through the night sky until the inferno at the warehouse was nothing more than a tiny point of light on an infinite black canvas.

There was a tug, a presence, something telling me to let go. I wanted to. Anything to make the pain end. But then her voice broke through the mindless haze, clear as a song on a silent night.

Mi brujita bonita, calling me home…

Gray, I mouthed, but no sound came out. I felt the beating of my heart in my chest, the blood running through my veins, strong and clear once again. I smelled the antiseptic scents of floor cleaner and medicine and gauze. My skin crawled with an itch so deep I was sure it would never fade.

But I was alive. I knew it with every fiber of my being. I was alive.

My head was heavy, my body trying to drag me back into a deep sleep, but I fought it. Where had I ended up? I had to see. Had to know. Slowly, I forced my eyes to open, recoiling at the sudden flood of white light.

I tried again. A peek. A little wider. Shapes and shadows emerged before me, filling in the light. Molecule by molecule, it seemed, my surroundings finally solidified.

I was in a bed, taped up with bandages, wearing nothing but gauze and a flannel sheet covering my lower half. It smelled like me. It smelled like Gray. The room was familiar, as was the woman keeping vigil at my bedside.

Gray, I mouthed again, but no, it wasn't her scent.

The woman beside me was my sister, seated in a chair next to the bed, her back ramrod straight, her hand resting on my forearm. Her face was turned in profile, her gaze focused on something outside the window.

She hadn't seen me yet, and I took the stolen moment to watch her. To re-memorize the shape of her face, the color of her hair. She had a few years on me, but when we were children, people used to think we were twins.

Same golden skin. Same wavy black hair. Same smiles.

It was a long time ago.

I finally shifted in my bed to let her know I was awake, and her head snapped toward me immediately.

I grinned, the last of the lingering fuzziness clearing from my mind.

Elena gasped at the sight of me, slapping a hand over her mouth. A smile peeked through around the edges of her fingers, making the skin around her brown eyes crinkle.

A flood of silent tears leaked down her cheeks.

"*¿Que pasa?*" I teased, testing out my voice. It was cracked and raw, but the words came out anyway. "*Jesús, María, y José.* You look like somebody *died*, Elena."

At this, my sister burst out laughing.

Dios mio, that was a good sound to come home to.

"You *asshole*," she said, smacking my shoulder, but she was still laughing. "You had us all scared out of our minds, thinking we'd be planning a funeral this weekend, and now you're cracking jokes?"

"What better time for a laugh than when you're standing on Death's door?"

"Speaking of Death's door," she said, "where is your friend Liam? I've got a few choice words for him, too."

Liam... At the sound of his name, a new memory surfaced, but I couldn't hold on to it. He'd been there that night, I was sure of it now. Helped me somehow. But that was all I had.

"I haven't heard from him," I said, still chasing that memory. But it was gone, like so many others from that night. Perhaps that was for the best. "As far as I know, he's still tracking Jonathan in Gray's realm."

Elena narrowed her eyes, but if she knew more, she wasn't saying a word.

I sat up a bit, and Elena propped an extra pillow behind my head. That, too, smelled like Gray, and I glanced around the room, searching for her, though I knew she wasn't here. The scent of her on my sheets was fading.

"She's resting," Elena said, answering the question before my lips had even formed the words. "For the first time in days. It took all of us multiple attempts and a few threats to convince her to finally leave your side for more than just a quick bite to eat and a trip to the bathroom."

"So she's... okay?"

Elena smiled. "Tired from the ordeal, but yes, Emilio. Now that you're here, we're all okay."

"And the witches? Reva? Haley and the others?"

"All present and accounted for. Getting stronger every day. I should know—I'm feeding and housing them. All this time, Emilio, I had no idea how much these women could eat!"

"You love it, and you know it."

"Guilty as charged. It's been a long time since I've had a full house. As chaotic as it is, it's also kind of nice. Big meals. Late-night talks. Fighting over the bathrooms." She took my hands in hers, her smile slowly slipping away. She held my gaze a moment longer, then looked out the window again, her attention drifting back to whatever she'd been watching before I'd woken up.

Wind howled against the side of the house, lashing the windows with heavy, wet snow I'd only just begun to notice—fiercer than any storm I'd ever seen in the Pacific Northwest.

"Wow," I said. "How long have I been out?" I was sure it'd been months. I'd probably missed Christmas, missed New Year's. It might be past Valentine's Day for all I knew.

"Three days," Elena said. "In and out of consciousness as your body healed."

I blew out a breath. Three days? That was a relief. "What's with the snow?"

"They're saying on the news it's a once-in-a-lifetime storm," Elena said, though something in her voice had changed. Was that *fear* I detected? "It started in the Bay and has been working its way westward ever since. Most of the state is feeling the impacts." She rattled off snowfall amounts and temperatures, wind chill factors, all the facts and figures as if she were a weather reporter. But she was holding back the deeper truth. I could practically smell the lies of omission in her blood.

"Elena. What aren't you telling me?"

She shook her head, turning her gaze on me once again and forcing a smile. "There's plenty of time for catching up and making plans of attack now that you're awake. Right now, I want you to focus on healing. Can you do that for me?"

She swept the hair from my forehead, a gesture so unexpectedly sweet and motherly it made my throat tighten. She must've seen the emotion in my eyes, but this time she didn't look away or change the subject or feign some excuse about getting dinner started. Instead, she held my gaze, her own deepening with a mix of shadows and regrets and memories and even, most shocking of all, love.

"What are you thinking, Lainey?" I whispered.

The sound of her childhood nickname was foreign to us both, and the shock of it showed in her face. But still, she didn't break our connection. Not this time.

"I was thinking about that old saying about anger and forgiveness," she said. "How holding a grudge is like drinking poison and waiting for the other person to die."

I hadn't been expecting such a dark turn, but I shouldn't have been surprised. All evidence pointed to the fact that I'd nearly died in the warehouse that night. It made sense that my sister would be thinking about all the unsaid, unsettled things left between us—things we'd ignored for two decades. Hell, I couldn't be certain, but as I lay on that concrete floor, blood leaking out of my organs, I was pretty sure my own stockpile of regrets had flashed through my mind.

"For so many years," she continued, "I pretended you didn't exist. Did you know that?"

I shook my head. How could I know? The last thing she'd ever said to me was "Leave me, and don't ever come back," a broken whisper from a broken woman whom I would've done anything to make whole again. Until I'd called her about the Landes murder and Jonathan's connections in Raven's Cape, we hadn't spoken a word to each other in two decades.

"It's true," she said. "It was the only way I could let go of even a *fraction* of the rage I felt toward you." She closed her eyes and shook her head, pressing her lips together so tightly they turned white. "Whenever anyone asked about my family, my home, I told them I'd been an only child, adopted by a couple in America when I was very young."

I sighed, my heart breaking. My for-public-consumption backstory had been similarly constructed, similarly terrible.

The only person I'd ever told about Elena was Ronan, and even he didn't know the whole story.

"That night at the warehouse," she continued, her face going a few shades paler, "seeing you on the floor like that, the blood… I thought I'd lost you, Emilio Alejandro Alvarez. I thought I'd have to see that name carved into a tombstone. And for the first time in twenty years, I realized you *hadn't* stopped existing for me. You never will."

Tears glazed her eyes, her pain so raw and real I had to look away. "We share the same blood, Elena. That alone connects us, even if we'd never spoken again."

"No, it's more than that." She wiped her eyes. "I spent so long wishing you'd never existed, and then I almost got my wish the other night. I was a monster, I realized. A fool. All that hatred, all that wasted time and energy, none of it ever brought my baby back. And now I was going to lose my brother on top of it all. When I got home that night, I went to my room and prayed. I prayed to *Jesús* and *Madre María*. I prayed to the saints. I prayed to the ghosts of Mamá and Papá and my husband and daughter. I prayed to every goddess I could name, and when I ran out of goddesses, I moved onto the gods, and then the universe, and then the stars, and anyone or anything else that would listen. Because in that moment, when I looked down and saw your blood covering my hands, I knew in the depths of my soul that I didn't want to lose you. Not again. No matter what happened in the past."

The force of her emotions hit me like a wave, and I closed my eyes, nearly drowning in the guilt I'd kept at bay for so many years. It was a constant force, and now it surged, as dense and heavy and dangerous as a black hole, threatening to drag me under for the last time.

"Emilio," she said softly, her hand against my cheek, and I opened my eyes to find her face streaked with fresh tears. "I don't want to waste any more time pretending I don't have a brother. We've lost so many years already."

"So many I've almost lost count." I swallowed the thickness in my throat. "I'm sorry, Elena. I'm so sorry. I was sorry then, and I've never stopped wishing for a time machine to go back and do it all differently. I never meant…"

I trailed off. She'd heard variations of this apology many times, and it hadn't changed anything.

I almost expected her to turn her back again. To order

me out of her life, out of Raven's Cape, never to return. I wouldn't have blamed her.

If it weren't for me, her family might still be alive.

But instead, she looked at me, the look in her eyes more vulnerable and hopeful than I'd ever seen, and said, "I want to let you back in. I just… I just don't know how. All that time, all that anger, still so many questions that I know you don't have answers for… There's a wall around my heart when it comes to you, and I can't find a way to crack it. Not yet."

I took her hand in both of mine and held it close, grateful beyond words that she'd shared that with me. For so long, I thought she was lost to me, and I'd tried to make my peace with that, though I'd never succeeded.

And now, she'd given me new hope, no matter how fragile. No matter how distant.

"So what do I do, Meelo?" she asked, her voice cracking on my old nickname. "Let you in, even after everything?"

"I can't answer that for you, Lainey." I pressed a kiss to her hand. "But I'm glad you want to try."

"But where do we go from here?"

"Nowhere. We just stay here. Right here. Take it day by day. Maybe one of those days, we'll find the first crack in the wall." I smiled, reaching up to smooth away the last of her tears. "Or maybe you'll get tired of me and decide to add some more bricks, make it even stronger, add some turrets and battlements on the top, a couple of armed guards, a cannon, a cauldron of boiling oil…"

"Okay, okay, I get it." She rolled her big brown eyes, a

faint smile touching her lips. "You watched too much American TV as a child. I tried to warn Mamá, but she never listened."

"Day by day," I repeated, my tone serious again. "Fair enough?"

She tucked her hair behind her ears and nodded, her smile growing a fraction wider. "Day by day. Yes, I think I can manage that," she said, and the heaviness that had descended between us dissipated in an instant, burned away like fog in the morning sun.

"He's awake?" A familiar voice called out from the doorway, and I turned to find my *brujita*, tears filling her eyes as she clasped her hand over her mouth, just like my sister had done. It made me smile.

"And doing much better now that you're here," Elena teased. "Hmm. Look at that color in his cheeks! It's like someone just flipped him over and gave him a shot of adrenaline right in the—"

"Arm," I finished for her.

"Sure, Meelo. If you say so." She gave me a wink, smoothing her hand over my cheek once more.

"I'm… I'm sorry," Gray said. "I didn't mean to interrupt. I can come back later."

"Don't be silly." Elena rose from her chair and stretched. "We were just finishing up."

"For now," I reminded her.

"*Sí, mi hermano.* For now." She smiled one more time, her eyes bright, her shoulders squared. It was like a weight had been lifted, one we'd both been carrying for far too long.

I didn't dare admit it out loud, but that smile of hers did more to heal my wounds than all the medicine and bandages in the world. For the first time in twenty years, Elena had given me hope that she might one day forgive me. And in that forgiveness was the seed of something even more powerful: if my sister could find a way to forgive me after everything I'd done, maybe I could find a way to forgive myself, too.

"Elena," I called out, just as she reached the door.

She squeezed Gray's hand, then turned to look at me over her shoulder. "*Sí?*"

"Empanadas for dinner tonight. Lots of 'em. Piles and piles. With extra chimichurri."

"So demanding, this wolf! As if I'm his personal chef!" She let out a put-upon huff, but I saw the covert little wink she'd flashed at Gray, and I knew without a doubt there'd be a feast waiting for me tonight.

FIFTEEN

GRAY

It'd been so long since I'd heard Emilio's voice, I was afraid this was just another dream. Tentatively, I reached out to stroke his cheek, rough with several days' worth of stubble. His black hair was getting long, curling over the tops of his ears in a way I suspected he'd hate if he could actually see it, but to me he was beautiful. Warm and alive and really, truly here.

"No need to wait for an invitation, *querida*." He opened his arms, waving me in for a hug despite the bandages wrapped around his chest. "I know you want a piece of this."

"But your injuries…"

"Paper cuts compared to how it feels not being able to hold you. Especially when you're standing right next to me, smelling like strawberries and sunshine and everything I want to be close to for the rest of my life."

His voice had faded to a whisper, his eyes serious and

intense, and in that moment, every last protest died on my lips. I leaned in close and buried my face against his chest, not bothering to keep the tears in check. They soaked right down through his bandages—tears of relief, tears of joy, tears of love, tears for every emotion I'd been struggling to keep in check since the moment I'd seen him fall beneath Orendiel's silver blade.

"Don't you ever scare me like that again," I whispered.

He cupped the back of my head. His hand was big and warm and strong, and right now, it felt like the only thing keeping me from falling off the edge of the earth.

He was here. He was really, truly here.

"I'll do my best, *mi brujita.*"

"That's not good enough." I lifted my head so I could look into his eyes. "I'm serious, Emilio. What we're building here... It doesn't work without you. *I* don't work without you."

He said nothing at that, only nodded, the depths of his brown eyes so beautiful it almost hurt to look at them. I leaned in close, brushing my lips across his mouth, my kiss as gentle as a breeze.

But before I could pull back, his hands were in my hair again, holding me close as he deepened our kiss. I parted my lips, and his tongue swept across mine, unleashing a soft moan from deep inside me as his sweetness flooded my senses.

It was so precious, so special. And I'd come so close to losing it.

Never again.

Without breaking the kiss, I slid into the bed beside him, leaning against his body, threading my hands into his hair. Heat emanated from his skin, and I breathed in his vanilla-and-pine scent, welcomed the scratch of his stubble against my chin, memorizing every sensation. This kiss was the first of the rest of our lives, the second-chance welcome-back embrace I'd been dreaming about, and I intended to carry it with me always. Forever.

He shifted beside me, pulling my leg across his hips, his hand sliding up the back of my thigh. *God,* I'd missed his touch, missed the feeling of being small and safe and well-protected in the arms of my big, muscular wolf, and under his powerful grip, it wasn't long before I'd forgotten all about his injuries.

We kissed long and hard, slow and sensual, teasing and gentle, every kind in every way until I could no longer feel my lips. When we finally broke for air, I turned over on my back, my head bent against his, staring at the ceiling and thanking all the forces of the universe for making this possible.

"Now look what you've done, *brujita,*" Emilio teased.

I followed the line of his gaze down to the sheet draped over his hips, now tenting upward.

"Hmm." I nuzzled his neck. "That looks… uncomfortable."

"I'm not so sure about that. Would you like to try it on and find out?"

"Please." I laughed. "Spare me the crass jokes. Now you sound like Asher."

"Hey, I faced down Death and got another chance. If you think I'm going to waste any more time holding back my thoughts—even the dirty ones…" He turned toward me and kissed me again, a soft moan rumbling in his chest.

Desire flooded my core, but I didn't dare act on it. I'd just gotten him back, and from the dark circles under his eyes, I could tell he still needed a lot of rest.

The patient himself, however, had other plans.

"What do you think, doc?" he asked, turning on his hip. His hard length pressed against my outer thigh, and it took every ounce of willpower I had not to slide my hand beneath the sheet and touch him. "Is this wolf cleared for physical activity?"

"I'm not a doctor, Emilio," I said.

"Maybe not. But you can *definitely* make things better for me."

I gave him a playful eye-roll. "Who *is* this wise-cracking, innuendo-dropping beast in my bed, and what have you done with sweet, kind Emilio Alvarez?"

"You really want to know? Fine. I've fallen in love with a *bruja*, that's what I've done." His voice dropped to a sultry whisper as he traced my lips with his fingertip. "And nothing will ever be the same again."

I gave in to the magnetic pull of his words, of his eyes, leaning into his embrace once again. Each kiss was deliberate now, intense, as if he were kissing me for the very last time and wanted to memorize the taste of me.

"I thought I'd never see you again, Gray," he whispered.

"That night in the warehouse… It's a blur. But you were there. With me every step. I thought—"

"Shhh." I kissed him again, too scared to go down this path, to rehash the moment Orendiel's blade cut through the air, to revisit everything that had come after. But it was too much to hold back, and seconds later, I was breaking our kiss, my heart twisting, my eyes filling with tears at what tonight would feel like if he *hadn't* made it back. "I know," I said. "I know, because that night, when I saw the blood… I thought I'd never hold you like this again, or kiss you or watch the moonrise or eat a whole pan of brownies with you. It all happened so fast, and then Ronan was shouting at me to get the others to safety, and I just…"

I trailed off and closed my eyes, the memories still so fresh, so present.

"I'm so sorry, *querida*. To put you through that… I never… It was stupid."

"You have nothing to be sorry for, Emilio. You were there to help our friends. To liberate innocent witches. To help us restore the balance of power to our communities. You're a hero. You know that, right?"

"Hero? I could've ruined the entire mission." He shook his head, his earlier humor receding. "I was a fool. I left myself wide open for the attack—rookie mistake. But I saw Elena in the line of fire, and in that moment, all I could think about was saving her. I couldn't let her fall, Gray." His jaw flexed, his eyes going to some faraway place I couldn't see. "Not there. Not again."

"Not… again?" I placed my hand over his heart, my brow creased with confusion. "What do you mean?"

"Hmm?" He shifted his gaze back to mine, his eyes cloudy. Perhaps he hadn't meant to say all of that out loud, but now that he had, there was no taking it back.

"You said you couldn't let her fall again," I said.

"I… I did." He sat up higher in the bed, sliding an arm beneath my head, but not meeting my eyes. Instead, he watched the window, the snowflakes piling high along the bottom edge. It was a Darkwinter-induced storm, they'd told me. Fae magic meant to isolate the residents of Blackmoon Bay. Eventually, it would do the same thing here.

But right now, safe in the arms of my wolf, I thought it was beautiful.

After what felt like hours, Emilio leaned over and kissed the top of my head. Then, speaking softly into my hair, "Do you know why I became a cop, *querida*?"

I shifted onto my hip, trying to look into his eyes, but he was back to watching the snow fall.

"We never really talked about it," I said. "I guess I just figured you wanted to help people. Supernaturals, especially."

"I did. I do," he said. "And I'm good at it, Gray. I feel like I'm really, truly meant for this work."

"I *know* you are."

"But that's not why I do it."

I waited, slipping my hand beneath the sheet to find his. He laced our fingers together, and I squeezed him tight, sensing that he needed the reassurance.

"I... I'm atoning," he said. "I never put it into words before, but I see that now. I wanted to help our kind in Blackmoon Bay because I couldn't help them in Mendoza."

"Atoning? That's a strong word, Emilio."

"Not strong enough."

"But... atoning for what?"

He finally tore his gaze away from the window, turning to look at me once again. What I saw was shocking; there was so much pain and regret in his eyes, it scared the hell out of me. This man had faced death, come back from it. Yet whatever he was thinking about now had been more traumatic than even that. I had never seen him so wounded. So ashamed.

"Emilio," I whispered, squeezing his hand even tighter. "What is it? What's wrong?"

"Do you remember that night," he said, "when we got the call about Reva? When you and Elena were having a midnight snack?"

"Of course." I was still carrying the weight of my conversation with Elena—the things she'd revealed to me. Even after everything we'd endured since that night, her story still haunted me.

Her husband—her true mate—had been slaughtered, along with her three-year-old child.

"She told me that her husband and daughter had been killed," I told him, though I suspected he'd heard as much. He'd interrupted us to tell us about a call from the RCPD— that Reva was waiting for us at the station. Still, it seemed like he needed me to say it again. To make absolutely sure I knew where the rest of this conversation was headed. "She said the two of you barely escaped Argentina with your lives. That even your parents... Everyone... I'm so sorry, Emilio."

My words were useless, but I had to say them. I *was* sorry. They'd lost their parents, their family, their pack. Sometimes I wondered how they even found the strength to get out of bed in the morning.

"We lost everyone we loved except for each other," Emilio confirmed. "But Elena... Did she tell you why?"

"Not specifically. Just that your pack had been betrayed."

"It's true," he said, and by the sadness in his voice, I suddenly knew what was coming next, even before he said the words. I wanted to press my fingers to his lips and stop him, to kiss away his confessions before they escaped, to preserve his and Elena's private grief and the trauma of what was obviously a very personal, very terrible situation.

But when he met my eyes again, I saw the truth: Emilio *needed* to say these words. To confess.

Perhaps, I realized, it was the very first time he'd ever felt able to do so.

"Our pack *was* betrayed, *querida*," he said. "By me."

SIXTEEN

"These roads are absolute shite," Beaumont grumbled.

"Be glad you're not the one driving." I took my foot off the gas again and peered out the windshield, trying to keep a little distance between our vehicle and the taillights in front of us—the van Lansky and Jael were in. But the task was proving futile. They were sliding around as much as we were, and even though the plows had been through recently, the snow was accumulating faster than they could keep up.

"This is insane," Haley said from the backseat. "I've never seen so much snow."

"That's because it's totally un-fucking-natural." I clicked on the wipers, trying in vain to keep my view clear, but it was useless. The snow was falling in big gobs, reflecting the light from our headlights until it looked like we were doing warp speed through outer space. The woods didn't help— the pines were several stories tall, their branches thick with heavy, wet snow, blocking out any ambient light we might've picked up from neighboring towns.

Our plans to lure the Darkwinter Knights out of the Bay had been temporarily put on hold in light of the crazy storm, and for the last couple of days our focus had been shoring up the house and making sure we had the supplies we needed to wait out the weather.

The five of us had just finished up a major supply run in Baldersville, a few towns down the highway from the Cape, middle of fucking nowhere. We'd tried all the stores in town closer to Elena's place, but they'd already been cleaned out. Same story everywhere we stopped along the highway until we'd gone about two hours out of our way and spotted a well-lit plaza with a couple of big chain stores —it'd felt like a fucking oasis in the desert, and we dove right in. The weather hadn't been as bad down there, either. But now that we were getting closer to the Cape again, forced onto the back roads due to highway closures, it was a frozen shitshow nightmare.

"I'm starting to think we might need a contingency plan," Beaumont said as I slowed down again. We were only doing about fifteen miles an hour now, crawling like sloths along the road, our little caravan the only fuckers crazy enough to venture out on a night like this. But we had no choice—with so many people staying at Elena's, we couldn't risk running low on anything, especially with this insane fae-mojo weather. "Maybe we should find a place to stop for the night."

"And day," I reminded him. "If we stop now, we won't

be able to leave again until the sun goes down tomorrow."

"Better delayed and safe than frozen solid," he said.

"Look around. There's no guarantee this is going to lighten up. For all we know, conditions will be a hundred times worse tomorrow night."

"It pains me to say this," he grumbled, "but you make a fair point."

"Hey. We'll make it," I assured him. "Elena will beat our assess if we don't. She's got a whole feast planned, and I'm already working on my toast."

We'd just finished loading up the vans with everything on our list—bottled water, flashlights and batteries, matches, candles, every kind of food imaginable, blankets, sheets, pillows, air mattresses, extra clothing, coats, boots, winter gear, toiletries, paper products, herbs and crystals for some more warding magic, and of course, the all-important cases of booze everyone had begged for—when I'd gotten Elena's call. All five of us whooped and cheered in the parking lot at the welcome news that our wolf pup was awake and finally out of the woods.

Haley had insisted on running back into the plaza for a get-well gift, despite the fact that Emilio had already *gotten* well. Still, she'd gone ahead anyway, coming back out fifteen minutes later looking like a walking hospital gift shop. The woman had picked out at least four dozen roses in just about every color of the rainbow, all arranged in a giant vase she could barely get her arms around, three big-ass "Get Well" helium balloons trailing behind her. Looped over her elbows were two more shopping bags—one full of stuffed animals, the other crammed with boxes of choco-late-covered, well, everything.

"Seriously, Hay? Seriously?"

"What?" she'd asked, taking her time arranging all that shit in the back seat. "He was practically in a coma. He needs to be surrounded by bright, cheery things. Plus, he loves chocolate. Everyone knows that."

I peered into the other bag. "And the stuffed… cats?"

"Oh, those are for the witches. Kind of an inside joke."

"You've just thought of everything, haven't you?" I teased, but even I was smiling at that point. Girl really knew how to bring the silver lining.

The balloons bobbed beside her now, the massive rose bouquet strategically balanced on her lap. The whole van smelled like old lady perfume, but I wasn't about to tell *her* that. Besides, she was right—it was a good idea. Emilio would love everything about it, the big fucking softy.

My gut twisted as my mind tried to serve up a replay of the night he'd been attacked, but I shut that shit down fast. Our wolf was okay. He'd fucking made it through the jaws of death, the crazy bastard. All because Gray had never lost faith that he would.

"I don't like this," Beaumont said suddenly, scanning the road ahead. "Something feels off."

"You think?" I reached for the console, trying to crank up the window defogger. "We're driving through a blizzard in a tin can with half-bald tires, on a sheet of solid ice, through the pitch-black woods, and I'm not even sure we're going the right way anymore."

"Thanks, as always," Beaumont said, "for the optimism. However, that's not what I'm talking about. Something doesn't feel right. Out there."

I tried to follow the line of his gaze out the side passenger window, but I didn't want to take my eyes off the road for more than two seconds at a time. "Just a storm, Beaumont. You never seen snow before in your fancy-ass London house?"

"No, I haven't. But that's not—"

"You see anything weird out there, Hay?" I asked her.

"Yep. I spy something… white." She tapped her window, then said, "Well, look at it this way, guys. If we crash into a ditch and have to sleep out in the woods overnight, at least we're well-supplied."

"Awesome!" I flashed her a thumbs up in the rearview. Her sunny disposition was practically a foreign language to me—I swore the girl had a physical aversion to bitching and moaning. "You can be in charge of setting up camp, okay, Bright Side?"

"You got it! Your tent will be the one next to the bear den. I'll be sure to stock it with plenty of chocolate first." She gave the back of my head a playful smack.

I laughed. Since Gray couldn't touch me without starting a fire, I was pretty sure she'd given Haley carte blanche to knock me around on her behalf whenever the opportunity presented itself.

"No fucking with the driver," I teased. "Unless you wanna end up in a ditch."

"Pass," she said.

Silence drifted in, and for a while, the only sounds in the van were the squeak of the wipers on the windshield, the slow grind of the tires on the snowpack, and the occasional clank of bottles in the back.

"We seem to have lost Lansky," Beaumont finally said.

I narrowed my eyes and peered out the windshield again, as if I could see anything through the wall of white in front of us. Son of a bitch, he was right. "Yeah, I don't even see the taillights anymore," I said. "How'd they get so far ahead of us?"

"Maybe they didn't," he said. "I doubt they'd speed up in these conditions. Perhaps they found a place to pull off."

"Let me try Jael." Haley dug out her phone, but that idea turned out to be a bust. "Shoot. No service. Sooo… anyone got a flare gun?"

"It's the trees," I said. "This stretch of road is pretty spotty for cell phones."

"You think they're okay?" she asked. "What if—"

"Fuck! Hold on!"

There was no warning. No time to course-correct. By the time I crested the hill and saw Lansky's taillights swerving off the road, we were already on a collision course with the jackknifed semi he'd clearly tried to avoid. We hit a fresh patch of ice on the downslope and the steering wheel jerked from my hands, and then we were spinning like a kid's toy, picking up speed as we careened downhill toward the wreckage, rose petals of every color falling around us like snow.

SEVENTEEN

GRAY

It was one of those moments where you're lying totally still, holding your breath, willing your heart not to beat, and suddenly you feel the ground shifting beneath you, dropping away.

I was so certain I'd known what Emilio was going to say, so sure I could name the ghosts that had haunted his eyes every time I stared into them for more than a moment.

I tried to save them, I thought he'd say. *But I couldn't. Or, I should've been able to warn them. I should've seen the signs. Or maybe, I was just a scared kid. I ran and hid instead of being brave, and I've carried that shame ever since...*

But to say that it was his fault? That *he'd* been the one to betray them?

I swallowed hard, willing my muscles to remain still, hoping he couldn't scent the rush of pure shock flooding my body.

"Before we came together on this case," Emilio contin-

"

ued, tightening his arms around me as if he were scared I'd bolt, "Elena and I hadn't spoken for nearly twenty years. Did you know that?"

"Not… Not really," I said, willing my heart rate to return to normal. My skin felt hot and prickly, but not because I was afraid of Emilio or anything he might've done in the past, no matter how terrible.

No. I was afraid—terrified—that when he finally confessed his greatest regrets, I wouldn't have the words to make it better for him. To give him the absolution he'd been seeking most of his life.

"I knew that you'd emigrated here together after separating from your pack, but that was basically all," I said. "Ronan never said much about it."

"No, he wouldn't have. He doesn't know the whole story anyway—just the end." A warm sigh escaped Emilio's lips, stirring my hair, and he pressed a lingering kiss to the top of my head. "Actually, I guess I can say now that Ronan's part *wasn't* the end. For a long time, I feared it was, but my sister… Things are in flux right now. There's so much… I don't…"

I felt the sudden vibration in his chest, slowly turning into a tremor that shook the bed, and I realized he was trying—and failing—to hold back a storm of sobs.

All my words, all the right things to say, all the comforting thoughts, everything failed me. I didn't know what to say, what to do, how to help him, so I did the only thing that felt right in that moment—I snuggled closer to him and wrapped my arms around him, drawing his head to my chest, stroking his hair. I channeled all my love for him into this moment, sending it to him, strengthening him, trying to let him know without words that it was okay to let go. To let every horrible, ugly, scary, fucked-up thing go.

He seemed to sense it, and he clung to me as he wept, burying his face in my shirt, his tears damp on my skin as they leaked out in an endless river. Soon, my own tears followed, my heart breaking for the lost wolf he'd been, the family he'd left behind.

Of all the guys, Emilio had always been the most sensitive, the most compassionate, the most in touch with the emotional side of things. But I'd never seen him so vulnerable, so exposed. Whatever had happened in Argentina, whatever guilt and shame and grief he'd endured, he'd stuffed it into a bottle and shoved it into the darkest part of his soul, keeping it locked away… Until tonight.

When he finally ran out of tears, my wolf stilled in my embrace, but he didn't pull away. Didn't roll over or try to mask his pain or pretend it was something else, or worse— apologize for the show of emotion, like so many men would do. Instead, he held me closer, inhaling my scent, his breathing finally smoothing out again.

Our bedroom overlooked the backyard, and outside our window, the wind howled like a banshee, ushering in another moonless night. A fresh blanket of snow had descended on Raven's Cape, the windowpanes murky with frost. Throughout the rest of the house, we could hear the chatter of the witches, their laughter, their bickering, the occasional clink of dishes and silverware being set out on the table, Elena calling for wine and rum and a little more garlic in the sauce. It didn't take a detective to figure out that she'd be preparing a feast tonight; Emilio had come through the worst of things, and everyone whose lives he'd touched wanted to celebrate.

But right now, tucked into our bed, there was only me and my wolf, safe and warm and well-hidden from the happy chaos unfolding in the rest of the house, and for a long time we clung to each other without words, twin flames flickering in the window on a dark night, illuminating the way home.

I had no warning for just how dark that night was about to get.

EIGHTEEN

DARIUS

I blinked the fog from my mind, focusing on the skull-shaped indentation in the passenger window next to me. *My* skull shape, I realized, rubbing the side of my head. Blood trickled from a gash above my ear, but it was already healing.

Fortunately, I had a hard head, and though I was a bit dizzy, it seemed I was no worse for the wear.

"Ronan? Haley?" I sat up slowly, still trying to get my bearings. Both of the front airbags had deployed, and everything around me was coated in dust and rose petals. "Everyone okay?"

"Motherfucking piece of shit bullshit asshole snow! Fuck this shit! I fucking hate winter!" This, from Ronan.

"So the eloquent demon is still with us," I said. "Excellent. Haley?"

"Still with you," Haley piped up from the backseat, her breathing a bit erratic, but otherwise sounding like herself.

"Which is more than I can say for Emilio's presents. What the hell happened?"

"We hit… something." I unhooked my seatbelt and tried to open the passenger door, but it refused to budge.

"A fucking semi, that's what we hit." Ronan wrenched open the driver's side door and stumbled out. "A semi that had no business being out on this back road, especially in a storm."

Haley and I joined him outside, the three of us standing in the middle of the road, trying to piece together the puzzle. The snow was falling heavily; we had to constantly brush it from our eyes.

"The van is toast," Ronan said. From the looks of things, we'd slid down the hill, slamming sideways into the back of the rig. The passenger side took the brunt of it, the back end of the van securely wedged underneath the truck. Half of our supplies were scattered around the wreckage.

"So glad I picked the left side to ride on," Haley said, shivering. Whether it was the frigid night air or the realization that she'd just narrowly escaped death, I couldn't tell.

I took her by the shoulders and looked her over, checking her head, her neck, her arms, but she waved off my ministrations.

"You'd be the first to know if I was bleeding," she said.

I let out a brittle laugh. "Indeed."

"Hey!" someone shouted from the other side of the semi. "Ronan, Darius! That you guys?"

"Lansky," I said.

"It's us," Ronan replied. "You guys okay?"

"A little banged up, but we'll live. You?"

"Same. Anyone check the guy in the truck?"

"Not yet," Lansky called back. "We're a little stuck at the moment."

"You got phone service?" Ronan asked.

"Negative."

"Alright, we're coming to you. Hang tight." Gingerly, the three of us stepped around the wreckage and made our way around the back end of the semi, following the sound of Lansky's voice. It was slow going on the icy road, with visibility at a minimum, and the danger of more vehicles sliding down that hill.

Fortunately, it seemed we were the only ones risking a drive tonight. Well, us and the semi, which seemed extremely out of place. Something about it didn't feel right. Not just the fact that it was out on a back road in this storm, but something else I couldn't quite put my finger on.

The feeling of unease that'd crept up on me after we'd left the plaza had never really left, and now it intensified, putting all of my senses on high alert.

We found Lansky and Jael trying unsuccessfully to climb out of a ditch, their van tilted nose-first at such an extreme angle that its back wheels had lifted off the ground. Ronan and I helped them up the slope, everyone slipping and sliding on the rapidly accumulating snow.

"I swear that truck appeared out of nowhere," Lansky said. His eyes were still wide with shock, and I could smell the adrenaline surging through his blood. "One minute the roads were empty, nothing but this crazy snow. I'd just downshifted to tackle that hill, then all of a sudden, I'm hitting the brakes and swerving to avoid something that just… It just *appeared*."

"He's right," Jael said. Other than the falling snow flattening his hair, the fae prince looked as dignified and unruffled as ever, his yellow eyes glowing faintly. "I, too, saw nothing until the very moment of near-impact."

"Sounds like more of Orendiel's magical bullshit to me," Ronan said. "Let's check it out."

"I'm going to do a damage assessment on our supplies," Haley said. "Hopefully, I can salvage a few things from our van."

"Good idea," Ronan said. "If we can get Lansky's out of the ditch, we might be able to drive it back. Ours is definitely a lost cause."

As I scanned our perimeter, keeping my heightened senses attuned to any vehicles that might've approached the top of the hill or any other threats coming our way, Ronan, Jael, and Lansky checked out the cab of the truck.

Ronan stepped up and peered inside the driver's side window, shaking his head. "Driver's definitely dead."

"Let's get him out," Lansky said, and Ronan hauled open the door.

The man inside—human, by the scent of him—toppled lifelessly into Ronan's arms, his limbs as stiff as those of a weeks-old corpse.

"What the fuck?" Ronan dragged the guy to the ground, propping him up against the truck's massive front wheel. "There's not a scratch on him, but he's a human popsicle."

Jael crouched down and checked for a pulse, then shook his head. After a beat, he closed his eyes and said, "This man did not die from exposure or natural causes. This is fae magic at work."

"Darkwinter?" I asked, approaching the body.

"Worse. The spell that took this man's life force has a dual signature belonging to two extremely powerful fae." Jael got to his feet, his typically smooth face creased with deep lines of concern. "Fenlos and Talia."

"The bloody *council*," I said. Emilio had known Talia would turn up in all of this again. He just hadn't known how.

"The bloody council," Jael echoed.

"Looks like they're not hiding behind their bullshit pretenses anymore," Ronan said.

"No," Jael confirmed. "This spell could've easily been camouflaged, even from me. They wanted us to know of their involvement, and to draw the next logical conclusion."

"Which is?" I asked.

"That if the two highest-ranking members of the fae council are blatantly using their magic to sabotage us in a battle against the Darkwinter and the hunters, then the *entire* council has already chosen sides. It's just as Emilio feared."

Lansky crouched down to check the body. "Yeah, this guy's been dead at least two weeks. Which begs the question..." He stepped around the front of the cab to the other side of the road, then returned. "How did he get here? He's got no visible injuries and a fae magical signature. His truck literally appeared out of nowhere—there are no tire tracks on the other side of the road, and the only tracks on this side are from two vehicles—mine and Ronan's. Highway patrol has closed just about all the roads. No one else is out in this shit right now."

That was it, I realized. The thing that'd been bothering me about this. There were no tracks through the snow. The truck hadn't been driven here. It was put here magically.

Lansky blew heat into his hands, spinning around to take in the rest of the scene, putting the pieces together. "Jael, you said these fae wanted you to detect their signature—you're the only one of us who could."

"Yes, they know by now I'm working with you. Orendiel would've told them about my involvement in freeing the witches from the warehouse. The public fight Kallayna and I staged would also lend credence to the fact that I'd betrayed them all, including my sister."

"Okay," Lansky said. "So they know you're on our side. And they also knew, somehow, that we'd gone for a supply run today, and that we'd be taking *this* exact route back, even though we didn't take it on the way out, and there are three other routes we could've taken to avoid the highway closures. This is a setup."

"No, not a setup," I said, catching a new scent on the frigid air. Lansky's eyes suddenly widened—it seemed he'd caught it, too. "An ambush."

It was a sharp animal odor, but not completely natural. Shifters, I figured, though not a type I'd ever encountered before. "There," I said, nodding at a faint movement I'd just caught in the woods bordering the road. I was likely the only one who could see it through the snow. "In the trees."

"Haley, get in the van!" Lansky barked, and drew his weapon as the big cats shot out into view.

There were six of them, snow-white but for their reflective blue-green eyes. Their body shape gave the impression of mountain lions, but these creatures were about four times larger, with thick, corded muscles and powerful jaws that looked like they could crush bones with very little effort.

"Why aren't they attacking?" Ronan asked as the beasts came to a stop at the edge of the road about fifteen feet from us.

"Because you've got a witch in your pocket, dumbass," Haley said, and immediately, the scent of human blood filled my nostrils. I turned to see that said witch was not in the van as Lansky had ordered, but kneeling down in the middle of the road, squeezing blood from her fist into a small pentagram she'd traced in the snow, her other palm facing out toward the shifters, as though she'd stopped them by her will alone.

When she'd squeezed the last drop of blood from her fist, she pressed the wounded palm against the symbol. The snow around it glowed briefly, then melted.

Before I could even *ask* what that was all about, she got to her feet, turned her palms face up, and began to chant, slowly pacing out a circle around us.

Spirits and guides, ancestors all

I call on you now, each one and all
I offer my blood in exchange for protection
Delay this attack from every direction
Let all who dare breach this circle I cast
Fall back to the moment of three minutes past.

She repeated the mantra several times, not stopping until she'd completed a full circle around us, magically cutting us off from the shifters.

"It's a confusion spell," she explained when she rejoined the group. "It's not much, but it's all the blood I can spare on short notice."

"What's with the three minutes thing?" Ronan asked.

"Each time they hit the boundary, their minds will revert by three minutes, so they'll feel like they haven't initiated their attack yet. It's essentially a time loop—it should make them retreat and start over. But seriously, guys. This is like, blood magic 101 stuff—totally makeshift. We've probably got about ten, fifteen minutes tops before it wears off."

Lansky took another look at his van. "We need to get that thing on the road. It's our best shot."

"On it," Ronan said, and Lansky and I followed him down into the ditch. Physically, we were the strongest and best able to push it out. But that meant leaving Haley and Jael unprotected—a prospect I didn't like one bit.

"Hold the circle, you two," I said. "The moment you sense the magic weakening, give us the signal."

"You think those things can understand us?" Lansky asked, jerking his head toward the beasts across the road.

"I want to say no," I said, "but I'm inclined to err on the side of caution these days."

"Alright. On three," Ronan said.

We crouched down and grabbed the bumper.

"One, two—"

All three of us jumped the gun, but after a few more attempts, we finally got the job done, shoving the two-ton van out of the ditch and back onto the icy road. It skidded to a stop, looking as tired as the rest of us undoubtedly felt.

Jael helped us out of the ditch, and we headed over to inspect the vehicle that would hopefully get us home.

"Can't believe the airbags didn't blow on this one," Ronan said, knocking on the hood. "You guys slid in face first."

"Yeah, remind me to bust Hobb's balls about that later," Lansky said. "He was supposed to take it in for a re-install after the dealer sent out a recall notice, but he blew it off." He crouched down to take a look underneath, inspecting the damage. "Okay. Aside from the obvious cosmetic shit, the front axle's bent, and the bumper looks like it's folded in against the front right tire. But if we go real slow and don't take any sharp turns, she'll get us home."

"Assuming she starts," Ronan said, wiping the icy slush from his eyes. All of us were wearing caps of snow three inches high. Poor Haley's teeth were chattering, but bloody hell, the woman was still smiling.

I left Ronan and Lansky to deal with the van while I checked on Haley and Jael.

"Five minutes," Haley told me. "Spell's fading."

"It's some spell, though." I put my hand on her shoulder and leaned forward, peering into the snowy woods. None of the shifters had moved from their posts, not even to attempt a breach. "They're completely immobilized."

"They're not the most predictable creatures, that's for sure." Haley shook her head. "I'm not sure if it's my spellwork, or something else keeping them at bay."

"Let's not look a gift horse in the mouth, shall we?" I winked at Haley, then turned to Jael. "Anything you can do?"

"I'm afraid not," he said. "Though not for lack of trying. Their minds have been secured against manipulation—likely they're only susceptible to Darkwinter influence."

"Darkwinter?" I asked. "So these aren't Jonathan's hybrids?"

"No way," Haley said. "Jonathan was too much of a loose cannon to make something this dangerous and, I don't know. Coordinated? They haven't attacked yet, but look how they're standing in formation like that. It isn't accidental. They're watching our every move. I wouldn't be surprised if there are more of them further down the road."

She was right. They'd positioned themselves at even intervals, and when I looked closely, I saw the slightest movements of their eyes, following Lansky's footsteps as he approached.

Jael and Haley were right. These weren't Jonathan's rotting, broken creatures. They were powerful, genetically altered, fae-made beasts bred for a purpose we could only begin to guess at.

We needed to get out of there.

"Bad news," Lansky said. "Engine won't turn over."

"Two minutes," Haley warned, and immediately I felt the shift in the energy around us, like an electrical current surging, then fading. At the edge of the road, one of the big cats took a step.

"Fuck," Ronan said. "This is about to get ugly. Anyone got weapons?"

"Nothing that would help against these creatures," I said.

"Can't you shoot them?" Ronan asked Lansky.

"Doubt it." Lansky drew his weapon again anyway. "These aren't silver bullets. They won't work on shifters."

"Might not kill them," Ronan said, "but maybe you can make them bleed."

Haley took a step backward toward the van. "Now or never, boys. Thirty seconds and we're totally exposed."

"Stay alert." Lansky took aim, firing off three shots into the chest of the closest beast.

The creature didn't even flinch, and if it'd bled at all, it'd been such a minuscule amount that not one drop had stained the snow.

"Great. Apparently, they heal faster than regular shifters, too," Lansky said, holstering the useless gun. "Guess we're doing this the old-fashioned way."

"Haley," I said, catching his meaning. "Now might be a good time for you to get in the van. You too, prince. See if you two can get it started."

The moment we heard the van door slam shut, we struck.

From the corner of my eye, I caught the dark gray blur of Lansky's wolf form, Ronan right on his heels. The shifters were just coming out of the spell-haze when we took down the first two—Ronan and Lansky on one, me on the other. I barged into him, biting, slashing, disemboweling. His blood tasted ashy and bitter, laced with some kind of chemical, but I drank deeply anyway, needing the fuel and—yes—needing to put on a show of dominance.

The wolf and the raging, black-eyed demon made quick work of their foe, Lansky mauling him with his massive claws while Ronan tore off hunks of white fur and flesh with his bare hands. The bullets hadn't made a dent, but the damned things were finally bleeding now. The three of us had no intention of letting them heal.

I scanned ahead for my next shifter meal, but was shocked to see the rest of the pack backing off.

Were they… retreating?

"Why aren't they attacking?" I growled, wiping the blood from my mouth.

Lansky pawed at the beast he and Ronan had shredded, drawing my attention to a black metallic object that appeared to be fused to its collarbone. It was circular and flat, about the size and shape of a watch face.

I tore the bone clean out of its carcass so Ronan and I could take a closer look.

"I'm guessing it's some kind of behavioral control device," he said. "Or tracker. I bet they all have them."

"Maybe that's why they're holding back," I said.

"If that's the case, then someone is watching. Someone's controlling them."

"Let's take them out," I said, already anticipating the bitter tang of blood on my lips.

But the big cats were already disappearing, loping away into the snow-packed forest on silent paws.

*　*　*

"I don't believe they weren't trying to kill us," Lansky said later, stepping into what was left of his clothing. While Haley and Jael had finished loading up the salvageable supplies into Lansky's van, Ronan, Lansky, and I had done a full sweep of the area, tracking the shifter prints a good mile out in all directions before the trees became too dense to continue. "Not for a second. Six cats that size against three of us? They could've done a hell of a lot more damage."

"We hit the first two pretty quickly, though," I said. "My sense was they weren't expecting our initial attack."

"No way. They knew *exactly* what we were up to. Exactly how we'd react. I'm telling you, guys. These aren't normal shifters operating on instinct. They're following orders in real time."

"Detective Lansky is right," Jael said, securing one last box of food in the back of the van. "My belief is that Darkwinter is trying to unhinge us a bit. Consider it—Orendiel suffered a massive defeat that night at the warehouse, and he knows we're gathering strength here. What better way to keep us off guard and second-guessing our strategies?"

"Psychological warfare," I said. "Dark fae expertise."

"It is," Jael agreed, "and this is just a *taste* of what he might unleash. What he's already begun unleashing in the Bay. By his actions tonight, he's virtually guaranteed that whatever his actual capabilities, we're going to imagine much, much worse. Hybrid shifters? No. Try electronically controlled hybrid super-shifters. A violent attack on our home? Yes, but let's add in a minor attack that cuts off the food supply during a storm. The point is, we don't know what he's fully capable of or what he's planning, and it could be virtually anything. That's how dark fae operate. He's counting on our fear of the unknown. Humans especially are conditioned to operate on worst-case-scenario fears, and that fear makes it much easier for the fae to manipulate their targets."

"Obviously, that glitter-dicked asshole has never dealt with *me*." Haley leaned out the driver's side window of the van, now idling in the center of the road, ready to go. "I'm all about the *best*-case scenario, which at the moment is the prospect of ushering dozens of beautiful empanadas into their final resting place in my belly. Now, if you all don't mind… Can we *please* get the fuck out of here?"

NINETEEN

EMILIO

The ghosts that had laid siege to my heart had lingered there long enough. If Elena and I had any hope of reconciling, if I had any hope of being a brother and friend to the guys, if I had any hope of being the man Gray truly saw when she looked at me with those pretty blue eyes, I needed to evict them.

And I needed to do it now, before they slipped out of the light and into the dark corners once again.

"My sister and I were very close growing up," I began. "But at some point, she got involved with a new crowd, and she started spending all her time with them. Camping trips, road trips, last-minute parties I was never invited to. I hardly ever saw her that summer, and when I did, she was merely coming and going, picking up a change of clothes, bribing me not to tell my parents that her new friends weren't… our kind."

"They only wanted you guys to hang out with other wolf shifters?" she asked.

"They weren't like that with me, but my sister was the alpha of our generation, poised to take over leading the pack for our father. By the time she was thirteen, she'd already been promised to the alpha of a neighboring pack—a guy named Franco, who also happened to be my best friend—and it was just accepted that they'd eventually marry and mate as adults. But that promise was made years earlier—nothing she'd ever taken seriously. And these new friends of hers… They were human. They had no idea what she was. But I figured out pretty quickly that one of them was becoming more than a friend."

"As in…?"

"As in, she fell in love with him, Gray. A man named Jonah Shiley. He was the only one she'd told about her true nature."

Gray sucked in a breath. "She married Jonah. He was the forbidden love she told me about."

"Eloped, actually. None of us knew about it for a whole year. We'd thought she was living with a roommate, but it turned out that was just a girlfriend covering for her and Jonah whenever we planned to visit. She was nineteen years old, and he was twenty, and there was no telling them about the ways of the world or pack hierarchy or anything that even remotely implied their love was wrong."

"Because it wasn't," she said defensively, and I realized the subtext of my words.

Gray was a human witch. I was a wolf shifter. And

nothing about us—about her touch, the way she looked at me, the way my heart seemed to grow big whenever she walked into the room—felt wrong.

"No, that's not what I meant, *querida*. You're right. Their love wasn't *wrong*. It was just... against the rules. My parents loved us, but they were also extremely practical and extremely loyal to the pack. When they found out about the marriage, they basically disowned her. I saw her even less than before, as if that were possible. I missed her, you know? Missed getting into trouble together, missed her teasing me, missed just... Just hanging out and being goofy with my big sister."

"I'm sorry," she said, and I felt her own sadness wash through her. I wondered if she were thinking about Haley, or the other sisters she'd been separated from as a baby. Unlike me, Gray hadn't really known or remembered them. She didn't have anyone to miss.

I wrapped my arms more tightly around her, holding her close. When I finally felt her sadness retreat a bit, I continued.

"Anyway, the family she was promised to—Franco's kin —they didn't take the news too kindly. My buddy dropped me, and our family became pariahs. People started disrespecting my father, then outright challenging his authority. Kids at school were fucking with me. It sucked. So there I was, basically still a kid, no sister, no friends, total outcast.

"Then the inevitable happened—I got jumped after school one day, five wolves, tore my ass to shreds—Franco and his brothers. They would've killed me, too, if this other pack hadn't shown up and saved me. They fought off Franco's crew and helped me patch myself back up."

I remembered them now, new in town, mysterious, all muscle and swagger. Chasing off Franco and his guys as if they were little field mice. I'd worried they'd beat me up themselves for being so weak, but they didn't say a word. Just took me home to one of the guys' apartments, patched me up, fed me. And from then on, they were always around.

"They saved me that day," I continued. "And they protected me every day after. Pushed me to get stronger, smarter, to develop my instincts. Basically, all the things my father should've been doing, but he was too busy defending our territory to worry about me.

"My sister got pregnant later that year, and once again, we didn't know a thing about it until Maya—" I stopped suddenly, my throat closing up over her name. My niece's name. I hadn't said it out loud since we'd left Argentina—Elena had forbidden it, even before she and I split. Hearing it now, feeling it, it brought everything rushing back in crystal clear, high-definition images. The good, as well as the bad.

Maya's first tooth. The sound of her sweet little laugh. How she couldn't say my name, so called me "Em-ee-o" instead.

My eyes blurred with tears, my throat stinging with the scream that wanted to claw its way out.

But Gray nestled in closer, her breath soft against my

bare chest, and from her I took just enough strength to continue.

This, too, was part of the deal. No one said exorcizing these ghosts would be easy or painless.

With a cracked voice, I said, "Maya, my niece. My sister showed up on our front porch three days after the baby was born, this little pink bundle in her arms. My parents melted. And just like that, she was part of our lives again. Maya and Jonah, too."

I stilled again, taking a moment to gather the rest of my thoughts. This was the inevitable turn in the road, the part of the story where the darkness began to seep in, and I felt it mirrored inside me now like a wisp of black smoke curling up from my gut, thickening around my heart.

"People heard about the happy little family," I said. "That's when the threats started."

"Against Elena?"

"Well, at first they were more generic. There were rumors of a rival pack moving in to the area from the north, looking for a challenge, and Franco's family was more than happy to fan the flames. They started spreading lies about my father, about his ability to manage and provide for the pack. Someone threw bricks through my parents' windows painted with curses and crude, violent images. They cut the brake lines of my father's car—fortunately, he'd only made it down the driveway before he figured it out. They slaughtered the chickens and cows on my parents' land. My father started getting anonymous calls and emails demanding that my sister be tossed out of the pack, stripped of our protection. When he refused, the threats escalated. This went on for a couple years, but my parents always managed to stay on top of things, to not lose hope.

"Then one day, someone physically assaulted my sister in the grocery store parking lot, trying to get at the baby. She fought the guy off and Maya was unharmed, but that was the last straw. My father decided my sister and her family needed to go into protective custody."

"Holy shit," she whispered. "How did he even set that up?"

"Well, he was a cop—no surprise there, right?" I laughed, grateful for the chance to relieve some tension. "In our family, you were two things: a wolf first, an officer of the law second. He'd always known it was only a matter of time before Elena and I followed in his footsteps."

I swallowed through another painful lump of emotion. My father hadn't lived long enough to see either of his children follow in his footsteps.

"Anyway," I said, "he had some help from a high-ranking shifter friend a few jurisdictions over, and they made all the arrangements. He and my sister staged a big public blow-up, and he officially disowned her, basically banishing her from the town. A few days later, we got them set up with new IDs in a small mountain town about an hour-and-a-half from where we lived. Other than my father and his friend, I was the only other person who knew the location. Even my mother couldn't know—that'd been her choice. She was too worried she'd break down and go visit them, blowing their cover."

Gray shook her head, her silky hair brushing against my skin. "That must've been the hardest thing for her to do. Especially after all the ups and downs she'd had with Elena, and finally getting close again, only to have to let her go…"

"Oh, she was miserable," I said. "My father, too. Our family was torn apart, and there was nothing we could do about it—not if we wanted to keep them safe from the threats and attacks. My sister didn't even dare send us letters or pictures—we were all so worried they'd be traced back. My mother started drinking. My father buried himself in his work, taking overnight shifts and walking beats he'd long since graduated from, just to avoid the emptiness at home."

"What about you?" she asked.

What about me…

It was a loaded question, the answer weighted with so much guilt and pain I felt it now, eating away at my insides, flaring up all over again. For this was the root of it. The domino that fell and knocked down all the others.

My hand began to sting, and I realized Gray was gripping it so tightly, her fingernails were making half-moon indentations in my skin. Gently, I extracted myself from her grip, wrapping her hands in mine instead. It seemed we were both waiting for the other shoe in this painful story to drop. The difference was, I knew what was coming.

And I needed to anchor myself to her. To hold on for all I was worth as the memories came at me full force, the fiercest, most brutal waves that hit me full-on and pummeled me against the shore.

I could still feel the old resentments, the shamefully hot burning in my gut when I thought about what Elena's choices had meant for our family. I loved her, I loved Maya, and even Jonah was starting to grow on me. But because she'd broken the rules, she'd broken our family, too. I lost my sister, but I also lost my parents. She'd cost me my sense of home and place and belonging. She'd cost me my friendships and dignity and standing in our pack. She'd cost me everything. That's how it'd felt.

So when my friends—the guys who'd looked after me when Franco went crazy on me—started showing up again, I welcomed it. We were all a little older at that point, a bunch of wild-eyed wolves looking for trouble. I'd started drinking with them, staying out all night, looking for girls, generally disturbing the peace. There was always some party to go to, always some ruckus to cause.

Stupid boys.

Telling Gray about it now, I could see all the signs. All the fucking clues. But back then, I wasn't much different from my sister with her friends—no one could've convinced me that any of it had been a bad idea.

"One night," I went on, "the guys took me out to this expensive new club in downtown Buenos Aires, insisting they pay for everything, that they wanted to show me a good time since I'd been so down about my father disowning my sister. I drank a lot that night—more than I ever had—and we were all just letting off steam. I started opening up a little more about my fucked-up situation at home, and next thing I know, I'm telling them about the threats and how my sister wasn't really disowned, just relocated for her protection."

I felt the shift in Gray's body immediately, her muscles tensing, her heartbeat kicking up. Even she could read the writing on the wall—the message it cost me absolutely everything to finally translate.

And by the time I had, it'd been far too late.

She pressed a kiss to my shoulder, warm and comforting. It was like she could sense me slipping under the waves and wanted to pull me back up again before I drown.

"It's okay," she whispered. "I'm right here."

I gripped her hands tighter and squeezed my eyes shut, forcing myself to watch the scene unfolding like a movie. It would be—I promised myself right there, right in her arms as the storm raged on outside our window and inside my heart—the very last time I watched that movie. The very last time I forced myself to relive it.

"They listened attentively," I said, "asking for more details, their eyes full of fake concern. They said how sorry they were—that they'd had no idea I was dealing with all this shit at home. They reminded me how they'd had my back with Franco's crew, and how I was like family to them. How that automatically made my parents and sister their family, too. How they wanted to help me protect her. A few more drinks, and I believed them. I'd felt like I'd been carrying that burden on my own for so long, it was a relief to get help. A relief to know that this big, strong, ragtag pack could fight for us. That they could put an end to the threats and bring my sister and her family home where they belonged."

Silent tears leaked from my eyes again, but I didn't bother to wipe them away. Like the ghosts, like the movies, they needed an outlet, too. And through it all, Gray just held me, kissed me, touched me, let me know without words that she wasn't going anywhere. Wasn't judging.

"By the time we left the club," I said, "the boozy feelings had faded, but the sense of relief had only intensified. I felt damn near euphoric. I couldn't wait to go home and talk to my parents—see what we could do to bring these guys into the fold, strengthen my father's position as alpha, and put our family back together.

"They drove me back to the house, but as soon as we turned down my road, I knew something was wrong. Then we saw the firetrucks at the top of the driveway, and a blaze of orange that lit up the sky." I reached for the bottled water on the bedside table, taking a long swig. The long-remembered taste of acrid smoke and the scent of burning animal flesh curdled in my mouth.

"The guys stayed by my side that whole night," I continued, "waiting for the fire chief to come out of the ashes and tell me the answer to the only question I cared about—whether my parents were inside. But I knew before he'd even spoken the words. The house and outbuildings had been torched. The remaining animals had all burned alive. And my parents... my parents died in their bedroom closet, huddled together until the very end."

By now, Gray's tears were flowing, too, running like a tiny river down the side of my chest. My need to comfort her overwhelmed my own pain, and I stroked her cheek with my thumb, pressing a kiss into the top of her head. I would never be able to express how much this meant to me—that she'd been willing to listen, to feel this pain, to help me carry it.

"I knew I had to get to my sister. That she and her family would be next, if they hadn't already been found and targeted. The guys drove me there as fast as they could, breaking just about every traffic law on the way. I never once hesitated to tell them the address."

I took another slug of water and a deep breath, forcing myself to unclench the muscles that'd tightened like piano strings. This was it. The worst part. The last and most treacherous and most deeply buried memories, the ghosts with the sharpest teeth and claws, the ones who'd fight me every step of the way as I tried to finally release them.

"It was my fault, *querida*," I said, my words like broken glass in my throat. Each one cut deep, cost me something, but I couldn't stop. Not until every last one was out. "All those years with the rumors about the rival pack, it was them. My so-called friends. They were in league with Franco's family the whole time, and they'd been working me for years, slowly laying the trap. I took the bait, because they made me believe—no, scratch that. I *let* them make me believe—that they could help me. But when we finally got to Elena's home, the second we got out of the car, I knew. I just knew, and there wasn't a damn thing I could do about it.

"Two other cars pulled in immediately behind us, full of shifters I'd never seen before—bigger, angrier, their eyes wild with bloodlust. To them, it'd been a hunt years in the making, and they'd finally cornered their prey. I knew it that instant that these monsters were responsible for the fire at my parents' home, and now they'd come for my sister's family, too.

"I ran inside and woke up Elena and Jonah, trying to get them out, but we were the little field mice now. The monsters loped into the house like they hadn't a care in the world, a dozen guys against the three of us. Elena and I didn't even have time to shift—it all happened so fast. It was… It was a slaughter, Gray. The pleasure they took…"

The scene flashed behind my eyes once again. The sound of Elena's desperate screams as they'd ripped Maya from her arms. The way Jonah had dropped to his knees and begged, tears streaming down his face. The blood splatter arcing across the bedroom wall as they'd cut his throat. The soft, muted cries as the biggest of the pack had smothered Maya against his chest, pressing all the air from her tiny lungs and discarding her on the bed like a rag doll. They beat the shit out of me and Elena both, leaving us for dead. Lying on the bedroom floor, barely conscious, we watched their filthy boots stomp out of the house, the sounds of their laughter and whoops of victory like another round of blows to the head.

"Then I smelled the gasoline. Saw their silhouettes outside the window, flickering behind the orange flames that rose up suddenly from the base of the house. Their laughter went on and on... I swear it was still ricocheting around my skull even after I heard all their cars peel out."

The only reason we'd survived that night was thanks to the kindness of an elderly neighbor, who'd risked his own life to drag us out of the fire mere moments before the house crumbled.

"Elena and I woke up two days later, side-by-side in the local hospital, both of us in utter shock. Part of me feared the pack would be back to finish the job, but then I realized they'd left us alive on purpose. They let us go, because they knew we'd never pose a threat again. They'd defeated our family, killed our alpha. Elena and I were broken wolves without a pack—like some pathetic cautionary tale that would go down in the history books as a lesson to anyone that might try to challenge their dominance in the future.

"The moment we were released from the hospital, we went into survival mode, fueled entirely by shock and adrenaline. We had some money—some accounts my parents had set up when we were kids—and we used it all to pay off the right people, get passports and all the papers and tickets we needed to get to the states and disappear. From Los Angeles, we made our way north, seeing the forests and mountain ranges that reminded us of home. We found work and a cheap house to rent in a small seaside town called Raven's Cape, and for a little while, we lived in relative peace, haunted only by our own demons and the nightmares we never spoke of out loud."

"Raven's Cape," Gray whispered, lifting her head and glancing around the room. "This was your house?"

"No," I said with a faint smile, smoothing the hair from her forehead. The side of her face where she'd been resting against my chest was pink, her eyes still glassy with tears. "Elena has significantly upgraded since we lived together. The house we'd rented before isn't even there anymore—it was probably condemned and put out of its misery."

Gray settled back against my chest again, and for a while we just lay together in silence, the snow still swirling outside, the sounds of the household drifting in along with the mouthwatering scents of Elena's cooking: ground beef and onions frying, parsley and garlic being chopped up for the chimichurri. My stomach rumbled, and Gray let out a soft laugh, trailing her fingertips back and forth across my abdomen.

"It was a mistake, Emilio," she said softly. "A terrible mistake. You didn't intend for anyone to get killed. You thought they'd help keep your family safe."

I appreciated the sentiment, even though I suspected she knew her words would offer little comfort. When you'd carried a matched set of luggage stuffed to the gills with guilt, self-blame, and regret for two decades, it wasn't a simple matter of dropping the bags on the curb and moving on just because someone said you could.

"Of course I didn't intend for anyone to die, *querida*, but that doesn't change the outcome. What does intention matter in a situation like that? If a drunk driver kills someone you love, and later says they didn't mean it, does that change how you feel? Does it ease your pain or change the fact that you've lost someone forever? Does it bring them back?"

"But a drunk driver... You could argue that's negligence."

"You could argue that what I did was negligence, too. A drunk driver is blinded by alcohol and overconfidence, and they make a shit decision in a moment. I was blinded by a lot of things back then, too. Anger. Resentment. A fierce need to prove myself to a pack where I'd never be alpha. And a deep, endless ache for the family that I'd once had. If I'd been thinking clearly, if I'd kept my promises to protect my sister's secrets, perhaps..." I trailed off. Those thoughts, too, were part of the haunted house of horrors in my mind. And as such, they needed to be brought out into the light and released along with all the rest.

"Elena and I stuck together in America out of necessity, and Elena was still so fragile. Shock, mostly. I knew I couldn't leave her, even though I was terrified of the day she started asking questions.

"It took six months, but then it happened. The grief... It was like walking through mud. When it finally started to recede, just a little bit, her mind cleared up. The story wasn't adding up. She began asking more questions—hard ones. Ones with complicated answers I didn't want to give her. I dodged, redirected, distracted her, tried to convince her it was unhealthy and we had to let it go, had to board up that part of our lives and keep focused on the future. What a load of bullshit that was."

"How did she finally find out?" Gray asked.

"I'd gone out to pick up a pizza, and when I came back inside, she was sitting at the kitchen table with a half-spent bottle of pineapple vodka and that faraway look in her eyes she'd often get, her hands in her lap. I held up the pizza box and made a joke about how we could've just gotten pineapples on the pizza instead of having to drink them. She laughed, but there was something wrong with it. It was totally foreign, like it belonged to another person. A chill went down my spine. Then her smile died, and she lifted her hands and pointed a gun at my chest."

Gray gasped.

"'It was you,' Elena whispered. All the blood drained out of me, and I knew she'd finally figured out the truth. Enough of it, anyway. Enough to know who'd led the wolves to her door. And my God, *querida*, I'd never seen such despondence. It was like the last thread holding her together just snapped.

"'I've got two silver bullets in here,' she said. 'One for you, one for me. That's how it has to be, Meelo.' I didn't even try to argue with her. She was going to kill us both. I was certain of it. And the worst part of it was, I wanted her to. I saw the emptiness in her eyes, and in that moment, I really believed death would be the better option for both of us."

A shiver raced through Gray's body, and she reached for

the sheet and pulled it up to our shoulders. "What changed her mind?"

"You know how you say there's no coincidence?" I said.

"Yeah, that's a lesson I've been forced to learn over and over."

"Okay. So here's where shit gets *really* insane."

"You mean it gets worse?"

"Not at all. It gets better." At this, a smile slid over my face. She was going to like this part of the story—a little levity, a slightly happier-than-expected ending. "That was the night I met our boy, Ronan."

TWENTY

GRAY

"What?" I bolted upright in the bed, sure I'd misunderstood him. "Ronan just happened to show up on your doorstep at the exact moment you and your sister were about to die?"

"As crossroads demons are known to do, I guess," he said. "See, Elena had told me she was going to kill me, and then she was going to kill herself. It was *going* to happen, the forces already set in motion. I saw it play out like a movie, and I knew there'd be no talking her out of it—not even if I'd wanted to. My sister has always been stubborn— you might have picked up on that."

I let out a soft laugh. I *had* picked up on it. It was one of the things I really, really liked about her.

"Anyway," he said, "she flipped off the safety, steadied her aim. And I nodded and told her I was sorry, and that I loved her, and I understood why she had to do this. Then I closed my eyes, waiting for the bite of that bullet. Praying it would be quick, but knowing it wouldn't. Silver poisoning is… unpleasant."

I shuddered again, remembering his tortured body in the warehouse, the way the silver had eaten through his flesh and bones, slowly killing him. A hundred years could pass, and I'd never forget that sight. The fear. I only hoped that *he* hadn't remembered it. That he'd passed out long before the full gruesomeness of his predicament had set in.

"But instead of the pop of a gun," he continued, "I heard Elena gasp. I opened my eyes to see her staring at a point just past my shoulder, her mouth hanging open in shock. So I turn around, and there's this brooding, black-eyed demon leaning back against our kitchen counter, cracking a beer and tossing the bottle cap into the sink. 'Oh, don't mind me,' he said, taking a swig. 'Just here for the show. Continue, please.'"

Emilio's soft smile turned into a full-on laugh, and the sound of it unleashed the floodgates. It was like a needle popping a balloon that just kept expanding and expanding, and now I laughed, too. The things he'd shared with me had been so dark, so tragic, I marveled at the fact that we still remembered how to laugh—that we could do it so soon after talking about everything else. But I cherished that laughter, too. It felt like my wolf and I had been lost in a dark, dangerous forest together, so certain we'd never find our way back to the light. And now here we were. Laughing.

I closed my eyes and took a moment to send a prayer of thanks to the universe.

What bodies, these. What magic. What love.

Then I laughed even harder as the picture of Ronan sharpened in my mind. "Oh my God, he's *such* a drama queen!"

"Well, he knows how to make an entrance. I'll give him that."

"But how did he get there? How did he know what was going on?" I had so many questions, all of them rushing out at once. "What was he even *doing*?"

"To put it bluntly, Elena was about to commit murder *and* suicide, and apparently, this is one of Sebastian's favorite combos. Not to mention the fact that I had the most guilty conscience of anyone alive. I guess he thought we were good candidates to go darkside, so Ronan was dispatched to negotiate a deal for our tarnished souls and carry us back to hell."

"But you *weren't* good candidates, obviously."

"Oh, you should've seen Elena's face! The mere idea of working for the Prince of hell got her all riled up again..." Emilio shook his head, almost like he still couldn't believe the turn of events. "You might say Sebastian gave her back the will to live. Ranting and raving at Ronan the entire time about how presumptuous he and his boss were, she emptied out the bullets and chucked them out the window right then. And when she turned back to meet my eyes, there was so much rage and disgust and fire—fire I hadn't seen in years. In that moment, I knew she'd survive. Not because she'd get over it or forgive me or forget what'd happened in Argentina, and not because she'd find a healthy way to deal with it. No. I knew that the anger in her now would fuel her for as long as it took."

Emilio blew out a breath, the earlier levity slipping away again, just as I knew it would. Humor existed even in the darkest corners of a tragedy, but wounds like this didn't just disappear after a good laugh. This was the first time Emilio had ever talked about all of this—I felt that, deep in my bones. He still had a long way to go to releasing his shame and all the pain that came along with it, and to putting the pieces of his relationship with Elena back together, if that was even a possibility. But he'd done the hardest part tonight—starting the process. Speaking the words. Freeing himself from having to carry it alone.

"After giving Ronan a piece of her mind, and telling him he owed her three bucks for the beer, she looked me dead in the eye and told me to pack my bags and leave the Cape. She said she never wanted to see me again.

"Just the fact that she'd survived the night, that I'd survived the night, that all felt like a gift, and I didn't want to take that for granted. I knew I'd caused her so much pain already, I just… Honoring her wishes—leaving, for good— it felt like the only decent thing left to do."

"So you ended up in the Bay," I said, connecting the dots. "Ronan helped you."

"You know he has a thing for strays." Emilio laughed again—not quite as exuberant as the last one, but a laugh nevertheless. "He offered to help me get set up in the Bay, and the rest, as they say, is history. I got a job on the force, met Darius soon after that, did some consulting with him.

He was still practicing law back then, before he traded all that in for Black Ruby. Ronan and I didn't see each other all that much—he had his work, and I had mine, and our paths crossed only on occasion, but we always had that unspoken bond. And he knew, without my ever having to say as much, that when the time came when he needed me, I'd be there. No question."

I let the magnitude of his words settle over me. "So before I came into the picture, you guys weren't really all that close?"

"Well, yes and no. Like I said, we had that unspoken bond. But when you did come, it brought us closer once again. And then when Sophie passed away and you started coming into your powers and everything else happened, well..." Emilio sighed. "Now I can't imagine Ronan *not* being a part of my life."

I poked him in the ribs and smiled. "So you're saying that my craziness is the glue that bonds you guys?"

"No, Gray," he said seriously. "You coming into our lives and bringing us all together like this... It's the best thing that's ever happened to me. And I'm pretty sure the rest of the guys feel the same way."

"Me, too," I said, holding his gaze, still marveling at all he'd been through, at everything he'd survived in order to end up here. In my arms. In the home of a sister he'd once thought he'd have to turn his back on forever.

During one of our infamous brownie sessions, back before anything romantic had happened between us, Emilio had told me, *People do all sorts of misguided things when they're trying to protect the ones they love, querida. Let's just say I know something about that.*

At the time, I'd sensed that he'd endured some terrible losses in his life, that he'd carried a truckload of regrets. But I'd had no idea the depths of his pain.

I'd seen real glimpses of it in his eyes tonight, felt his broken heart in the tears that'd soaked my shirt.

But when he looked at me now, his eyes were clear, flickering with something new and shiny. Something that brought a warmth to my chest I couldn't even describe.

Hope.

"Tonight," he said through new tears, "just before you came in here, was the first time since Elena had pointed that gun at me that she gave me any indication that we might have a relationship again." He smiled faintly, lowering his eyes and focusing on a loose thread in the sheet. When he looked up at me again, he said softly, "*Querida*, I died that night, didn't I?"

It took me a beat to realize he was no longer talking about what had happened between him and Elena, but the warehouse battle. The sudden shift nearly gave me whiplash; it felt as if I'd been yanked back in time, back to those ugly moments of seeing him lying in a pool of his own blood.

"You... you'd been badly wounded in the fight," I began, my throat thick with emotion. "Cut with a silver blade. Bleeding..."

"Badly wounded enough to die, then." He shook his head, as if trying to clear away new cobwebs. "I remember trying to shift out of my wolf, and I couldn't. Not all the way. I remember having all the heightened senses and instincts of the wolf, but the pain felt like a man's pain. The fear was... indescribable."

"There was a while there where you got kind of... stuck," I explained. "You couldn't quite shift one way or the other. Ronan and Elena didn't know how to heal you."

"So how *did* they heal me?"

I pressed my fingertips to his lips and shook my head. I wanted to shush him, to tell him there was no point in revisiting that awful night. That the important thing was that he did survive, never mind the hows of it all.

But secrets and lies were the twin snakes that kept looping back to bite us, time and time again. Whether it was Emilio lying to his sister about how her family died, or Liam lying to me about our relationship, or Ronan keeping my deal a secret, or me lying to him initially about what I'd done to Bean... Secrets like ours were heavy burdens, and eventually, they came crashing down on us, and the truth slithered out, all the more venomous for the time it'd had to fester.

I made a vow right then and there that I'd never lie to the men I loved. Not even to protect them.

"The warehouse was burning," I said, "and I was on one side with Ash and Darius and Jael, along with the witches we'd just liberated. We were running for the exit, and I just... I saw you go down. I got to you as quickly as I could, but you were... you were in bad shape."

I told him the details, as best as I could remember.

"Ronan promised he'd save you, and so I left. We had to get the witches to safety. So I came back here with Ash and Darius and everyone else, and we just waited for word from Ronan and Elena. When they finally showed up, you weren't with them. Ronan said that Liam arrived in the form of the great raven to claim your soul. He saw it leave your body. You were… mutilated." I shivered as the images flooded my mind again, unbidden. Emilio lying in all that blood, his chest cleaved open, his body shifting between man and wolf, stuck in limbo. "Liam took you, but Ronan and Elena didn't know where. You were just… gone."

Snuggling in close, I told him the rest of the story—how I knew he wasn't totally gone from us. How Haley and I did the blood spell and I'd tracked them to my realm. How I'd fought Jonathan, how when I finally found Emilio and Liam, it looked as if they'd been waiting for me. I explained the ritual Liam had guided me through, trying to remember all the details—the moonglass, the magic, the feel of his soul as I gently guided it back home.

"And together," I finished up, "Liam and I brought you back. I'm not sure what happened in the realm after that— there was a strange earthquake sort of event, but then it stopped. And you called for me. That's when we knew you were okay. I took your hands in mine, and then… Well, the next thing I knew, I was waking up in this bed next to you, and Haley was shouting for Ronan and Elena, and someone told Lansky to call the medics back to the house. I was fine the next day—just needed a little rest after the energy expenditure from calling up and using so much magic. You needed a little more time." I kissed his shoulder again, dropping my voice to a whisper. "And here you are. Back with me where you belong."

Emilio was silent for a long time, and though I was dying for his thoughts, I let him be. It was a lot to process, coming back from the brink of death.

"I heard your voice," he finally said, a little awestricken. "Felt your presence all around me. I felt this... this energy pulling me toward the gates. I guess some part of me *knew* I had died—that I was supposed to go through them. But suddenly you were there, your spirit. It was pulling me, too. And no matter how strong the call coming from the other side of that gate, I knew I didn't want to go through it. Not as long as you were standing on the outside, calling me home."

"As if I'd *let* you leave without me." I tried to laugh, but Emilio seemed to be stuck in that moment, uncertain of how to feel about the whole thing.

"Gray, that kind of magic... There's always a cost."

I offered a faint smile. I'd said something similar to Liam when he'd made the moonglass. "Doesn't mean it isn't worth it."

He nodded, but I could tell he wasn't convinced. He brought my hands to his mouth, pressed a kiss against each palm. When he looked at me again, he said, "What was the price, *querida*?"

"I don't know. Honestly. I connected with Liam briefly last night—He's still in my realm, still hunting Jonathan. He told me he's been called to appear before... Well, I think he called it a cosmic tribunal? We don't know exactly what that means for us yet."

"Maybe nothing," he said.

"Maybe nothing," I echoed, but the words felt as thin as the frost on the edges of the window.

"Gray, you shouldn't have—"

"Don't even think it."

"But—"

"I have the power to raise the dead, Emilio. To manipulate souls. I don't know why that power was entrusted to me. Or how it even works, exactly. Or what my bigger purpose is in all of this. I don't even know if the Silversbane prophecy is legit, or just some wishful thinking by generations of witches desperate for answers and hunters even more desperate to get their hands on that kind of mojo. But I *do* know that I can't lose you. That in that moment, I was facing that very real possibility of having to say goodbye to you forever. So yes, maybe there *is* a bigger consequence, an astronomical price tag we can't even imagine, and it'll drop on us all like an atomic bomb when we least expect it. But I would do it again in a god damn heartbeat. You know why?"

He didn't say anything. Just turned his head away, his eyes focusing on the ceiling.

"Because I love you," I said softly. Taking his face between my palms, I turned his head toward me again, stroking my thumbs over his cheeks. "You snuck up on me, Emilio Alvarez. From the very first, you showed me so much kindness and compassion during Sophie's murder investigation. You supported me even when I violated police procedure. You bought me shower poofs and baked me brownies and watched the moonrise with me. You protected me. You let me into your heart. And somewhere in all of that, through all the insane stuff that's happened between the first time you showed up at my house with your messy bed-hair and San Francisco T-shirt, and right this very moment, I fell in love with you. *That's* why."

Another tear escaped down his cheek, but still he hadn't spoken. His brown eyes seemed to darken.

Emilio was healing remarkably well, especially considering the extent of the original damage. Elena was right—his color was looking good, and the wounds crisscrossing his body were no more than battle scars now, his skin red and raised, but completely healed.

Still, the experience had clearly changed him. He'd died that night, and I'd brought him back. Despite the fact that he'd just unburdened himself of one of his greatest secret shames by telling me about his past, there were new shadows swimming in the depths of his eyes.

It seemed to me that he'd aged, somehow. Not physically, but... cosmically.

"I don't know how to ask this," I began. "So I'm just going to blurt it out. Are you pissed that we brought you back? Or freaked out or... I don't know. Confused? I need you to be totally honest with me."

At this, he immediately shook his head, surprising me.

"You brought me back to my sister. To a chance to set things right between us—a chance that she is finally willing to consider after twenty years of stone-cold silence. You brought me back to my brothers. To my life's work. To the new friends and partners we're making here in Raven's Cape. And most importantly, you brought me back to *you, mi brujita.* To the woman I fell *madly* in love with. So sure, I could sit here on this bed and tell you that what you did was wrong, unnatural, that it never should've happened, that I was supposed to die that night and you should've let me go." He closed his eyes and let out a deep breath, and when he looked up at me again, his gaze was full of fire. "But that would make me a damn liar, because there is *nowhere* else I'd rather be than right here in your arms."

He slid his hands into my hair and pulled me against his mouth, stealing my breath with a wild, feverish kiss that had me wishing we had the house all to ourselves. I wanted him to claim me in every room, in every way, both of us running around naked and howling up at the moon and celebrating the fact that we'd survived another crazy night.

But for now, that kind of celebration would have to wait. I was grateful for the kissing, anyway.

I finally pulled back to catch my breath, my lips stinging with the intensity of his welcomed attack.

"You're blushing, *querida,*" he teased. "Something on your mind?"

"Maybe." More heat rushed to my cheeks. I felt like a kid with a crush, and I loved every minute of it. "It's just… You… you fell in love with me, too?"

"You think I buy shower poofs and twelve bottles of fruity conditioners for *every* woman I meet?" He grabbed me by the arms and flipped us so that he was on top of me, the sheet between us barely hiding his desire. "What kind of—"

He cut off abruptly, taking a deep whiff of the air, his face twisting with concern. I felt the change in his body immediately—his muscles stiffened, then bunched, and I recognized the movements for what they were.

He was about to shift.

"Emilio, don't!" I gripped his arms, his muscles hot beneath my touch. "You're not totally healed yet."

Without a word, he jumped up from the bed and headed for the door, naked and stumbling as he went.

"Wait!" I shouted, chasing him down the hall, nearly tripping over Sunshine and Sparkle on the way. "You're still healing! You can't just—"

"The guys are in trouble!" he shouted, barely avoiding a collision with Elena, who seemed to be on the same trajectory toward the front of the house. Someone managed to haul open the front door just in time, and the pair launched themselves out, transforming into wolves before their feet even touched the snow-covered ground.

TWENTY-ONE

GRAY

The question about whether Emilio could fully shift in his current condition was swiftly answered.

They were magnificent together, two sleek, black wolves streaking across the bright white snow like arcs of dark lightning. I was so mesmerized by their power, their grace, that it took my mind a minute to process the sight unfolding before me.

The team that had gone out for supplies in two relatively newish vans was now stumbling out of a single, completely jacked-up van that had somehow gotten wedged into a snowbank at the end of the driveway.

Haley, Jael, Ronan, Darius, and Lansky—I counted them twice just to be sure. They were all there. All standing on their own two feet.

But three of them were covered in blood.

"Ronan!" I ran outside, following the path of the wolves

to the end of the driveway, where Emilio and Elena were frantically sniffing around the van and the perimeter of the yard. Sparkle and Sunshine joined them, tracking some unknown threat.

"It's not our blood," Ronan said, and I stopped just before him, reaching out to touch his jacket for a quick second. He lowered his head to catch my eyes. "Hey. I'm okay, Gray. We all are. I promise. Which is more than I can say for half the shit we bought and one of the vans, but hey. Priorities, right?"

I nodded, the adrenaline spike slowly fading. "What happened?"

"We—" Ronan began, but his attention suddenly shifted to the super-hyper wolf circling us, wagging his tail and yelping like a puppy.

"What? Look at *you*!" Ronan let out a full-on laugh, dropping to his knees to grab Emilio's huge wolf head. He scratched him behind the ears and brought his face close, inhaling Emilio's scent, his eyes full of emotion. The whole thing was so adorable and touching, it basically turned my insides into a puddle of goo.

"Who's back in action, huh?" Ronan wrestled Emilio to the ground, teasing him like he really *was* a puppy. "Who's the biggest, baddest wolf that ever was? Who's a good boy?"

The two of them went at it, rolling around in the snow until Emilio finally pinned Ronan by the shoulders. He licked his face from chin to forehead, and then, shocking us all, shifted back into his human form.

Asher and a crowd of witches had gathered on the lawn now, and all of us busted up laughing at the sight of a very hot, very naked man straddling a very stunned demon.

"Dude, are you fucking *kidding* me?" Ronan shoved Emilio off and got back to his feet, dusting himself off. "I didn't miss you *that* much! For fuck's sake, put some clothes on."

"No!" McKenna shouted. "Don't cover up on our account, hot stuff."

"Seconded," Kasey, another witch from the prison, called out. Elena had bought everyone new phones, and she had hers out now, probably filming a livestream of the whole thing. Not that I blamed her.

"Even *I* got a little buzz from that display," Asher said, kicking snow at Ronan.

Emilio smacked Ronan on the shoulder. "You love it and you know it, hellspawn."

"I feel totally violated," Ronan said, but he was grinning like an idiot. Rubbing the snow from his hair, he said, "Shit, it's good to see you walking, brother."

"Good to *be* walking."

"All sorted?" Darius asked. Then, without waiting for a reply, "Excellent. Perhaps you might consider dressing, preferably before that summer sausage of yours turns into a cocktail wiener? It *is* ten below out here, you daft bastard."

Emilio wasted no time in hauling Darius in for a hug. Unlike Ronan, Darius took the "violation" in stride.

"You look much better than the last time I saw you," Darius said, his voice heavy with relief. He might not remember everything about Emilio, but he'd come to care for him all over again. That much was obvious.

"Unlike you guys." Emilio wrinkled his nose. "What *is* that stench? I thought I smelled shifters. Elena and I bolted out here, thinking you'd been attacked."

"We were waylaid by a pack of hybrid shifters," Darius said. "Mountain lions. The whole thing was a mind-fuck cleverly disguised as an ambush."

"Orendiel?" I asked, snapping my fingers for my hounds to come back. Though the wolves had decided we weren't under immediate attack, my hounds were already patrolling the street in front of the house. I couldn't blame them—they'd been cooped up most of the day on account of the snow. Seemed it was lightening up a bit now, though.

"Yes," Jael said, coming out from behind the van with an armload of grocery bags. "Along with his associates on the fae council. They left us a message."

"I don't care what it takes," Lansky was barking into his cell phone, pacing in the snow alongside the van. "Get a team up there. I need barricades between the seven-mile marker and the twelve. That whole section is officially closed until they can clear out the vehicles and the body. No, no ID. Let the M.E. figure it out."

"Body?" I asked.

"Girl, you have no idea." Haley handed me a package of toilet paper about the size of a small condo, then returned to the van to retrieve some kind of crate. With a bright, trademark-Haley smile, she said, "The good news? The alcohol survived the crash. I repeat, the alcohol survived the crash."

TWENTY-TWO

In celebration of our wolf pup's triumphant return from the land of the near-dead, Elena had outdone herself in the culinary department, setting up a massive buffet in the dining room featuring all of Emilio's favorites from the homeland. It was so good to be home, to be surrounded by everyone I cared about… All the Orendiel bullshit began to fade into the background.

Liam was still in the Shadowrealm, and part of me actually missed the guy, despite my feelings about what he'd done to get Gray's soul back from hell. The longer I'd sat with it, the faster my rage had started morphing into something pretty damn unfamiliar to me.

Gratitude.

We'd all done things to keep her safe. To keep each *other* safe. I couldn't fault him for that. Not when I caught her blue-eyed gaze across the table, the soft smile on her lips just for me. The woman still loved me, even after everything.

I gave her a wink, then reached for my glass. We may have been temporarily without everybody's favorite surfing philosopher, but we still had a lot to celebrate tonight. It was the first time the rest of us had all been together in a long-ass time, and that alone deserved a toast.

So all around the dining table and spilling into the living room, we raised our glasses of whiskey and wine—and chocolate milk for Reva—and for the span of one incredible meal, we allowed ourselves to relax. To drink. To laugh. To just be.

But by the time the dinner dishes were cleared and the coffee and *tres leches* cake appeared, the mood had shifted. It was like we all sensed it at the same time—an invisible threat, still hanging over our heads, still lurking just outside the door.

"I feel like we're still missing a lot of pieces to this puzzle," Gray began, sneaking something under the table to one of her hounds. "But we can't sit around waiting for answers that may never come. Especially not after what happened to you guys on the road tonight. We need to make a plan of attack."

"Attack?" Reva set down the bite of cake she'd been about to take, the color draining from her face. She looked up at Gray, who was seated next to her. "I thought you guys were done fighting. Everyone's here. Everyone got out. Even Emilio is better."

Gray ran a hand over Reva's fuzzy head. "We didn't get

everyone out, sweets. Jonathan had been keeping and tormenting other supernaturals besides witches. We can't just turn our backs on them."

"I know, but… What about their own people? Why does it have to be you guys?" The poor kid looked terrified, and I couldn't blame her. These witches had become her family. We all had, in a very short time at that. She didn't want to lose a single one of us.

"Because we know about the situation," Gray said, "and together, we have the power to do something about it." She took Reva's hand in hers and smiled, her whole face lighting up with pride. "It's kind of like when you guys were stuck in the caves. You were the only one who knew another way out, and even though it was a huge personal risk, you took it. You slipped away from the guards and snuck out right under their noses. Right?"

"I guess."

"Look around, Reva. All these amazing witches sitting here tonight? That smart-ass demon over there snarfing down his fourth piece of cake, even though everyone else hasn't even had one yet?" Gray grinned at Asher, who laughed with his damn mouth full, then shrugged and shoved in another bite. "They're all here because of you. Because they were in trouble, and you had the power to do something about it, and you did it. No questions or second-guessing."

"I'll drink to that." McKenna raised her glass again, nodding at Reva, and the rest of the witches and Ash followed suit.

Reva's cheeks glowed pink once again, and she nodded and took another big gulp of her chocolate milk, looking about six years old instead of sixteen. Damn, sometimes it was easy to forget she *was* just a kid—one whose sense of security and normalcy had been stolen from her, time and again. By Norah. By whoever shit-ass adults abused or just plain lost track of her in the first place.

We're not gonna let that happen again, kiddo...

"One thing's for sure," Ash said now. "The whole lure-them-out plan is shot to shit. From what you said about those mountain lion shifters, they've definitely got eyes on us. No way they're taking the bait."

"Agreed," Beaumont said. "So that's where our plan of attack comes in. It seems we'll have to take the fight to them after all."

"You talking about the Bay?" Emilio asked. He gestured for Elena to pass him the cake, and cut himself a hefty slice. I still couldn't believe how good he looked—even better than before the fight at the warehouse. The fact that he was even sitting here with us was a damn miracle. But smiling? Happy?

"You still thinking about our roll in the snow?" he asked, and it took me a half-second to realize he was talking about me. The whole table erupted in laughter. "You're looking at me like you want to make out or something."

"There's not enough whiskey in this whole town to make that happen." I lifted my coffee mug, which was half full of the stuff anyway, and grinned, taking a big gulp. "I was just thinking that the whole coming-back-from-the-brink-of-death thing is a good look on you."

"And I'll drink to *that*." He lifted his mug and stretched across the table to clink it against mine.

"We're all drinking to that." Elena laughed and reached for the bottle of whiskey at the center of the table, topping off her own coffee, then passing the bottle to Gray. Around the table it went.

When we'd all settled down again, McKenna said, "Okay, so how can we bring the fight to the Bay? Jael said there's no way in, not even by a sneak attack. We can't even get close."

"Anyone got any ideas?" I asked. "Any magic we haven't thought of, spells we could use, weapons, something…"

Reva raised her hand. "Oh! I have an idea."

I bit back a laugh, totally picturing her in school, squirming out of her chair to answer the teacher's question. *Pick me! Pick me!*

"If it's your idea, it's bound to be good," Gray said, and Reva grinned. "Let's hear it."

"What if I did something with my shadow traveling? I don't know anything about disabling fae magic, but I might be able to get into the city astrally and snoop around. Maybe I could, like, spy? Find out what kind of spell they're using or what else is happening over there? Anything could help."

"It's… possible." Jael tapped an elegant finger against his coffee mug as he considered it. "Since she wouldn't be physically trying to get into the Bay, the magic wouldn't necessarily register her presence. She may be able to slip through."

"Wouldn't they have accounted for something like that, though?" Haley asked. "Seems like a pretty big flaw in their security."

"But they don't even know about her," Ash said. "You saw this little badass in the caves, Hay. She snuck out right under their noses, and they never gave it a second thought."

"Shadow traveling *is* quite rare," Jael said. "I don't believe we've come across a witch with that power in decades. It's unlikely that Orendiel and the hunters would've concerned themselves with something like that— they can't possibly account for all variables. They're more focused on Gray and the other supernaturals sitting around this table. Honestly, they may not even realize how strong the rest of the witches are. They may believe they're still in a weakened state after the prison ordeal."

"Yeah, underestimating us is kind of a hunter specialty," McKenna said. "Dicks."

Elena reached for the coffee carafe, topping off a few of our mugs. "Okay, in theory, I like Reva's idea. We can protect her physically, and she can sneak into the city with her shadow mojo. But she still has to get close to the Bay, and I'm not sure how to do that. Between the storm, the road closures, and the risk of exposure to Darkwinter spies, it'd be a pretty big gamble."

"Well, it's not so much the distance that's a problem,"

Reva said. "I was able to get to Gray in that fireplace, right? And that was while I was here in the cave prison, and she was staying at the safe house near the Bay. So, it's the same distance, basically."

"So you think you can do it from here?" Elena asked her.

"Not at the moment. I mean, I could *get* there, sure. But I don't think I could hold a clear connection for very long. Like that time with Gray, I was only able to get a few words out. Same with Emilio the first time I traveled to see him in the woods."

"Right," Emilio said. "It'd felt like a bad connection. It was easier for me to pick up on it in my wolf form, but even then, it was spotty and didn't last very long."

"And for this to work," Elena said, "you'd need more time in there. Not just to spy, but to be sure you weren't seen in the process. If they spotted you, even astrally, they'd know about our secret weapon, and you'd be on their radar in a big way. I won't take that risk."

"I can do it," Reva said. "I know I can. I just need to practice. I need to work on sustaining the connection and keeping it clear."

"We can all help her with that," McKenna said, and the other witches nodded. "It's not like we're going anywhere with this storm, anyway."

Elena finally agreed. "Let's see how the practices go. We'll check in a couple of days and figure out next steps."

"Okay, so that's a good start," Gray said, passing Asher yet another piece of cake. I didn't know how that bastard wasn't four hundred pounds by now. "Hopefully, Reva's insights can help us track down Orendiel and pinpoint his base of operations. That way, if we can figure out how to break the magical security, we'll know the primary target in the city."

"I still feel like there's someone higher up pulling the strings," Emilio said. "Not just the council, but someone else. Someone with much bigger aspirations."

"Bigger than wiping out supernaturals from the inside out, and stealing witches' power?" Gray asked.

"I mean, those are major things," Emilio said. "But hunters have always wanted that. And no offense, Jael, but you can't tell me the fae are totally cool with witches and other supers having magic. That's always been a sore point with the Council."

"Snobs," Asher fake-coughed into his hand.

"No, you're right," Jael said. "I'm afraid my kind has always held a bit of an elitist attitude toward magic. But most of us have made peace with the fact that we have to share it. Most of us have no interest in subjugating witches —or anyone else for that matter."

"Still," Emilio said, "*some* of you do. Darkwinter, specifically. So this is really nothing new for them—it's just happening on a much bigger scale. But at the end of the day, Orendiel is still just a soldier. And so are Talia and Fenlos. I'm telling you guys, my gut says there's more to this than just a coup."

The house fell silent, all of us sipping our spiked coffee, nibbling on the last crumbs of cake. I sensed the mood shift again, the hope we'd built up slipping dangerously close to despair once again.

Not tonight. No fucking way.

"Look, guys," I said. "The other night, Beaumont said we can't let fear and speculation sidetrack us, and he's right. We need to stick with the known quantities, and right now, that's Orendiel and the Bay."

The vampire nodded at me across the table. "Thank you, hellspawn. I didn't know you'd been listening."

I grinned at him. "What can I say, bloodsucker? I'm full of surprises." Then, to the rest of the group, "So we're in agreement? Gather intel on Orendiel and the Bay, figure out a way to get in there and neutralize the Darkwinter Knights, and take it from there. With enough witches on our side, I'm pretty sure we can show those hunters *and* the dark fae straight to the fucking door."

"With enough witches?" At this, Gray's eyes suddenly lit up. "Wait. I might have an idea on how we can get in."

"Don't keep us in suspense, Cupcake," Asher said.

"We all know that witches help keep the power balance in check," she said. "That's why it was so easy for Orendiel's Knights to destabilize the Bay and lock it up with fae mojo. Most of the witches had been imprisoned, murdered, or chased out, leaving the city wide open for a new power to slip in."

"Yes," Emilio said. "By the time we left the Bay to come here, the power structure was already crumbling. That's when we started seeing a rise in supernatural-related crimes. The Bay was essentially falling apart before our eyes, and there wasn't a damn thing we could do about it."

"So... What if we could counteract Darkwinter by restoring some of the power balance in the city?" she asked.

"What do you mean?" McKenna asked. "How?"

"We've got about two dozen witches in this house alone." Gray rose from her chair, her excitement building. "I'm sure we could bring even more into the fold if we put the word out in the Cape and some of the neighboring towns."

"You know, that's not a bad idea," Elena said. "We can check in with Verona Braden—she owns the metaphysical shop where Delilah was last seen. If anyone would know how to get in touch with the witches of Raven's Cape, it'd be her."

"Here's what I'm thinking," Gray continued. "We start putting the word out. Get everyone together. Bide our time a bit, train, figure out when it's right for Reva to slip in there and poke around. Using her intel, we'll narrow down our main targets and anything else we need to know. Then, assuming we get a large enough contingent of witches, we ride out to the Bay, see if we can break that spell with our own collective magic."

"And once we're in," Haley said, "we take back our city. Fuck yeah, Desario."

"Storm the castle, so to speak," Darius said. "Excellent. I'm told I own a club in Blackmoon Bay. And a rather nice car."

"I can attest to that," Gray said, her cheeks darkening in a way that set a flare of jealousy straight into my chest.

Really? In Beaumont's car?

I grabbed my drink, drowning the flood of images that thought unleashed. It's not that I was jealous she'd been with him.

It was that she still *could* be with him. He may not remember everything about their relationship, but he could still touch her.

My heart burned with a now-familiar ache, but I shoved it way down. Regret had no place at this table. We were so close to figuring this shit out. Close to taking back what was ours.

"I think," Emilio said, reaching for the bottle of whiskey once again, "we've got ourselves a plan. A damn good one. And that calls for another round."

Everyone cheered and banged on the table, laughter exploding like fireworks once again. And for a minute I closed my eyes and soaked up all the warmth and let myself believe this was home. That we were all part of a big, crazy, obnoxious family celebrating a holiday dinner that we'd make last all week.

It's almost enough to ease the pain of our reality.

"Personally, I think it calls for a group hug," Haley said, rising from her chair and waving everyone close. "Come on, guys. You too, grumpy demon over there. Bring it in."

She was talking about me. I got up and joined the knot of people that'd formed at the head of the table, never losing sight of Gray.

I stood as close as I dared. I caught a hint of her scent, a touch of her sweater brushing along my forearm as I reached in to hug Ash. But all I could think about was touching her. Holding her in my arms. Pressing my lips to her forehead and promising her that everything would work out. That we'd be okay, just like always.

I couldn't do that, though. Couldn't even graze her skin without burning her. It was the ultimate fucking punishment.

And after everything we'd been through together, all the shit we'd somehow come out on top of, this would be the thing that would finally break me.

The others let out another collective cheer, the celebration kicking back into high gear as more hugs and more booze got passed around, and I grabbed a jacket and one of the hounds and slipped out the back door unnoticed, out into the snow-globe night where I could temporarily lose myself in the backwoods, breathe in the icy-fresh air, and—for a little while, anyway—pretend I wasn't dying inside.

TWENTY-THREE

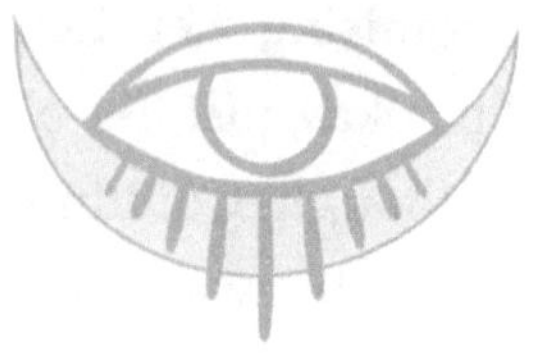

GRAY

The morning after our insane feast, the hounds and I found Elena in the kitchen at dawn, cracking dozens of eggs into a huge bowl. The sun was giving us a rare show, the snow finally letting up a bit, and the light streamed in through the kitchen windows, illuminating her like an angel.

After everything Emilio had told me about what they'd gone through—about what Elena had lost—it was hard to look at her without getting choked up.

"I know I look good from the back," she called over her shoulder. "But damn, girl. Take a picture or something."

I laughed, the knot of emotion loosening. She'd probably scented me long before I'd even approached. It was hard enough to sneak up on a regular shifter, never mind a cop shifter.

"Girl, did you even go to bed last night?" I asked.

"I did. But I was wide awake an hour ago, so I put on the coffee and got to cooking."

"Again?"

"Honestly?" Elena laughed. "I love cooking. Besides, it's easier than doing dishes."

I glanced around the kitchen, taking in the mountains of dishes piled up on the countertops, plates and mugs practically spilling out of the dishwasher. Other than Reva, we'd all gotten a little tipsy last night, caught up in celebrating Emilio's recovery and enjoying a little fun before tackling the challenges ahead.

"You want some help?" I asked her.

She looked at Sunshine and Sparkle, panting and excited, and then at me, taking in my puffy coat, snow boots, and the huge, fur-lined hat I'd found that made me look like a Russian soldier. "Looks like you three already have plans."

"I promised them a walk in the woods this morning." I scratched behind Sparkle's ears, and she let out a little yelp of pleasure. "But I can be back in fifteen minutes to chop or wash or whatever."

"No, Gray. It's a beautiful day, and who knows how long it'll last? You need some fresh air and alone time." She offered me a warm smile, then nodded toward a basket covered with a towel. "Take two blueberry muffins to go."

I reached for the basket. "Two? These things are huge."

In response, she leaned her head out the kitchen doorway, calling across the dining room to a pile of witches in the living room, most of them crashed out on the air beds and sleeping bags they'd brought back from the supply run. Elena had set some of the beds up in the basement downstairs, but most of them had wandered back up here some-time in the middle of the night. It seemed they'd gotten used to close quarters in prison and didn't want to be separated.

I couldn't blame them. Now that I had my rebels back under the same roof, I didn't want to be separated from them, either. The five of us had crashed in the room Emilio and I had shared, Ronan taking a sleeping bag on the floor, lest we accidentally bump toes and start a fire.

"Haley!" Elena shout-whispered, as if that wouldn't wake up the entire room. "Haley! Get dressed."

"Hmm?" came the groggy reply, and like a litter of kittens piled up in a box, the rest of them stirred, too.

"Get up, girl," Elena said, and Haley's head finally popped up from the pile.

"I'm up, I'm up." She stifled a yawn, slowly getting to her feet and picking her way across the floor. "What's going on?"

"Gray needs your help outside with the hounds," Elena blurted out, and I almost smacked her. "I don't want any of you wandering out there alone. Even during the daylight hours."

"No worries. Give me five minutes." Haley stretched, then disappeared into the bathroom.

"What is *wrong* with you?" I asked the minute Haley was out of earshot. "I thought you said I needed alone time!"

"You do—alone time with your sister. You have to tell

her, *loca*," Elena said. "You keep putting it off, and you're going to miss the chance and regret it forever."

I opened my mouth to argue, but Elena was right. If anyone knew about regret and potentially rocky sibling reunions, it was her.

Still, I wasn't ready. Telling Haley she had not just one but three sisters, that I was one of them, that we were all part of some ancient witchcraft legacy, that our mother had tried to kill us... The conversation was a lot more involved than dropping one simple truth-bomb about a long-lost sister.

"Aren't you happy that she's your sister?" Elena asked, cutting right to it, as usual. "Don't you want her to share that joy?"

"I'm thrilled," I said, because I truly was. "It's just that... I don't know. I guess I keep waiting for a sign from her. Like some kind of guarantee that she'll feel the same way."

"Oh, Gray." Elena wiped her hands on the towel tossed over her shoulder, then cupped my face. "How could she not?"

I shrugged. I know it seemed obvious to her, but I'd been alone for so long, I felt totally clueless about how female friendships worked, let alone sisterhoods. Sophie was the first and only female friend I'd ever really had, and I'd kept her at a distance, too. It was kind of ironic that she was the one to bring Haley into my life. And though Haley and I had gotten pretty close since Sophie died, I had no way of knowing how she truly felt about me.

What if it totally freaked her out? Or worse—what if she already knew we were sisters, and didn't want to tell me because she didn't want the burden that came along with that? The obligation?

What if *she* didn't want to claim *me*?

"No, no, no. Don't do that." Elena whipped me on the butt with her towel, recapturing my attention. "You're overthinking it, Gray. You need to just tell her, get it all out, and let things unfold naturally from there. Haley will listen. She'll—"

"Listen to what?" Haley appeared in the doorway looking as fresh and perky as if she'd already downed half a pot of coffee. She was all bundled up, just like me, her cheeks pink, her eyes bright. We looked like a pair of snow-beasts about to embark on an Arctic adventure.

"I'll... tell you outside," I mumbled. My heart fluttered with fresh nerves, but they weren't necessarily bad ones. Just... nervous ones.

Brilliant, Desario. Really.

Haley shrugged, then spotted the basket on the counter. "Ooh, muffins!"

"I already got one for you." I laughed, catching Elena's eye. Yeah, it was time.

Thank you, I mouthed.

Elena winked, then shooed us all toward the back door, Sunshine and Sparkle practically peeing themselves with excitement.

"Brunch will be ready in an hour," she said, "so don't go

too far. I'm counting on you two to referee the bacon plate. You know how guys are about their meat."

Haley cracked up. "Gray *is* the expert on guys and their meat."

Holding back a laugh of my own, I shoved her out the door before she could make any more jokes about my arrangement with the guys.

"Don't knock the meat-lover's sampler platter until you've tried it," I said.

"*Knock* it? Seriously? Girl, I'm over here trying to figure out where to order my *own* sampler platter." Haley giggled and linked her arm in mine, and together we followed the hounds into the woods, Elena's laughter trailing us all the way there.

TWENTY-FOUR

GRAY

The snow out back was hip-deep in parts, and though Haley and I had to push ourselves to plod through it, it was no match for the hounds. They bounded around like a couple of pups, carving figure eights in the thick layers of white as Haley and I fought for every breath. When we finally reached the shelter of the backwoods, the snow leveled off, and we scouted around for a good place to take a muffin break.

"There," she said, pointing out a huge nurse log lying in a copse of trees, mostly untouched by the snow.

We sat on the log side by side, unwrapping the muffins while the hounds waited at our feet, their hypnotic eyes fixated on our every move.

"Haley," I began, at the same time she said, "Can we talk about the hounds?"

We both laughed, then she said, "I'm sorry. You go first."

"No, it's fine. They're kind of new to the family. Courtesy of Sebastian."

She hadn't spent much time with them yet—other than for a few brief hours with Emilio last night before dinner, they'd hardly left my side since we'd all escaped the warehouse.

"So basically, they're your jailers?" she asked.

"More like my protectors," I told her. "And my friends. I don't think that's how Sebastian intended it, but that's how it worked out. Right, girls?"

They wagged their tails and licked their chops, probably thinking I was about to hand over the muffin. Not happening.

"Their cuteness is definitely in the eye of the beholder," Haley said, narrowing her gaze on them. "But I have to admit… they're kind of growing on me."

"They have that effect."

"Can I…?" She held out her hand tentatively, and Sunshine nudged it with her nose.

"Be my guest. Looks like they like you."

She stroked Sunshine's muzzle, and of course, Sparkle wanted in on the action too. Soon they were competing for her affection, plodding around the woods in search of sticks and rocks and other gifts for their new friend.

Sparkle came back with a huge, snow-packed pine bough about the size of Haley herself, and we both cracked up.

"I'm so honored, Sparkle," Haley said. "What a beautiful gift. I shall treasure it always. From a great distance."

The sun peeked through the clouds overhead, rimming the snow-covered pines around us in a golden glow, and a calmness came over me. The sound of my sister's laugh filled me with pure happiness, and suddenly I felt lighter, knowing that the moment was right.

It was time.

"I need to tell you something, Haley," I said softly. "It's important."

She stopped petting Sparkle and glanced up at me, expectant. "Everything okay?"

"More than okay. You're… you're my sister."

"Oh my God, I'm *so* glad you said that." Her eyes filled with emotion, and she leaned over to pull me into a hug. "I feel the same way, Gray. I know we got off to a rough start at Norah's place, but that was just growing pains, you know? We make a kickass team. Remember that time at the morgue, with that security guard? I wonder what he's—"

"Haley." I pulled out of her crushing hug and grabbed her arms, blinking the happy tears from my eyes. She was such a crazy witch, in the best possible way, and she was mine. All mine. How did I get so lucky? "Listen to me. You're my sister. My *real* sister. As in, we have the same biological parents. The same blood. The same grandmother —Deirdre."

Haley's eyes widened. For a moment, she went totally still. She didn't breathe, didn't make a sound. I held my breath, too, worried she was about to bolt on me, or laugh, or just… not react at all.

But then she just started laughing again, happy tears

like mine streaking her cheeks, and I let out a big, fat sigh of relief.

"Sisters?" she asked, bewildered. "But… how?"

How? I wanted to make a sex joke. Like, *Well, Haley, when a mommy and a daddy love each other very much…*

But I couldn't. Our mother *hadn't* loved our father. She'd murdered him. She'd made four babies with him, and then snuffed out his life, nearly snuffing out ours, too.

"There's… more," I said.

Haley was still beaming. "I'm all ears. Tell me everything."

"No, I mean more of *us*. Our parents had four daughters. Somewhere out there in the world, we've got two other sisters. We were all separated as children and raised separately to keep us safe, because there's this whole prophecy thing and our mother wanted our magic and… God, this is a long story."

My heart was in my throat, my magic buzzing beneath my skin as I thought of our mother again. Even the hounds picked up on it—they bounded back over to me, pressing against my legs, sniffing all around.

"It's okay, girls. Mama just needs to chill." I blew out a frosty breath, then steadied myself, waiting for my magic to settle. When it did, I turned to Haley and told her the whole story—as much as Deirdre had told me, anyway: The Silversbane Prophecy, and our mother's visions about it during her pregnancy. The four of us. How she'd desperately wanted our magic. How Deirdre believed she'd killed our father. Our near-drowning at her hands, and all the ways our lives had irrevocably changed as a result.

"Drowning…" Haley closed her eyes, her voice soft in the winter air. "When I was younger, I used to have this recurring dream. There were four little girls—sometimes I was one of them, and other times I'd be watching them like a movie—you know how dreams are weird like that. Anyway, the girls were always dressed in white, and we were always walking through the woods. Sometimes we'd pick berries, or build a tree fort, or look for cool rocks. That part was slightly different each time, but the dream always ended the same way. Whether I was one of the girls or just an observer, we'd reach the river, and then one by one, we'd vanish. I was always the last one left standing—or I'd watch the last one standing, and she'd become a spitting image of me. And in that moment, I'd be overcome with this feeling of such loneliness…" Haley shook her head. "Sometimes the feeling would stay with me for hours after waking up. Like, some part of me knew that something was missing."

"Something *was*. All of us—we were missing from each other." I put my arm around her shoulder, and we bent our heads together, our breathing synchronized.

"I grew up with good parents," she said. "But they died in a car crash fairly young. My mom's mom—Nona—she raised me after that, but she passed away when I was a freshman in college. I couldn't afford the tuition. I ended up in the Bay—like a lot of witches without a family."

"You had a family, though. We both did. We just didn't know about each other."

Haley nodded, snuggling in closer. "I guess that's why I ended up joining Bay Coven. I wanted that family. That sisterhood. It didn't turn out exactly as I'd hoped, though."

"But it did," I said. "Never mind Norah. You got Sophie out of the deal. And Delilah and Reva and all the others. And after that, you got all the sisters you kept safe in the prison."

"No, you're right."

"You also have me, Hay. And guess what? Now that I've found you, I'm not planning on letting you out of my sight again."

"And I can't escape you, even if I wanted to." She reached down to pat Sunshine's head. "You'd send these two to hunt me down."

"Don't tempt me."

We sat in silence for a moment, both processing things in our own ways. I sensed Haley had a million more questions, as did I. Deirdre might be able to fill in some of the gaps, but the last time I'd seen her was when I'd come back from the realm with Emilio. Once we knew Emilio was out of the woods, she'd said her goodbyes, telling me she had to check in with Sebastian and would be back when she could.

I hadn't heard a peep from her since.

"There's a lot more that Deirdre hasn't told me yet," I said, "but we'll figure it out. We'll find the others."

"We're sisters," she said, her smile widening. "I still can't believe it. And we've got two more."

"Do you think they're in a coven?" I asked. "Or practicing magic at all? I wonder if they're in Washington, close to the Bay. Deirdre said we'd all be drawn there eventually, but right now it's like looking for a needle in—"

Two low, dangerous growls stopped my stream-of-consciousness babble, raising the hairs on the back of my neck.

"Sunshine? Sparkle? What's going on?"

"Do you feel that?" Haley held out her hands, then hopped off the log, looking around the woods as she rubbed the chill from her arms. "It's like it just dropped by about twenty degrees."

"Now that you mention it, yeah." My breath, which had been a thin white mist all morning, was now a dense cloud. I stood up and peered through the trees, looking for a patch of sunlight I was sure had been there seconds earlier.

When had it gotten so dark?

"What time is it?" I asked. "How long have we been out here?"

Haley glanced at her watch. "It's only half-past eight. Less than an hour."

"We'd better head back."

Overhead, the treetops swayed and creaked, dumping another load of snow on the forest floor. And then... silence. Stillness.

Not the good kind.

A chill crawled across my skin. The dogs closed ranks,

flanking me and Haley. Then, they began to bark, but there was no one around—not that I could see.

"Something's not right." I closed my eyes and reached out for a connection with the earth. But for the first time since I'd gotten back in touch with my witchcraft, I felt nothing. It wasn't just that I couldn't sense the earth's magic or draw up the energy. It was like there was no energy there at all. Something was actively blocking it.

"We need to go," I said urgently. "Now."

But it was too late. We'd been spotted. Not by a person or shifter or fae magician.

By something else entirely.

TWENTY-FIVE

GRAY

"What's happening?" Haley's eyes widened. "It feels—"

A gust of arctic wind stole the rest of her words, and she gasped for breath, her lips turning snow white right before my eyes.

Holy. Shit.

"Haley! Move your ass!" I grabbed her hand and bolted, dragging her behind me. I had no idea what was happening, but I felt the frigid air close on our heels as if it were an actual monster chasing us through the woods. Without breaking my stride, I glanced over my shoulder to make sure the hounds were following, and the sight behind me threatened to steal my breath, too.

It was as if the woods had been hit with a tsunami, but instead of sweeping over the landscape with water, this one was invisible, and it turned everything it touched to ice. Glittery silver-white crystals solidified behind us, freezing the air in a narrow path that wound through the trees, heading right for us.

It was no more than fifty feet away.

"Move!" I shouted, tugging her forward. "Faster!"

This was no ordinary storm. Not even the freakiest weather event could explain it. All I knew was that if we didn't beat this thing to the house, we were going to be encased in ice.

We were going to die.

"Haley, faster!"

With a burst of new energy, she pushed forward, linking her arm in mine as we hauled ass toward the backyard. My lungs burned, my lips cracking and bleeding from the cold, my fingers and toes already going numb, but the harder we pushed, the further away the yard was starting to feel.

"We won't make it!" Haley shouted. "There's too much —" The wind howled between us, carrying away the rest of her words.

She was right. That thing was coming too fast. We were already bordering on exhaustion, and the backyard would be another trudge through hip-high snow. We had one last recourse, a realization we both seemed to reach at the same moment.

Magic.

"We need to connect blood!" she shouted. "Bite your hand!"

Still running, we each bit into the soft webbing between our thumb and index finger, drawing blood. Without speaking, we clasped hands again, pressing our wounds together.

I felt the touch of her blood immediately; my magic sparked to life in response.

"Channel my power!" she shouted. "Now!"

Holding onto her hand for dear life, I stopped and turned toward the invisible enemy, raising my other palm and calling on the last of my reserves, drawing on whatever power I could from my sister. I felt her own magic move through me, much liked Darius's power had when we'd fought the memory eaters in the Shadowrealm.

An electric bolt of bright blue magic shot from my outstretched palm and slammed into the icy torpedo heading our way. It exploded in a shower of sparks, and for a moment, everything stilled. I bent over at the waist, trying to catch my breath.

"Calm before the shit-storm," I panted. "We need to keep going."

Haley nodded, still clasping my hand. The magic had bought us a precious few seconds, but it'd weakened us both severely, and now we stumbled awkwardly through the trees and out into the yard, pushing ourselves beyond all physical possibilities.

Everything below my waist was numb.

Sparkle and Sunshine were barking like mad, clearing a path ahead of us.

Slowly, the back deck came into view and the sliding glass door opened. Emilio and Asher bolted out, their eyes wide with shock.

"Get back!" I shouted at them, knowing the ice-missile was already back in motion. "Move!"

They ignored me, both of them leaping off the deck and charging toward us at lightning speed. They reached us at the same time, grabbing us by our jackets and yanking us backward, half-carrying us back to the house. They practically threw us onto the deck, where Ronan and Elena were already reaching for us, hauling us in through the doorway. All four of us plus the hounds tumbled inside, and someone slammed the door shut behind us.

We all watched in horror as the white path that had been targeting us spread out, then crested, peaking as a giant wave that towered over the house.

"Everybody, duck and cover!" Elena shouted. "Away from the windows!"

Then the wave crashed. It broke upon the house, shaking it down to the foundation. Windows shattered. Shelves rattled, dishes crashed to the floor, door frames cracked under the pressure of trying to stabilize the walls.

And then, just as quickly as it had burst on the scene, the mysterious vortex was gone.

Gingerly, we all got to our feet, rounding up everyone inside and making sure no one got hurt. Miraculously, everyone was okay—just completely freaked.

Outside, as far as we could see, the entire property and the forest beyond—was encased in ice, a child's fairytale wonderland that would've been beautiful if it wasn't so absolutely deadly.

"What the hell is happening?" I asked, still panting. My heart was in my throat, hammering so hard I wasn't sure I could even speak around it. "Is this all Darkwinter's doing?"

"No," Jael said. "The magic that made this is much more ancient. Much more deadly."

"What the fuck is it?" Ronan asked.

A familiar voice echoed across the house, his ominous words sending a chill down my spine that had nothing to do with the ice palace outside.

"It seems the price of our actions in the realm has just gone up," Liam said. "And our debtors are ever eager to collect."

TWENTY-SIX

GRAY

"I've been banished to the material plane," Liam said. "Delivered, in essence and body, to your doorstep. I fear my arrival is what brought about your current predicament."

I picked a path across a sea of broken glass in the kitchen, slowly making my way over to Liam. He was in his human form, dressed in dark jeans and an olive green V-neck sweater that made his blue eyes look even more ethereal than usual. To say I was happy to see him was an understatement, despite the bad news he'd brought. Despite all the things that still lingered between us.

He'd brought Emilio back to us. And now he was here.

I pulled him in for a tight hug, my heart still pounding from the ordeal we'd all just been through. He seemed surprised by the contact, stiff in my arms, but I didn't care. I'd missed him. Having him here... Well, it felt like the band was back together again. There was no other way to put it.

"How can the ice bomb be your fault?" I asked, pulling back to look him in the eye. "And what do you mean, you've been banished here? You can't travel to the Shadowrealm?"

"In this form, I am unable to travel *anywhere* now, unless it's on foot or by other normal means of transportation." Liam lowered his eyes. "My powers have been temporarily suspended. I can still take on my raven or owl forms, but that is the extent of my magic. Even as an avian being, I must remain tethered to the material plane. I can no longer manipulate soul energies, travel to or between realms, or perform any of my sacred duties as Death. For all intents and purposes, I'm human."

"Human?" I gasped. Liam had wanted a chance to live out the rest of his life as one of us, but something told me this wasn't what he'd had in mind. "But if you're here, without your powers, who is serving as Death?"

"There is none," he replied somberly.

"But how can that be? For how long?"

"I know not. For as long as it takes the Old One to reach a decision, I suppose."

"So you're on probation, huh?" Asher chuckled. "Never thought I'd see the day *you'd* break the cosmic rules, Spooky."

If Liam was surprised by *my* hug, he was downright shocked by Asher's uncharacteristic display of affection. Ash tackle-hugged the poor guy, nearly knocking him onto his very human—and very nicely packaged in those jeans, I noticed—ass.

"I am… pleased to see you liberated," Liam said, awkwardly patting Asher on the back. "I am pleased to see all of you, though I wish it were under better circumstances."

He broke free, then looked at Ronan, who nodded in greeting. Liam's gaze finally came to rest on Emilio, and the two locked eyes for a long moment, a silent understanding passing between them.

"Where's the vampire?" Liam asked.

"Basement," I said. "Sleeping. Someone should probably go check on him."

"I'll go," Elena said. "I need to check in with the department, too. I want to know if anyone else was affected by this—"

"Arctic missile," Haley said. Then, to Liam, "Yeah, so getting back to that… I thought Darkwinter created the storm? But Jael said it was some kind of ancient magic. Now you're saying it's *your* fault?"

"The dark fae did indeed create the storm, but due to my predicament, it is now growing even larger and more brutal than they'd envisioned. My arrival here seems to correspond with the polar weapon that targeted this precise location. It was as if the stripping of my powers had an immediate and equal reaction on the material plane."

"I thought it was targeting us," I said. "Haley and I were in the woods, and everything just turned into this insane winter wonderland."

"Only not so wonderful," Haley said. "More like a winter wasteland."

"I believe it was drawn toward my energy," Liam said. "Understand… The suspension of my powers is not just about human souls. I am Death, the Great Change, the Ultimate Transformation. Without me, life energy such as that which balances nature cannot—well—transform. We will now experience a state of perpetual winter, compounded infinitely by unchecked fae magic and spellcraft, and a complete power imbalance resulting from the disruption of the witch communities here. All of those forces have conspired in this moment to bring about the destructive forces you've just witnessed."

I leaned back against the kitchen counter, trying to stabilize myself. "This is insane. You all know that, right?"

"I'm afraid there's more," Liam said. "The longer I'm stuck here, powerless, the worse those inhabitants of the material plane will suffer. Living souls will not be able to pass on in death."

"What, like no one can die?" Asher asked.

"People will still die. And their souls will vacate their bodily vessels. But I won't be available to guide them, to call upon my ferriers, to move them through the transition. The souls will wander on the material plane as ghosts, trapped, and growing increasingly confused and frantic at their inability to move on. The more restless a spirit becomes, the more dark energy it draws to itself. That's when you begin to see poltergeists and hauntings, non-demonic soul possessions, things of that sort. That happens now with restless spirits, but consider it on a mass scale, where *all* spirits are restless."

"Humans will go insane," Emilio said. "They will absolutely break with reality."

"Yes, that is my prediction as well," Liam said.

"So we've got a winter weather lockdown," I said, "with the possibility of random, deadly, unpredictable events like what we saw today. We've got ghosts, possibly angry ones. We've got hauntings and possessions. And that's on top of the militarization of cities by the dark fae and the hunters."

"It's a lot to face," Haley said. "But remember what Ronan and Darius said. One thing at a time, deal with the known, figure out the rest as we go."

Footsteps echoed up the basement stairs, and I turned to see Elena emerging from the doorway, cell phone in hand. "No reported injuries from the arctic blast," Elena said. "Not in Raven's Cape, anyway. And Darius is fine, too. Sleeping like a vampire. I decided to let him be. He'll have a busy night ahead of him—as will the rest of us."

"So you got through to the department?" Emilio asked.

"Mayor's office, actually," Elena said. "It seems that what happened here was localized to my property—a rare weather anomaly, they're calling it. But another band of heavy snow is moving in fast, and the rest of the region is still dealing with the accumulation and frigid temperatures we've already experienced. The governor has declared a state of emergency. They're requesting federal aid, with military intervention a strong possibility, should things continue on this trajectory."

"But that means more humans flooding into the Cape," I said. "Right into the path of danger."

"That's exactly what that means." Elena's lips pressed into a grim line.

I looked around the kitchen, cataloging the damage. Broken glass. Broken windows. Cracked walls. Outside, I thought of all the living creatures that must've been buried under that ice fall, and my heart broke.

The full implications of what Liam and I had done in the magic realm were slowly sinking in.

"This is my fault," Liam said.

"No," I said. "It's mine. I'm the one who tracked Emilio to the Shadowrealm. It was my decision to bring him back. You were simply honoring my wishes." I turned to look out the back door, beyond the edge of the property where the trees now sparkled like diamonds in their icy prisons. "I risked all of you... All of this... I put everything on the line to bring Emilio back." I turned back to face them, their outlines blurred by my tears. When I found Emilio's warm gaze, a smile touched my lips. "But I won't apologize for it. I'd do it again in a heartbeat, for any one of you."

"As would I," Ronan said.

"Ditto," Asher said.

"Same," Haley said. "Come on, Gray. Really."

"That isn't up for debate, love." Darius peered out from the other side of the basement door. It seemed he didn't want to sleep through the excitement, after all, but he still couldn't risk sunlight exposure. "All we've left to do is deal with the outcome. How we arrived at that outcome is now irrelevant."

Emilio laced his fingers through mine, giving my hand a squeeze.

"Alright, we need to divide and conquer on this one," he said. "Let the governor coordinate with emergency services and deal with the human population. As for the rest of us, our job description hasn't changed. We need to stay on track with our plans."

"The mayor wants all hands on deck at the precinct," Elena said. "I don't see how I can refuse."

"No, don't refuse," Emilio said. "You, Lansky, and Hobb should do whatever you have to do to maintain status quo. We don't want to arouse any suspicion from the humans, so if coordinating from the precinct is what you'd normally do in extreme weather, then that's what you need to do now. But Elena, you need to be very, very careful out there. Don't travel alone and don't take any unnecessary risks. Your job is not worth your life. Are we clear?

Elena nodded. "We're clear."

"In the meantime, I'll reach out to Verona and start coordinating with the witches in the area," Emilio said. "It's more important than ever that we stick together on this."

"We've *always* been stronger together than scattered," Haley said. "It's time we start remembering that."

"It's happening." In a swirl of cold air, Deirdre stepped in through the front door, her coat and boots thick with snow, her eyes wide with excitement.

Either she knew something the rest of us didn't, or she'd finally gone off the deep end.

"I sensed a sudden shift in the universal energy," she

said, breathless. "Can't you feel it? I came as soon as I could. We have so much to prepare for, and very little time to do it."

"Deirdre, slow down," I said. "What's happening? What are you talking about?"

She beamed at me, locking me in her bright blue gaze.

I knew in a flash what she was going to say next.

"The Silversbane Prophecy, child. This is how it begins."

"With the blizzard from hell?" I forced out a laugh, but a bolt of nervous energy shot down my spine, and inside, everything was trembling.

"You've already begun gathering witches," she said, gesturing toward the sea of faces around us. "And now you will gather more."

"Okay, and then what?" I laughed again, but anyone in that room who knew me could've seen right through it. "I just stand on a chair, bang on a glass, and roll right into it? Like, Hi! I'm Gray, third daughter of a third daughter of a third daughter, Silversbane heir, destined to unite everyone. By the way, how do you all feel about uniting? Hope no one's got any plans tonight! Let's do some icebreakers!" It sounded ridiculous, even without my added snark. These women were strangers. Many of them had their own covens or had been practicing solitary for years. Who was I to come in and claim such a powerful legacy?

Who was I to unite them? To lead?

All the old doubts rushed in. But then Emilio squeezed my hand again, and Haley came to stand at my side, and

Ronan gave me a crooked grin, and Asher winked, and Darius offered a single nod of unwavering support.

And Liam's eyes blazed bright, just for a moment.

"Yes, Gray," Deirdre said, her own eyes softening. "You do just that. Perhaps with a little more finesse, but the principle is there. You tell them about yourself. Your magic. What you've learned. What's to come. Remember, child. Most witches are already aware of the prophecy. And while some have dismissed it as legend, many still believe. Many still hope."

Hope. That little word again, four letters and one syllable, strong enough to carry the most powerful essence we had.

But was *I* strong enough to carry *it*?

Maybe not on my own. But I wasn't on my own anymore. I had my rebels. My grandmother and my sister. Two more sisters still to meet. New friends like Elena, Lansky, and Hobb. And the kind, supportive smiles of all the witches surrounding me now. I hadn't even made time to learn all of their names, yet here they were, ready to cheer me on. Ready to trust me. Ready to help me carry that hope for our entire sisterhood.

My blood warmed, the magic settling into a comfortable hum. Suddenly, a sense of purpose rose inside me like a helium balloon, and I finally felt it. The energetic shift Deirdre had mentioned, like a warm wave of energy that radiated across my skin.

I smiled—a real one this time. "I think I'm… I'm actually ready for this."

"Sounds like shit's about to get real, Silversbane," Asher said with a big grin of his own.

"First order of business better be figuring out a new HQ," Ronan said. "Or shit's about to get *really* real. As in, fifty people sharing a bathroom real."

"Not to mention sharing a bed," Ash said.

Haley laughed. "As if you guys have a problem with that."

"We're very selective about it, though," he said, winking at me.

"Ronan's right," Emilio said. "We're already stuffed to the brim here. And now, with all the damage, it's not safe for any of us. We need to relocate. Tonight, if possible, before that next band of snow hits."

"Leave that to me." Elena hit a button on her phone and pressed it to her ear. "Start packing up, people. I know just the place."

TWENTY-SEVEN

EMILIO

"I hope no one is allergic to dogs." Verona Braden laughed as she reached for my arm, allowing me to guide her up the front steps and into the place we'd all be calling home for the foreseeable future. Roscoe, her golden retriever, followed behind us. I was honored he'd let me take over for him, temporarily standing in as Verona's eyes.

"I think it's pretty safe to say we're all dog people here," I said. "Elena and I are wolf shifters, for starters. In case you haven't figured that out."

Verona let out another hearty laugh. "Detective Alvarez, I can smell you a mile away. Same goes for your sister, and her partners as well."

"Hmm. I'll try not to take that as an insult," I teased. "Elena's not here, though. She'll be in later tonight."

"You carry her with you, Detective. Always." Then, holding out her hands as we entered the front foyer, "This place is lovely. Absolutely lovely."

Verona had her own ways of seeing a place, and her assessment was absolutely right. I still couldn't believe we'd scored it.

Apparently, one of Hobb's cousins owned a large stretch of oceanfront property about ten miles south of Raven's Cape and was in the process of building a bed-and-breakfast. The lodge had been completed earlier this month, but because of the freak weather, the family decided to postpone the public opening until springtime. So, after a decent amount of begging completely unbefitting to my alpha wolf sister—and the promise of a few more dates—Elena finally convinced Hobb to call in an old family favor.

Three hours later, we found ourselves moving in.

Nestled against the forest and facing the sea, the property had a rustic quality to it that I loved, with rough-hewn timber framing and dark pine walls, and huge bay windows overlooking the beach. Behind us, the landscape was thick with massive, old-growth pines and a canopy of lush foliage that protected us somewhat from the heavy snowfall and provided a sense of privacy and security.

The ocean was relentless, the frothy waves churning nonstop, creating a stunning soundtrack for all of us.

It felt good here. Clean. Alive. And perhaps most importantly, spacious. The main lodge was two stories high, with ten bedrooms upstairs and a professional kitchen, a huge dining room, and three other large living spaces on the main floor that we could further divide for sleeping and training areas.

"You're doing a good thing here, Detective." Verona

turned back toward me with a smile. "Bringing us all together like this."

"That means a lot coming from you," I said. When we'd first met Verona, she'd told us she'd been aware of the change in the air, the fear and rumors about another witch hunt already churning through her community. But she'd insisted that no matter what evil befell the Cape, she and the other witches could weather the storm as they always had.

Between the *literal* storm that'd hit, along with everything I'd shared with her about Darkwinter and the other information we'd been able to gather so far, she soon realized how deep this went. How much we *needed* to stick together—all of us.

I didn't mention anything about Gray or the prophecy. That was for my brujita to share whenever she was ready.

Verona had traveled with a small caravan of local witches she'd been able to persuade to the cause, and now they mingled with the witches we'd brought up from Elena's house, making quick, friendly introductions as everyone tried to make themselves useful and settle in for the long haul. Hobb had managed to sneak away from the precinct for a little while to help us get set up, but Elena and Lansky had their hands full at the RCPD, coordinating emergency response with the mayor and other local officials. She'd promised to drive up with Darius after sunset, but we didn't know how long she and the other detectives would be able to stay.

All of us had some long nights ahead.

The next couple of hours were a blur. Between assigning bedrooms and organizing our essentials inside the lodge, setting up and warding our perimeter outside, and figuring out dinner plans for our quickly expanding army, I'd only seen Gray in passing. She'd helped the witches find beds, cleanse and ward their spaces, and consolidate and inventory the food and magical supplies everyone had brought with them.

But I could tell from the tense, anticipatory mood that Gray had yet to fully introduce herself, or make mention of the prophecy. Of her heritage. Of how crucial it was that the witches join forces—not just to stay safe from the immediate threats of the storm and the hunters, but to unite. To fortify. To start looking ahead to a time when—hopefully on the near horizon—witches didn't have to hide or practice in the shadows anymore.

When they didn't have to fear for their lives, but could embrace them fully.

The first chance I had for a break, I tracked her down in the kitchen, where she'd been filling ice cube trays as if it were the most important task in the world.

She'd put her hair into a loose bun, and now I slipped my arms around her from behind and pressed a kiss to her nape, breathing in the strawberry-sweet scent of her skin.

"Hiding out?" I murmured.

"No. I mean, sort of." She leaned back into my embrace and blew out a breath, and I felt her heartbeat level out, her tense muscles relaxing just a fraction. "Okay, fine. I'm totally hiding out."

"Consider yourself busted."

"Busted, huh?" she asked playfully. "Does this mean you'll have to cuff me, Detective Alvarez?"

Dios mio, the thought of Gray in handcuffs… I bit her earlobe and groaned, an ache blooming below the belt that was only going to get worse. It'd felt like a thousand lifetimes since I'd had her to myself. Since I'd felt the press of her warm body, heard the soft sounds she made as we…

Cold shower, Alvarez. It's gonna be a long night.

She turned around in my arms and slid her hands over my shoulders. Her eyes were full of a new ferocity, a purpose. But beneath that, I sensed the current of her trepidations.

And I marveled.

The woman who'd chased me to the very edge of death and snatched me out of its jaws, breaking every last rule in the universe to bring me home… That same woman was still reluctant to claim her birthright. To stand up and claim herself.

How could she not know that the witches would follow her anywhere? That *I* would follow her anywhere.

"What if I don't know what I'm doing?" she whispered, answering my unspoken questions. "What if I say all the wrong things, or make the wrong choices, or lead them astray, or cause even more infighting? What if they hate me?"

"What if they do?"

The question took her aback, and she blinked up at me, surprised. "Then… then… I don't know."

"No, you don't, and neither do I. But here's something I *do* know. If you don't try, if you don't tell everyone what's coming and convince them that when the shit hits the fan, we all need to be standing on the same side, then we *will* fail. Wrong choices and infighting and their opinions of you will be the least of our problems." I grabbed her hands in mine and pressed a kiss to each palm, trying to send her all the love I could. To make her feel it. "This is life or death, *querida*. For all of us. You know better than most what we're up against."

She shuddered, and I saw the fears play out across her eyes. Hunters, dark fae, hybrids, perpetual winter, imprisonment, all the other things Liam had warned us about—most of them invisible and probably impossible to defeat.

"I don't say this to frighten you," I said. "I say it to remind you that you've already faced down a lot of those things, and you've come out swinging every time. Every day, your magic gets stronger, and so does this." I pressed my hand flat against her chest, feeling the steady beat of her heart.

Gray closed her eyes, blowing out another breath. After a beat, she turned away from me again, refocusing on her ice cube trays. "I guess I just need some time to figure out what to say."

"You *will* figure it out, though. I know you will. Gray, you're—"

"Alvarez, you got a second?" Hobb's voice cut in from the doorway. "Colebrook spotted something we need to check out on foot."

Liam had set off in his raven form a couple of hours ago to check out the area from above, keeping a particular eye out for anything that suggested we'd been followed or tracked. Fortunately for us, any attackers would have to come in through the forest, which was dense and slippery and difficult to traverse, or along the beach, which meant they'd be spotted quickly.

Assuming we could see them.

Still, Liam's bird's-eye view would come in handy. The shoreline up here was similar to the one near the original prison, with lots of rocky outcroppings and cave systems perfect for hiding.

"Be right with you, Hobb." I turned my attention back to Gray, hoping to give her one more kiss, one more vote of confidence.

But *mi brujita* was already gone, the ice cube trays abandoned on the counter half full.

TWENTY-EIGHT

GRAY

Even hidden away in the last bedroom in the farthest corner of the second floor, the ocean roaring all around me, Sunshine and Sparkle panting at the foot of the bed, I still couldn't drown out the sounds of the voices. Still couldn't breathe under the unspoken weight of the expectations. Under my *own* expectations.

Sitting on the bed I'd claimed, I stared at the Six of Wands card in my hand. In the deck that Emilio had given me, the card featured a man standing on top of a mountain behind a massive lion. In one hand he held a crystal ball, in the other, a flame-tipped wand. Five wands surrounded him, and overhead, two ravens circled in a blood-red sky.

The man in the card looked much more confident—not to mention qualified—than I felt, but the message was clear: I needed to be fearless. Bold.

I felt it inside me. I truly did. Deirdre was right—the time had come. All of us could feel it.

But I'd barely gotten used to the twenty-some witches in Elena's house, and now our makeshift coven was rapidly expanding, with more witches set to arrive in the coming days. Verona had done her job in putting the word out, and her network of witches had picked up and run with it, organizing volunteers with vehicles to drive out and pick up any witches within an hour's drive.

I wanted so badly to help them. To lead them. I felt it burning inside me, brighter than the fiery torches in the Six of Wands card. When I thought about what the Silversbane legacy actually meant to me, it wasn't about power or magic at all. It was about bringing people together. Mending old, generational rifts between women who probably couldn't even remember why their mothers or grandmothers had been fighting in the first place. It was about breaking down old structures and building something stronger. It was about eliminating any force or being that sought to keep us from doing just that.

And most importantly, it was about sisterhood.

For so long, I'd been a solitary witch, so deep in the broom closet I could barely *say* words like "witch" or "magic" without breaking out in hives.

Now I was part of something big. Something important. Something with life-or-death stakes not just for everyone here, but for witches and supernaturals everywhere.

The fire inside me surged, mixing with the magic and burning so hot, I feared I might just combust.

I swept the cards into a pile and tucked them back into

the box. There was no advice to be found in the Tarot tonight—nothing I couldn't divine myself.

Outside my door, I heard someone clomping up the stairs. The rhythm of the footfalls was a dead giveaway.

"Here's how it's gonna be," Asher announced to the entire lodge. Subtly had never been his strong suit. "I'm going in there. Anyone comes through that door who's not bleeding from a major artery is gonna get flatlined. Got it?"

His protectiveness brought a smile to my lips, and I opened the door, shooting him a glare I didn't really mean. "I'm fine, Ash. I just needed some space."

"I know. That's why I'm here."

"You know I need space, so you invited yourself up here to invade it?"

"I… Um…" He scratched the back of his head, clearly at a loss for words.

His slightly embarrassed smile was so endearing, I couldn't help but return it. "Damn you and your sexy incubus charms, Asher O'Keefe."

"You're not the first woman to say that, Cupcake."

"No." I arched an eyebrow. "But I'd better be the last."

"No question."

Laughing, I stepped aside to let him in. Rather than taking the invitation graciously, he marched to the end of the bed, clapped his hands once, then pointed at the door.

"Sunshine," he said, "Sparkle-butt, you know I love you. But you need to vamoose."

"Oh, good luck with that," I teased. "They only listen to me."

But my loyal hounds, traitors to their name, hopped up and marched out the door, which Asher promptly shut behind them.

"You're something else," I told him.

"What? You think you're the only one who can't resist me? I've got those girls wrapped around my finger like you wouldn't believe."

"So you've been bribing them."

"What?" He pressed his hand to his heart, mortally offended. "Sunshine and Sparkle and I have a deep relationship based on mutual respect and—"

"Bacon?"

Asher cracked up. "You know it."

"So what was the deal with Liam?" I asked, sitting back on the bed.

"He spotted a cave system not too far from here that looked like it could be trouble, but the shifters checked it out, and it's clear. Hobb's posting two guards there, anyway, just to be safe. Reva volunteered to go with them and do some of her shadow spelunking, but they squashed that idea pretty quick." Asher shook his head, smiling. "Crazy girl."

"Aww. She just wants to help."

"Yeah, I get it. But if she thinks we're letting her anywhere *near* a place like that, forget about it. Kid already spent enough time locked away in a cave."

"Where is she now?"

"I gave her my phone and my app store password, so I'm guessing she's hiding in her bedroom, running up my credit card."

I laughed. "You're kind of a softy, aren't you?"

"Don't let *that* get out." Asher sat next to me, and I leaned my head on his shoulder, taking in his fire-and-cinnamon scent. It stirred something inside me, doing nothing to cool the flames I'd been contending with before his arrival.

Despite the desire smoldering between my thighs, the mood turned serious; the weight of the moment felt impossibly heavy on my shoulders.

"Gray, I know what it's like when everyone is turning to you for answers you don't have," he said, his tone so suddenly gentle it made my heart squeeze. "When you're carrying the weight of the world on your shoulders because you know one wrong move can send the whole thing tumbling to the ground. I know what it feels like when you want more than anything to do the right thing, only you don't know what the fuck that thing might be. And most of all, I know you. Not as well as Ronan does. But I know you."

I lifted my head to meet his eyes, and he pressed his hand to my heart, fingertips grazing my collarbone.

"I see you, Gray Desario. I feel the dark magic pulsing through you. The doubts. What they're doing to you. I feel everything you feel, and if I could, I'd take it all away from you. Carry it so you wouldn't have to. Even the most painful parts."

"I know." My voice threatened to break, but I wouldn't fall apart. Not now. Not when everyone was counting on me. "I have to learn to live with it, though. To control it, channel it. It's my fate, right? Powerful Silversbane magic, and all the responsibility that comes along with it."

"Maybe so. But let me tell you a secret: Every once in a while?" He leaned in close, his breath no more than a faint whisper against my lips. "It's okay to fall apart."

Asher's words undid me, tender and unexpected and exactly what I needed to hear. I fell into his embrace, letting him wrap me up in his warmth. His strength.

He pressed his lips to the top of my head and said, "Let it go, baby. I've got you."

The emotion that I'd strangled back for weeks broke through the surface, finally erupting.

I wept shamelessly in his arms, releasing my heartbroken frustrations about Ronan's deal with Sebastian, my pain at all we'd lost when the memory eaters stole Darius's history, the betrayal I'd felt toward Liam, all the fears I'd buried when we'd come so close to losing Emilio. I wept for the women downstairs, for all they'd endured at the hands of the hunters and the dark fae, for all they'd lost before then, for all they'd grown up afraid to say and do and be. And I wept for the little witch I once was, the little girl full of magic and possibility, one of four magical sisters whose mother attempted to drown them out of petty jealousy.

When I'd cried enough tears to compete with the ocean outside, I looked up into his eyes once again, trying to find the words to apologize for the outburst. But there, reflected back at me, I saw so much love and support that in that moment, I truly felt like I could do anything. My crying turned into laughter, bubbling up from some deep, magical place inside me.

Wordlessly, Asher took my face in his big hands and kissed the tears from my cheeks. From my chin. From my neck.

It wasn't enough, though. With Asher, I was always hungry, always desperate for more.

He was kissing my cheek again, and I turned toward him, capturing his sensuous cupid's bow mouth, my core melting as his tongue slid between my lips.

We tumbled backward onto the bed, tearing off clothing as we fell, mouths and hands seeking warm flesh, seeking unmet desires, seeking love.

And then he was inside me, anticipating my every need once again, bringing my body to the very edge of my limits, making me cry for an entirely different reason.

TWENTY-NINE

GRAY

"Not that I'm complaining, Cupcake, but what are you smiling about now?"

I traced a path along the black symbols tattooed across Asher's chest, every muscle in my body relaxed and happy. We'd been locked away for an hour; eventually, someone would come looking for us, and I'd have to go back downstairs and face the music—more specifically, the magic. But for now, I was perfectly happy to hide away in a bubble of bliss with one of the men I loved, basking in the glow of all the ways he'd just made my body sing.

"I was just thinking about the day we met," I confessed. "Officially, I mean."

"At Bloodstone Park, across from Norah's place," he said.

"I'm surprised you remember."

"How could I forget? You were *so* into me. I thought I was going to have to restrain you."

"What?" I laughed, smacking him on the stomach. "I was so *not* into you! You were the biggest jerk I'd ever met. And that's saying something, because I've met a lot of jerks in my life."

"And *you* were wearing a tight pink-and-white hoodie that made you look like a giant cupcake. All I wanted to do was pin you down and lick off all the frosting."

I sat up, the sheet falling down to my waist. "Wait... *that's* why you call me Cupcake?"

Asher grazed his palm over my exposed breast, threatening to stir my body into a new frenzy.

"It suits you." He leaned forward and captured my nipple between his lips, his tongue sliding out to tease me. "Mmm. Very lickable."

"You are such a beast. You know that, right?" I laughed. "For your information, that sweatshirt was Sophie's. I don't own anything pink."

"As someone who just spent half the day hanging out between your thighs, I beg to differ. You've got plenty of pink—"

"Asher!" I smacked him again. Did this man ever stop?

He pointed at me, his grin stretching even further. "And now your cheeks are pink, too. Perfect."

"Now you're just trying to embarrass me."

"It's a skill. Seriously. Don't play a game of wits with me, Gray. You will lose."

"Say whatever you want, Mr. Big Bad Incubus. I know your secret."

"You think so, huh?" He kissed my jaw, my earlobe, his

soft lips buzzing over my skin and making me shiver. Somehow he'd gotten me horizontal again, the sheet around my waist mysteriously vanishing. He rolled onto his hip, propping his head up on his hand, watching me intently. "Which one?"

I trailed my fingers down his chest, down over the ridges of his abs until I reached his velvet-smooth cock. He was already hard again, but stiffened further at my touch, the beat of his heart pulsing just beneath his hot skin. "The one where your heart is almost as big as your—"

"*Almost,*" he said between kisses, groaning softly into my ear as I began to stroke him. "But not quite."

"Hmm. Lucky me."

"Lucky?" Asher rolled on top of me and grabbed my wrists, pinning them over my head as his solid weight settled over me. His cock teased my entrance, unleashing another moan from my lips despite my best efforts not to let him win.

"You don't even know the meaning of the word," he said. "But before the sun comes up? You damn well will."

I lost the ability to speak, my retort melting into a puddle of sighs as he rocked his hips and plunged inside me again. I felt his incubus hunger tugging lightly at my magic, and a rightness pulsed through my veins, warm and delightful and perfect. I loved the way we filled each other up, loved knowing that my magic could make him strong, could take care of him, just like he'd taken care of me.

I opened myself up to him fully, slowly sending out a warm pulse of magic, and Asher deepened our kiss, his body seeming to hum with it. He was close to the edge, thrusting in deep and perfect, faster and faster until I was certain he'd explode. But then, without warning, he stilled inside of me, pulling back to see my face.

In one big, impossibly strong hand, he cupped my chin, searching my gaze with an intensity that made me gasp. For a brief moment, I fell right into his ocean-blue eyes.

I saw his soul there. All the pain and regret and love and hope.

And he saw mine. I felt it, knew it. And for the first time in our relationship, I dropped every last wall, leaving myself completely open. I let him see it all—the brave, the scared, the shameful, the beautiful, all the parts of me that made up the whole.

"I've never wanted anyone like I want you," Asher whispered. He dipped his head and stole another kiss, stole my breath, stole my heartbeat. And I let him take it all, because in that moment, as he slid back inside me and finally brought us both over the edge of that cliff, as I fisted his hair and shuddered beneath him and sighed his name into the darkness, I knew without a doubt that I was his.

To protect.

To love.

Just as he was mine.

After a quick shower, we crept back into bed, sliding between the sheets and wrapping up in each other's arms once again. I felt him growing hard again, and I was certain we'd spend the rest of the night just as we'd begun it. But instead of slipping inside me, he turned me onto my side, snuggling against me from behind and wrapping me up in his embrace. With a fluttering of kisses on the back of my neck, he whispered, "You need to rest, Gray. It might be your last chance for a while."

I opened my mouth to argue, but a yawn escaped instead, and before I could even find the strength to rally for another round, I was fast asleep.

I didn't know how much time passed, but eventually, the soft, pleasant rumble of low voices woke me. I opened my eyes to find Ronan and Asher by the window on the other side of the bedroom, their heads close together, deep in conversation. Darkness had fallen, the moonlight illuminating their silhouettes. Ash was bare-chested, a pair of sweats hanging low on his hips. He had one hand on Ronan's shoulder, his other hand gesturing emphatically. Ronan's head was bent low, nodding at whatever Asher was saying.

My heart swelled. I loved them both so much. I opened my mouth to tell them just that, but before I could get a word out, Ronan's smile glinted in the darkness.

"Looks like Sleeping Beauty's finally awake," he said.

Both of my demons left the window and joined me in bed, Ash curling up behind me, snuggling in close, Ronan sitting on the very edge before me, careful not to touch me.

Though mere inches separated Ronan and me, it felt as if another person had wedged himself between us. That invisible, formless monster was a constant companion we'd always carry, reminding us of everything we used to have. Everything Sebastian had stolen.

It was a sharp contrast to the closeness Asher and I had shared tonight, and it lit me up with rage.

There *had* to be another way. But until we could find it, we'd take what we could, stealing glances, breathing in each other's scents, memorizing the sounds of laughter and voices and whispers, which had their own sweet cadence.

Keeping our voices low in the moonlit room, the three of us talked about the plans for the days ahead, which would be full of magical and combat training, Reva's shadowmancy practice, intelligence gathering, big speeches, and above all, constant vigilance.

After what felt like minutes but had probably been an hour, Ronan rose from the bed and stretched, wishing us both good night.

"There's room in here," I said, patting the space in front of me. "If we slept in our clothes, and didn't get too close…"

I trailed off. It was ridiculous that it'd come to this, and we both knew it.

"Emilio and Darius are on beach patrol tonight," Ronan said. "I should probably go check on them. Good excuse to take the hounds for a stroll, anyway."

"Aww, leaving so soon, demon?" Asher asked. Despite the teasing tone in his words, I knew he could sense how badly I wanted Ronan to stay.

I could sense the same feeling from him.

Ronan turned his back on us and opened the door. When he spoke again, his voice was rough. "You know I have to."

"Ronan," I said firmly, and he shook his head, refusing to look at me. I could almost feel the demons inside him, threatening to tear him apart.

Threatening to tear us *both* apart.

"He owns our souls, not our hearts," I whispered, and he finally turned around, locking his fierce hazel eyes on mine. "Stay with us tonight," I said. "Please."

Ronan closed his eyes and let out a sigh, but he finally pushed the door closed, sealing the three of us away in this perfect bubble once again.

With Asher still behind me, Ronan resumed his place in front of me, but this time he stretched out on his side, closer than he'd been before. His breath stirred the hair around my face, and he stared deeply into my eyes, reading me even as his own thoughts remained veiled.

"I wish I knew what you were thinking," I said softly.

"You know *exactly* what I'm thinking, Gray. I'm *always* thinking it. Same thing, every minute of every hour of every day." He lifted a hand to my face, keeping it just shy of actual contact. Heat radiated from his palm as he traced an invisible caress down my cheek. "Every time I see your face. Hear your voice. Feel your presence. All I can think about is how much I need to touch you. How it's eating away at me inside, knowing that I can't do it without hurting you."

Asher's body went rigid behind me, anger pulsing from his skin. "One day, I'm going to kill that Kentucky Fried fuck."

"You and me both, brother," Ronan said.

"There has to be a way," I said.

"To kill the prince of hell?" Asher said. "You bet your sweet little ass there's a way. And as soon as we figure it out, we're all getting a plane to Vegas, and we're going on a motherfucking crime spree. Because we're not just killing Sebastian. Hell no. We're taking out every one of his minions and burning his casinos to the ground, too. And after that, we're gonna piss on all the ashes."

Ronan laughed, shattering the dark, dense weight that had settled over us. "You've got it all planned out, huh?"

"I've got *sketchbooks* full of ideas. Just you wait."

"Okay, boys," I said, rolling my eyes. "I appreciate your vivid imaginations when it comes to tormenting Sebastian, and believe me, I'm all in. But when I said there has to be a way, I meant a way for us to be together tonight."

Asher's hand slid over my hip, his lips tickling my shoulder blade. "Now *there's* a sketch I'd like to see."

"Will you guys try something with me?" I asked.

Asher cracked up, and Ronan gave me a crooked smirk.

"Let's see," Ronan said, tapping his lips. "You're lying in bed next to a beautiful woman, who also happens to be naked, and she asks you if you'd like to try something with her. Your answer is... Ash, would you like to field this one?"

"Hmm, it's a tough one. I might need to phone a friend," Ash said. "But... No. Let's go out on a limb here and say..."

"Fuck yes," they both said, laughing so hard the bed

shook. Then, from Ronan, "What are you thinking, Desario?"

"I can't *wait* to hear this," Ash said.

"Sebastian is all about the fine print," I said. The idea was gathering momentum inside me, making my heart flutter. I gazed into Ronan's eyes, hoping this didn't freak him out. Hoping it would bring us closer, not push us further apart.

But some part of me knew it would bring us closer. That we needed this tonight, maybe more than we ever had before.

Be bold, girl. Fearless, just like the Six of Wands.

Okay, maybe Tarot *hadn't* been referring to the demons in my bed, but still. The fire inside me surged anew, reminding me that living a fearless life wasn't always about big, courageous acts of bravery in the face of life-threatening adversity.

Sometimes it was just about making a small, bold leap in the quiet space of your own heart.

"The deal specifically says you can't touch me," I said, and Ronan nodded. I tugged the sheet down and grabbed Asher's hand, pressing it to my bare breast, a slow smile stretching across my lips. "But it doesn't say you can't watch."

THIRTY

GRAY

Ronan's eyes darkened with lust.

"No," he said, his voice suddenly hoarse. He swallowed hard. "It doesn't say that."

Emboldened by the new intensity in his gaze, I kicked the sheet off completely and slid closer to him, bringing my lips within a hair's breadth of his. Everything about this moment felt dangerous and delicious, a heady mix that was already making me dizzy. Ronan's cloves-and-campfire scent called to something deep inside me, a familiar longing I'd associated with him ever since I'd started to have feelings for him—a longing that had only intensified since we'd finally crossed that boundary together.

"I want to do this for you," I whispered. "But only if you're okay with it."

He nodded, the tip of his tongue darting out to wet his bottom lip. My thighs clenched; that one little gesture flooded my core with so much heat, I thought we'd start a fire even *without* touching. I wanted nothing more than to slide my tongue into his mouth, to taste him, to unleash everything we'd been forced to hold back since we'd escaped the Shadowrealm.

"Take off your clothes," I said, arching back against Asher. "Both of you."

Ash slid out of his sweatpants, and Ronan followed suit, yanking the shirt over his head and kicking off his jeans and boxer briefs. My two fierce, beautiful demons stretched out on either side of me again, and Asher kissed my neck, swirling his tongue behind my ear, his fingers trailing slow circles down my ribcage, my hip, my upper thigh, then back up to my breast.

Both of them were hard as steel, Asher's cock pressing urgently against my backside, Ronan's so close to the apex of my thighs, if I closed my eyes and thought back to our last time together in the woods of the Shadowrealm, I could almost feel him inside me again.

"Touch yourself," I said to Ronan, soft but fierce, my breath hitching as a flood of raw desire coursed through my veins.

He did as I commanded, fisting his cock and stroking himself slowly, a soft moan escaping his lips.

Asher rolled my nipple between his thumb and forefinger, the sensation sending ripples of pleasure straight down to my core.

"Ronan," I breathed, as Asher increased the pressure on

my nipple, tugging and teasing, making me writhe. "Tell us what you want to see."

"I want to see your face," he said. "Your eyes. I want him to fuck you from behind and drive you absolutely wild... But your eyes are *mine*."

At those words, Asher growled in my ear, more than ready to comply. I arched backward again, and he slid inside me from behind, his hand on my hip as he slowly rocked against my backside.

My body was still buzzing from our earlier time together, my skin hypersensitive, but holy *fuck* he felt good. I bit my lip to keep from crying out.

Ronan's eyes blazed with new heat.

Asher grew harder inside me, his fingers digging into the flesh at my hip as he plunged in deeper, his teeth nipping at my neck, my shoulder.

Ronan leaned forward, dragging his nose through my hair and inhaling my scent, careful not to let our skin touch. His chestnut hair tickled my cheek, and I skimmed my fingers in front of his chest, feeling the heat rise from his body, our energies connecting even as our bodies couldn't.

"Touch yourself," he whispered, and I obeyed, slipping a hand between my thighs. I was hot and wet, two fingers gliding over my clit as Ronan stroked himself harder and faster, Asher's chest slick with sweat against my back.

Finally, I *did* cry out, the intensity almost too much to bear.

All three of us were getting close, the heat and energy

and magic rising between us, invisible tendrils pulling us close, wrapping us in a cocoon of love and desire.

Then Ronan sucked in a sharp breath, the space between his eyebrows creasing, his eyes glazing suddenly with emotion.

"You okay?" I whispered. "What's wrong?"

"It's torture, Gray. Watching you… My hands are on fire to touch you… I just… *Fuck*." His voice was raw, his chest rising and falling rapidly, his body trembling from the effort of holding back. "I'd fucking *die* tomorrow for a chance to kiss you tonight. To taste you just one more time."

I blinked back tears, the passion in his words threatening to unravel my heart.

Asher stilled behind me, resting his forehead against my shoulder blade. I knew without asking that he'd end this in a heartbeat if he thought we were causing Ronan pain. Both of us would.

"Do you want us to stop?" I whispered to the demon in front of me. My best friend. The man I loved. The one who'd agreed to this torment just for a long-shot, one-in-a-million chance at bringing me back from the Shadowrealm in one piece.

Ronan's eyes went demon-black, his voice a low growl in his throat. "Don't you fucking *dare* stop."

Ronan couldn't touch me, couldn't physically partici-pate beyond the closeness and the watching and the dark, desperate wanting. But I knew by the look in his eyes that he needed this. *We* needed this—this unexpected, unconventional way to be together, to break the chains Sebastian had tried to tighten around our hearts.

Asher shifted behind me, sliding in slow and deep.

My eyes fluttered closed, and I felt Ronan inch forward, the heat of his body reaching out to me once again.

Still stroking his rock-hard cock, he leaned in closer. "Don't close your eyes, Gray," he whispered. "Stay with us tonight. Please."

I smiled at the echo of my earlier words and did as he asked, my gaze locking onto his as the three of us continued to chase that pure, unadulterated bliss lingering just out of reach.

"Gray," Asher moaned, and I knew he was *right* there. In that instant, all of us were mere seconds from beautiful oblivion.

I increased the pressure on my clit, and my body tightened around Asher, my stomach muscles clenching, the now-familiar tingles gathering in my core.

"Gray... *fuck...*" Ronan's body tensed, and then he let go, setting off a chain reaction. Asher came hard inside me, his body shuddering against my backside, and with his gravelly voice in my ear and Ronan's gaze locked on mine, I finally let go, too.

The orgasm washed over me in a hot rush, stealing my breath as my body trembled beneath its power. I came for Asher. I came for Ronan. I came for all of us, my heart beating like a wild animal, my whole being alight with pleasure.

At the final gasp, I was finally permitted to close my

eyes, and the three of us lay in silence, floating on a cloud in some other sky, on some other realm.

It was one of the most intense experiences I'd ever had, and somehow, despite the fact that Ronan still couldn't touch me, I felt like it had brought us closer.

All three of us.

"I love you," I whispered. "Both of you. So much."

Asher tightened his hold on me, and I opened my eyes to see Ronan watching me close. Neither of them said a word. They didn't have to. I saw Ronan's love for me burning in his eyes, the fire of it more intense than the fire that sparked whenever we touched. I felt Asher's love surrounding me now, holding me close, keeping me safe.

Asher reached across my shoulder and wrapped his hand around the back of Ronan's neck. "You good, brother?"

Ronan gave him a silent nod and closed his eyes.

The intense moment between us had crested and receded, and the three of us finally broke apart, getting out of bed to stretch and change the sheets.

After another quick round of showers and a raid on the fridge downstairs, we crept back upstairs, stripped down once again, and climbed back into bed together. Ash took the middle this time, making sure Ronan and I couldn't get too close and accidentally set the mattress on fire. I curled up against Asher's left side, and Ronan did the same oppo-site me, meeting my eyes across the tattooed expanse of our incubus's chest.

There was nothing awkward about it; we were family.

The love we shared transcended all boundaries, and as we drifted off to sleep, I found a moment's peace in the knowledge that somehow, we'd find a way to transcend Sebastian's imposed boundaries, too.

We fell asleep quickly, and didn't stir again for hours.

Not until we heard the screams.

THIRTY-ONE

For hours I paced the rocky shoreline south of the lodge, my fingers wrapped around the handle of a fae blade we'd procured from the warehouse, all of my senses attuned to my surroundings. I tasted the ancient salt of the coastal air on my lips, felt the pounding of the surf beating in my chest, braced myself against the sharp bite of the wind on my face.

Despite the circumstances, I couldn't help but feel invigorated. Hopeful, even. Emilio had survived insurmountable odds to return to us, whole and unbroken. The witches we'd liberated from the hunter's prisons were growing stronger through practice and new, shared knowledge, combining their magics in unique and powerful ways that made victory feel a little more possible with each passing day, despite Liam's dire warnings. Gray was finally beginning to embrace her legacy, and though I suspected she'd need a little more time to fully claim her birthright, I felt the greatness in her, so close to the surface she practically hummed with it.

For the first time since I'd returned from the Shadowrealm without my memories, things were beginning to look up.

Other than the brutal cold and the frenzied state of the great Pacific, the night had been calm. Emilio and Elena were patrolling the southern end of the property, with Detective Lansky and another wolf shifter from the department keeping watch at the forest's edge. Two more shifters were posted at the mouth of the cave system Liam had discovered, and all was quiet there, as well.

But for an occasional wandering witch raiding the kitchen for a midnight snack, the occupants of our lodge had finally settled in for a good night's rest. After the energy and excitement of relocating to the lodge and settling in with the new witches and animal companions that'd arrived with Verona, it'd been a surprisingly peaceful evening.

So peaceful, in fact, that when a desperate scream broke through the rhythmic roar of the waves behind me, it took me a moment to comprehend what I'd heard.

Reva.

And she was in grave danger.

I spun around and caught sight of her cowering in the sand at the base of a massive sea stack. Her eyes were wide with fear, her whole body trembling in the wintry mist.

"Reva!" I knelt down before her, reaching out a hand to help her up. "How did—"

My words cut off abruptly as my hand passed through the mist. It wasn't Reva after all—only a shadow projection. Which meant her body was somewhere else, and I had no idea how to find her.

"Reva, where are you?"

"They're all around me!" she shouted. It didn't seem like she'd seen or heard me at all. "Leave me alone! I can't... Help! Somebody help me!"

I took off at a run toward the lodge, the ocean blurring in my peripheral vision, the icy wind tearing at my hair. I arrived on the scene at the same time as Emilio and Elena, the three of us tearing across the front of the property, straight for the forest behind the lodge.

"In the woods. There!" I shouted, catching sight of the melee just inside the tree line. Witches and wolves alike had teamed up against an enemy whose scent turned my stomach.

Vampires.

Gripping the fae sword, I charged into the trees, swinging at the first bloodsucker I saw, taking his head clean off.

I didn't even spare him a glance as I spun around, catching another one in the chest as Gray staked him from behind. He stumbled backward, and I beheaded him post haste.

"How many?" I shouted.

"A dozen at least," she said, yanking the stake from his back. The hounds were by her side, their fangs already dripping with blood. "Maybe more. We all bolted out here when we heard Reva screaming. The wolves had already taken some of them down—it all happened so fast, we—."

"Duck!" I hauled Gray to the ground and covered her with my body just as a vamp lunged at her from behind. Over-correcting for his miss, he slipped on the snow, and the moment he righted himself, a huge raven swooped in and clawed out his eyes. One of the hounds lunged at him, knocking him flat on his back. The other dove in to finish the job, gnawing at his throat, snapping the bones of his neck.

It was the most gruesome vamp-killing I'd ever witnessed, but I wasn't complaining.

Leaving the hounds to sniff out a new victim, Gray and I ran deeper into the woods, chasing the sounds of snapping wolf jaws and tearing flesh. Intermittent flashes of blue and violet light lit up the forest like a nightclub, magic sizzling in the blood-soaked snow.

"Reva!" Gray shouted, her stake at the ready. "Where are you? Reva!"

"Over here," I said, scenting the demons close by. "This way."

We caught up with Asher and Ronan, who'd just tackled a hulking bloodsucker with a ridiculous bright red mohawk. I did the whole world a favor and chopped his head clean off.

Gray and the incubus headed deeper into the pines in search of our youngest witch while I teamed up with Ronan on a pair of vamp females.

We made quick, bloody work of them, then circled back

around the edge of the forest, searching behind every tree for any other vamps lying in wait.

"Coast looks clear on this side," Ronan said, wiping the spray of blood from his face. He cocked his ear toward the woods again, the sounds of the skirmish finally beginning to fade. "Sounds like the worst of it is over. Fuck, that was intense. I was sound asleep."

"The wards held," I said, eyeing the lodge. Other than a single, one-way track through the snow from the back door leading into the woods, the rest of the area between the back of the lodge and the woods was still blanketed in unbroken snow. There were no footprints on the side or front areas, either.

"Our witches know their shit," Ronan said. "So. Local gang, you think?"

"Judging from their attire, no. None of them wore jackets or winter gear of any kind. I suspect that's what allowed us to get the upper hand so quickly—they came here looking for an easy score, but they weren't expecting the weather."

"Great. Vamp tourists." Ronan spit out a mouthful of blood, then dragged his sleeve across his mouth. "I'm guessing it means word is out that the council is no longer enforcing the rules. How long until this shit turns into a total free-for-all? Hell, maybe it's already happening in other places."

"Let's hope this was a one-off," I said. "It's possible these vamps are connected to the rogues we slaughtered at Norah's house. Hollis aside, some of those pricks were definitely out-of-towners. Not to mention the southern visitors Gray and I had the pleasure of entertaining at the morgue."

I shuddered at the memories. The female had been Gray's first kill.

"We're just making friends wherever we go, aren't we?" Ronan gave me a smirk that probably worked significantly better on Gray, but I appreciated it anyway. "Well," he continued, "at least we—wait. Wait, wait, wait."

"Did you hear something?" I asked, the sudden urgency in his tone putting me on high alert once again.

But Ronan hadn't moved. He just stood before me, his smirk turning into the brightest smile I'd ever seen on the demon.

And then he launched himself at me.

"Fucking hell, Beaumont. Fucking hell!" He hugged me so tightly, if I'd actually needed to breathe, I was quite certain I would've passed out. "You just remembered something, you scone-eating son-of-bitch! The vampires we iced at Norah's, Hollis, the morgue… You remembered!"

"I… huh. I supposed you're right."

"This is major. Major!"

He finally set me free, and I ran a hand over my head, trying to chase down those memories again, desperate to crack open a few more. But the moments from the fight at Norah's were already fading, Hollis's face slipping back into the shadows.

"It's okay," Ronan said. "Don't push it. You remembered something. That means it's all still in there. The rest will come."

"Let's hope you're right. I don't—"

"Here! I've got her!" The voice was Hobb's, and now he emerged from the trees, tattered clothing covering his body, a passed-out young witch cradled in his arms. "She's okay. Just a little spooked."

"Oh my God, Reva!" McKenna rushed over to inspect the girl herself. "What happened? How did you end up outside?"

"I just thought… I want to practice traveling," she said, stifling a sob. Tears streaked her dirt-smudged face, and she sniffled, her body still trembling in Hobb's arms. "The forest is so quiet, and it has so many shadows… I thought I could get a stronger connection."

"You thought wrong," Hobb snapped. "You could've been mutilated. You put all of us at risk, and—

"Detective," I interjected, giving him a stern glare. "Perhaps we should let McKenna take Reva inside and get warmed up."

"Come here, sweet pea." McKenna took the girl into her arms, swiftly shuttling her back inside the lodge.

"I found her hiding in a hollowed-out tree," Hobb told us, "half frozen, surrounded by four bloodsuckers. If the kid hadn't started screaming, we never would've gotten to her."

The rest of the group began trickling out of the forest, two and three at a time. The crew was a little scraped up and a whole lot exhausted, but for now, it appeared we'd all survived the latest attack.

"What the fuck was she doing outside by herself?"

Hobb asked. "Fucking kid. How many times did we tell her? No one goes outside alone. Especially not a fucking—."

"She's a sixteen-year-old child, Detective," I said. "One who is still learning to control a powerful magic none of us fully understands, and one who desperately wants to help the witches she considers family."

"Well, she damn near got herself killed, along with half my men. When that kid wakes up tomorrow, she's gonna have some serious explaining to do."

"Perhaps," I said, "you should seek explanations from your men instead. Despite their years of experience, not to mention their wolf shifter instincts, this child managed to slip beneath their careful net of surveillance, as did a nest of vampires—"

"We don't have the manpower to patrol the whole forest," he barked. "The vamps weren't anywhere near the lodge. I found the kid all the way on the other side of the creek."

"Again, I have to ask, how was she able to slip past—"

"Darius?" The whisper was faint, but panicked, the sound of it sending a bolt of fear down my spine. "I think… I fucked… up…"

I spun around just in time to see Gray collapse to her knees, her arm wrapped tightly around her midsection. Blood spilled out between her fingers, staining the snow a sickening shade of crimson.

"Gray!" I dropped to my knees before her, catching her just before she face-planted. "What happened?"

"Last vamp." She nodded toward the direction she'd come from. "Still alive. Staked him. But… not before he…"

"He's a dead bloodsucker now." Ronan's eyes turned black. With one of Gray's hounds on his heels, he grabbed my sword and took off running.

"Did he bite you, love?" I asked Gray.

She shook her head. "Knife. I was… stupid. Left my… inside unguarded…"

"Shh, it's okay. Let me take a look." Gently, I pulled her arm away from the wound, inspecting the damage. It was a nasty gouge about five inches long, slicing straight down beneath her breast. The blade had carved through clothing, flesh, and muscle. Milky-white slivers of rib shone through the gash, the wound pulsing with blood.

"Gray! Holy shit!" Haley emerged from the forest with Asher, both of them crouching down beside us. "Oh my God, what happened?"

"Stay calm," I told them. "She's going to be fine. Just give her some room."

"Beaumont…" Ash's tone was a warning, but I glared right back at him.

"Take off your sweatshirt, hellspawn. Put it behind her, then kindly back off."

He finally obeyed, and I turned my attention back to Gray, easing her backward onto the sweatshirt.

"I've got you, love. Try and relax." I leaned forward and brushed a kiss across her temple, a trickle of her blood coating my lips. It melted in my mouth, stirring my own blood to life. Something in my chest flickered, but I ignored it, focusing instead on the woman before me.

Using my fangs, I pierced the vein at my wrist, then held it over her mouth, allowing her a few drops before moving my wrist to her wounds.

It was an inelegant solution, but the best we had in the moment. Unlike when I'd healed her in the Shadowrealm, she was conscious now; my blood would burn inside her wounds like living fire. But once the pain subsided, it would bond with her blood, along with her magic, and start the healing process.

Too bad we don't have our own private cabin…

My eyes drifted closed, and in that quiet darkness I watched the memories of our time together in the realm like a movie I'd never tire of. There, in the cabin nestled in a snowy wood, was the first time I'd made love to her. It was the time and place where I'd fully, unapologetically fallen in—

My eyes opened with a start.

Memories. Real memories. More of them, coming in faster and more clearly now. Like the attack at Norah's house, saving Gray from the avalanche and all the time we'd spent in the cabin after had occurred *before* our final moments in the Shadowrealm.

Before the memory eaters had stolen my history.

"Thank… thank you." Gray was sitting up on her own again, wiping my blood from her mouth, when two things hit me at once.

I'd just saved Gray's life.

And I'd just remembered the absolute most precious piece of my own.

I took her face between my palms and tilted it toward me, capturing her beautiful blue gaze.

Then, as if I'd just figured out the answer to a complex question that had been plaguing me for years, I said, "Don't take this the wrong way, but I'm fairly certain I'm in love with you."

THIRTY-TWO

GRAY

"He remembered something, Hay." I measured out two more cups of dried lavender and another cup of amaranth flower into a glass bowl for Verona, who was busy in the common room sewing protective mojo bags. "Not just something, but a *major* thing."

Haley held up a finger to silence me, then continued counting the crystals spread out on the counter before her, piles of smoky quartz and black tourmaline that would also be sewn into the bags. Since the vamp attack three days ago, Verona and some of the other witches blessed with protective magical skills had been working nonstop, shoring up our defenses around the house as well as around our bodies.

No one had been seriously injured that night but me, and Darius had healed me on the spot. After Ronan had killed the vamp who'd knifed me, he, Darius, Emilio, and Detective Lansky scoured the forest, identifying and then burning all the vamp bodies and ensuring none had escaped alive.

Darius had been right—they were out-of-towners, a group from the Carolinas that he suspected had connections to the three that attacked us in the morgue the night we'd gone looking for intel on Sophie's murder. We couldn't be certain, but the detectives thought there might be some kind of supernatural bounty on my rebels and me. Lower-level vamps were fickle with their loyalties, and after the slaughter at Norah's house, it wouldn't have taken much for them to get the word out that Darius Beaumont was "a traitor" to his own kind.

With so many enemies breathing down our necks—known and unknown—Verona didn't want us taking any chances. "An unprotected witch is a sad story just begging to be written," she'd said.

Other than a freak hailstorm the following morning, our last couple of days had been fairly low key, and we'd spent them working on magic and spellcraft with Verona, inventorying our weapons and magical ingredients, and helping Reva practice her shadowmancy. After the attack, none of us wanted to let her out of our sights. Liam had been especially helpful in that department, spending long hours instructing her on the nature of physics, space-time, and astral travel. I didn't understand most of what they talked about, but he made her laugh and kept her out of trouble, and with his patient tutoring, she seemed to be gaining both confidence and skill.

"That's good, though, isn't it?" Haley finally looked up

from her task, her crystals all counted out into neat rows. "That means he's getting his memories back."

"What else *could* it mean?"

Darius hadn't remembered much—just snatches of the time we'd spent together in that cabin, the way he'd felt about me in those moments, and a little bit about the vamp attacks at the morgue and at Norah's place. Nothing more, and nothing since, but it was the first real glimmer of hope any of us had gotten that he might actually regain his memories.

"I don't know much about how memory works," Haley said. "I'm the blood girl, remember?"

I gave her my best, your-my-favorite-sister smile. "Speaking of being the blood girl..."

"*Gray*." She lanced me with an admonishing gaze. "I thought Deirdre was totally against the blood spell idea."

"Deirdre isn't here."

Haley and I still had so many questions for our grandmother, but since her first visit to Raven's Cape, she'd flitted in and out of our lives so often, she might as well be an apparition. Since the ice bomb and our subsequent relocation, she'd gotten slightly better at checking in by phone. But even then, whenever I tried to question her about the legacy or our mother or anything else having to do with the past, she suddenly had a hundred reasons to get off the phone.

Since I'd told Haley about our sisterhood and our bloodline, she hadn't even gotten time alone with Deirdre yet.

But our family dynamics, crazy as they were, would have to wait.

"She's just worried it will summon our ancestors," I said.

"Which will set in motion your end of the deal with Sebastian, imprison the ghosts of our relatives, and probably get you shipped off to hell where you'll spend the rest of eternity worshipping a glorified pimp who calls himself a prince."

"I appreciate your thorough and vivid imagination, Hay." I sealed up the jars of lavender and amaranth and set them back on the shelf with the other non-lethal herbs. "But I don't think it will work that way. Magic is all about intention. As long as we're clear on our desired outcome, we should be fine."

"Should be fine? You know that's just a stand-in phrase for 'I might blow everything to shit but I don't care because… *reasons*?'"

"Honestly? I don't even think the ancestor thing is Deirdre's main issue. She's just… I don't know. She thinks it's a distraction." I lowered my voice, crushing a bud of lavender between my thumb and forefinger. "She's worried that I haven't spent enough time with the other witches yet. She says if I'm going to lead them, I need to roll up my sleeves, get over my trust issues, and start participating as one of them."

"She has a point."

"I know, but she's also missing one. A big one."

"Which is?"

"We can do all the physical workouts Emilio and Elena come up with. We can learn sword fighting and martial arts. We can crush herbs and meditate and do group spells and swap secrets from everyone's books of shadows every single day, and yes, all of those things are important—I'm not saying otherwise. But they pale in comparison to the most powerful tools we have: Ourselves. Our bonds. Our own unique magic. Our instincts."

"Yes!" Haley pointed at me, a grin lighting up her face. "That's the kind of poster-worthy shit you should be saying to the group, Silversbane."

"Get me a bullhorn and some glitter cannons, and we'll think about it." I flicked the lavender bud at her, and she laughed again. "Anyway, I'm serious. Without his memories, Darius isn't whole. He still has instincts, but he doesn't remember his experience. All the things he's learned and honed along the way. All the people he's learned to trust—

"And learned to love," she sing-songed, batting her lashes at me.

"And love, yes. Love and friendship are bonds that strengthen magic, Haley. Witches, vampires, shifters, demons, fae, humans… We're all stronger for it."

Haley ran her hand over the neat rows of her crystals, a soft sigh escaping her lips.

"You're already saying yes," I said. "I can feel it."

She rolled her eyes, but then smiled, and I knew we were in business.

"Thank you, thank you, thank you!" I stepped around the counter and hugged her close, planting a big kiss on her cheek. "You really are my favorite sister. You know that, right?"

"I'm going to remember you said that when we meet the other two." She squirmed out of my embrace and made a big show of wiping my kiss off her face. "If this goes sideways, *you're* telling Grams."

I nodded, keeping my thoughts to myself. Because if this thing went sideways, Grams would be the least of our worries. Sebastian, on the other hand…

"Okay," Haley said. "Let me get this stuff to Verona. In the meantime, you put on the kettle and crush up some dried rosemary, forget-me-not, and vanilla bean."

"For the spell?"

"Those herbs are associated with memories, so I'm going to have you and Darius drink an infusion before we start. Can't hurt, right?"

"Good idea."

"We're also going to need black sea salt, water, six red candles, a sage bundle, and some matches. I'll ask Verona for some crystals to help keep out negative spirit energy. That should create a magical barrier against any of our dead relatives, *just* in case any of them get curious."

I was already rummaging through the pantry for the ingredients. "Is that everything?"

"Actually, we could use an assistant," she said. "This spell is pretty intense. Once we get into the ritual, it might be helpful to have someone on the sidelines keeping an eye on things."

"I would like to help, if you'll have me." Liam leaned

against the doorway, hands in his pockets, his casual stance completely at odds with the hope and excitement in his eyes.

Since we'd moved into the lodge, I hadn't spent much time with him, but his presence had been comforting. He'd been there when I'd brought Emilio back from the brink. He'd been there when I'd saved Asher's soul from the devil's trap in Norah's attic. It seemed fitting that he'd be there when we brought Darius back.

Looking at him now, at the flannel shirt buttoned crookedly, the messy blond hair, those bright blue eyes that never seemed to dim, I felt a flicker of hope and excitement, too.

"Liam Colebrook," I said with a grin, "you're hired."

THIRTY-THREE

GRAY

"How are you guys feeling?" Haley asked, checking her supplies one last time before finally shutting the door to the outside world. "Still good to go?"

Upstairs in the back corner bedroom I'd claimed as mine, Darius and I sat on the floor across from each other in the lotus position, gazing into each other's eyes. A thick red candle burned between us, carved with runes, its golden light reflecting in his eyes. Beside us, sage smoke rose from a stone bowl, purifying our space.

It was just after sunset and the room was dim at the day's end, yet for us, it felt like a beginning. A brand new day full of promise, potential, and possibility.

I was nearly giddy with it.

"Excellent," I said, and Darius nodded. He hadn't said much since we'd started, but I saw the hope in his eyes. He wanted this to work. Believed that it could.

"Liam," Haley said, "go ahead and serve the infusion."

Liam poured out two cups of liquid from a ceramic teapot on the dresser, passing one to each of us. The scents of rosemary and vanilla filled the room, wrapping me in a comforting embrace.

"As you're sipping your tea," Haley instructed, "I want you both to close your eyes, relax, and call up a particularly strong shared memory—one that comes to you easily, Darius."

His full lips parted into a grin, and my insides fizzed. "The cabin," he said. "Where—"

"TMI, vampire," Haley teased. "We don't need details. You guys just need to call it up for yourselves. In silence. Try to bring in as many sensory details as you can—sights, smells, sounds, tastes, feelings, intuitions, all of it. Once you've got that firmly in place, and your tea is finished, you can open your eyes again."

We closed our eyes, and I let my mind wander back to the Shadowrealm, back to the snowy wood where we'd found our perfect hideaway. I heard the crackle of the fire he'd built, felt the warmth of the flames against my bare legs and the soft T-shirt Darius had dressed me in. The scent of the cabin's bare wood interior mingled with the intoxicating whiskey-and-leather scent of my vampire, and my heart rate kicked up—both in the memory, and in the present moment. I drew in other details, too: the soft touch of his fingers on my skin as he'd traced circles across my forehead, calming me. The taste of his kiss, and the desperate need I felt for his touch. The warmth of his mouth between my thighs. The desire in his eyes when he'd finally claimed me, his words echoing in my memory... *You absolutely intoxicate me...*

My body was wound tightly, my breath coming in short bursts. I'd just finished the last of my tea, and I was certain I'd had a firm hold on the memory.

For me, those moments weren't going anywhere.

I opened my eyes and found my vampire with a hard-on.

He offered a devilish smile, but no apologies, and I couldn't help but laugh.

"I see we *were* thinking about the same thing," I said.

"I've been thinking about it every day since it came back to me, love. Dreaming about it, reliving it, replaying it. In fact, I'm considering commissioning Asher to make some sketches for me."

"Great," Haley said, and I flinched. I'd almost forgotten there were other people in the room. "Judging from the state of Darius's pants and the crimson flush on Gray's cheeks, I'm giving you both an A for that part of the assignment. Moving on."

Verona had given us several large crystals to help keep our magic contained and protect us from any potential visitors from beyond, and now Haley placed them in the corners of the room and on the windowsill—black tourmaline, labradorite, black obsidian. Next, she set the six red candles in a circle around us, standing a Tarot card against each one. They were all cards I'd consciously selected earlier from the deck Emilio had given me, hoping to draw on their particular energies for the ritual:

Six of Cups, for nostalgia and good memories, and a childlike faith that our blood spell would work as intended.

Judgment, symbolizing the rebirth of Darius as a whole being, memories restored and intact.

Three of Cups, a card of friendship and sisterhood, for the deep bond and gratitude I felt toward Haley.

Queen of Swords, to aid Darius with mental clarity.

The Lovers, representing our eternal bond, blood and heart and—though it was an odd choice of words, considering Darius was a vampire—soul.

And finally, The Star. I'd drawn it on the day Emilio and I had first been intimate together. The day Reva had turned up at the RCPD. It'd brought me a sense of calm and peace and hope, and I was channeling all those feelings again now, bringing them into the ritual that would bring my vampire back to me.

As Liam lit the surrounding candles, Haley knelt inside the circle next to me and Darius and unsheathed her athame, a slim silver dagger with a handle fashioned from raw quartz. She passed it through the sage smoke and whispered a few incantations in Latin, then used it to slice Darius's fingertip.

"Place a single drop of blood on Gray's tongue," she said. "No more, no less."

Darius did as she instructed, and I closed my eyes, letting the blood soak in like it had in the Shadowrealm. Again, I tasted the richness of it, smooth and slightly bitter, like dark chocolate without a grain of sugar.

A flood of images cascaded through my mind's eye. I gasped.

"Tell me what you see," Haley said.

"I can see Darius!" I said. "You… you're in London, meeting with clients in an old-fashioned looking office, with ornately carved furniture and shelves full of books and scrolls."

"Yes," he said softly, "I suppose that was where I practiced law."

"Now I see you at Black Ruby… You're filling out a liquor order. Wait, now you're unpacking blood from the deliveries. And now you're… Oh." My cheeks flamed again as I watched an image of myself through Darius's eyes. He'd just taken my blood, sealing our bond, and though he'd teased me with more sultry innuendo than I could handle, I sensed from the memory that he was practically on fire inside. I felt the strength of our connection surge through me, both in his memory of that moment and in my own mind right now.

The movie reel spun onward from there, forward and back, showing me glimpses of his past I could only guess at. Centuries, cities, faces, feelings, all of it spinning into a blur.

I opened my eyes, my heart threatening to burst from my chest. I couldn't process it all.

"His memories are still there, locked away in his blood," I said. "Or connected to it or… something. I don't know. There was so much… I'm sorry." My eyes filled with tears, my body suddenly overwhelmed with emotion.

Darius reached for my face, silently wiping a tear with his thumb. His own eyes were intense, his gaze heavy. I sensed a hundred thoughts forming in his mind, in his heart, yet he seemed unable to find the words to voice a single one.

Instead, he smiled, and I let out a breath, steadying myself again. Reminding myself that we were in this together. That this was absolutely going to work.

"No, that's a good thing, Gray," Haley said. "That means your theory actually holds water, and with a little luck and a whole lot of magic, we might be able to kickstart Darius's own recall abilities."

She held up her athame again, instructing us to hold out our hands, palms up.

"Essentially," she continued, "we need to recreate the blood bond, connecting you both in an unbroken circle. The idea is that your blood, your magic, and the magic of your existing bond will flow from one heart into the other, into the other, into the other, continuously, until there is no longer a separation between the two. Magically speaking, of course."

"If we need to recreate the bond," I said, "shouldn't Darius drink from me? That's how we did it initially." Memories of that moment in Black Ruby rushed back, stirring me up inside.

Across from me, Darius arched an eyebrow, his lips twitching with the effort of holding back a smile. He knew exactly what I was thinking about, exactly what that memory was doing to me. He could scent the desire in my blood.

"To create the unbroken circle effect," Haley said, "you'd both have to drink from each other, and that's a no-go. We can't risk turning you. No witch can survive the change."

I nodded. It was an old refrain, one all witches had learned from a young age. Though we were human, the magic in our blood didn't mix well with vampire blood. Other than the witch Jonathan had claimed to turn, for which we'd seen no evidence, none of us had ever survived an attempted change. I needed no further proof than Sophie and the other Bay witches Jonathan had murdered by injecting them with vampire blood.

I shook off the cobwebs of those old thoughts. Right now, I had to stay focused on Darius. On our ritual. On what it would feel like later tonight, holding my vampire in my arms, kissing him, talking about all the things he'd remembered.

We kept our hands steady, and using the tip of her athame, Haley carved runes into our skin, cutting just deep enough for blood to rise but not drip. It stung, but I welcomed the pain. It kept me focused on the moment, on its importance.

When she finished, Darius and I clasped hands over the candle between us, pressing our palms together and lacing our fingers tight. The moment we connected, my palms began to warm, then tingle, the sensation slowly spreading up my arms and into my chest.

"Do you feel it, Gray?" Haley asked, and I nodded, stifling a giggle. It made me feel light and happy inside, like getting laughing gas at the dentist.

"Now," she continued, "I want you both to gaze into each other's eyes and focus on your connection. See it reflected in your gazes. Note the different colors and facets in the eyes of your beloved. The exact shade and shape of the lips you've kissed so many times. The sound of breath, the scent. Feel the way your skin tingles when you touch, the way your fingers are so tightly entwined, the sting of the rune carvings. Imagine your blood flowing from your heart, Gray, down your left hand and into Darius's right. Darius, feel yourself receiving that gift of blood and magic from her, bringing it deep into your own heart, then sending it back out to Gray through your left hand and into her right. Imagine it's a circle of fire, spinning slowly at first, then heating, quickening, binding you together as it grows brighter."

Everything around us was silent but for the soft popping of the candles and the strong, wild beat of my heart. As I felt the magic working through us, my body warm and tingling, the circle of flames growing stronger, I gave in to the deep pull of Darius's gaze. The emotion reflected in his golden honey eyes was indescribable; the moment felt shockingly intimate, despite our company.

As the circle of flames continued to spin, Haley rose to her feet, then paced her own circle around us, chanting a spell as she moved.

Blood is the bond, blood is the key
To unlock the cage of these memories
What flows from one heart shall flow to the other
As mysteries past will soon be uncovered
Trust in this magic, trust in this love
Restore what was lost, below and above.

She repeated the verse three times, once for each circle she walked. As she chanted, the flames inside me heated, my magic spinning, twining, connecting. My heart was beating hard enough to burst, but each time I feared it would, I felt the magical rush of Darius's blood into my body, steadying me. With each circle Haley completed, more of Darius's memories surfaced, flickering through my mind only to rush away again before I could fully grasp them.

I hoped they were rushing back to him.

"Rise," Haley said, "keeping your hands clasped."

When we'd gotten to our feet, she said, "I want you to close your eyes and imagine the circle of flames slowing down, dimming, slowly fading like embers in a fire. Reclaim your magic, your blood. Feel it filling you up again, spreading throughout your body, renewing you. Once the flames have completely subsided and you feel whole again, you may release each other, and the ritual will be complete.

This part took a bit longer than the chanting, but Darius and I seemed to get there at the same time, slowly releasing each other. It was hard to let him go; after the deeply intimate moment we'd just shared, it felt like I was breaking the connection all over again.

Like I was risking losing it all.

When I looked into his eyes, I saw a flicker of sadness, and knew he'd felt the same way.

"Darius," I whispered, reaching for his face. If this was supposed to restore him, why did I suddenly feel so empty? So lost?

"I'm afraid I was right," he said softly, a smile tilting at the edge of his lips. "I *am* in love with you."

And then his eyelids fluttered closed, and Darius swayed on his feet.

THIRTY-FOUR

GRAY

"Liam," Haley ordered, and in an instant, Liam was at my vampire's side, catching him before he collapsed. Slowly and gently, he guided Darius onto the bed, pulling the blankets up to his shoulders, tucking him in.

My heart melted, and I blew out a breath.

"All part of the process," Haley assured me. "He just needs to rest now. How about you? Feeling okay?"

"I… I'm fine. Just a little dizzy. Nothing some OJ and chocolate won't fix."

"Here, hold this." She pressed a piece of smoky quartz into my left palm, folding my fingers around it. "It will help ground you. Take—"

I gasped as a new image jolted my mind, accompanied by a sharp burst of pain that had me dropping to my knees and clutching my head.

"Breathe, Gray." Haley knelt by my side, rubbing circles

on my back. "Deep breaths. Count backward from ten if you need to."

"There's another image," I said, trying to focus on it. On *her*, I realized. "A woman. I don't think she's from Darius's memories."

"A woman? What does she look like?" Haley asked. Her voice held a note of concern.

"She's sitting at a desk in the middle of a huge office, flipping through old books. She's wearing modern clothes —a black pantsuit, blue silk blouse. Her jacket has some kind of silvery-looking pin in the shape of a crown, with two swords crossing underneath."

Haley sighed. "Dark braid over her left shoulder, a little too much eye makeup?"

"You see her too?" I opened my eyes, slowing getting to my feet. Just as quickly as she'd arrived, the woman was gone, taking the head-splitting pain with her.

"Not at the moment," Haley said, "But I had a similar vision while I was chanting. When I saw her, though, there was with a younger woman with her—same color hair, glasses. It looked like they were packing up boxes together. Papers, files, office stuff."

"Why did we both see her?"

Haley shook her head, blowing out the candles in our circle.

"It's possible she's one of your ancestors," Liam said. "Despite the protective crystals, her essence may have been drawn here. Both of you possess very strong, very special magic, amplified by your bloodline. Working spells together is bound to have unforeseen effects."

"That would make sense," Haley said, "but I'm pretty sure the women I saw weren't dead."

"I'm with Haley on this one, Liam. It didn't feel like a spirit or even a memory, like when I'd seen people from Darius's past. It felt like we were spying on someone."

"Yeah," Haley said, "I didn't get the sense she knew we were there. She definitely wasn't watching us. The minute she appeared in my mind, I let her drift past, bringing myself back to my breathing and chanting."

A shiver rolled through my body, and I rubbed my arms.

"Not to worry," Liam assured me, resting his hands on my shoulders. "Shared visions are perfectly within the realm of possibility in a situation like this."

His warmth brought me back to the moment, a few tiny sparks zapping my skin where he touched me. That was one thing that *hadn't* changed—his effect on me. No matter what we'd gone through or what the Old Ones had done to his powers, Liam still had the ability to electrify me with the simplest touch.

"Sorry," he continued, releasing me, and immediately I missed the contact. Missed him.

Why did everything have to be so complicated?

"Anyway," he said, "sometimes witches inadvertently connect with the energy fields of others, especially during intense spellcraft. It's possible you picked up on a remnant of something that happened in this lodge in the very recent past, or something that's happening nearby as we speak. There are other properties in the area."

Liam's explanation made sense, and Haley and I shook off the lingering creepiness and set to work picking up the candles and other materials from our ritual. We decided to leave the protective crystals in place, and to leave the main candle burning—the one that had sat between me and Darius, casting his face in a warm glow.

I moved it to the bedside table, smiling at my sister and Liam. "I couldn't have done this without you. Both of you."

"Maybe not," Liam said with a wink, "but knowing you, you would have found another way."

"Are you calling me stubborn?"

"I am. And I believe it's one of the best qualities a witch can possess."

I laughed, then took my place in the chair next to the bed, where I'd remain until my vampire woke up. I wanted to be the first person he saw when he did.

I brushed my knuckles over his stubbled jaw, marveling at his grace, his beauty, the power of our bond. "So what happens now?"

"Now, we wait," Haley said. "He should remain in stasis for about six hours, and when he comes to, he'll likely be confused. The memories could rush back in a flood, competing with new memories or ideas about his identity he's formed since the attack in the Shadowrealm. Or it could happen more gradually, with bits and pieces coming back to him out of order, or melding together. Or it might not..." She trailed off, not bothering to voice her doubts, which I appreciated. Tonight, I had no room for those kinds of thoughts. His memories would return, even if it took months. There was no doubt in my mind.

"I'm just a few doors down the hall if you need anything." Haley leaned in to kiss my cheek, then saw herself out, shutting the door softly behind her. Liam stood at the end of the bed, hands in his pockets, rocking forward on his toes.

"You once told me that memories don't exist," I said to Liam, a smile touching my lips as I remembered the conversation. We were still at the safe house where Ash used to live, and my incubus and I had just survived an attack by zombie animals I'd inadvertently brought back from the dead. "That they're only stories we tell ourselves, and the way we let them change and shape us is our fatal flaw."

Liam let out a quiet laugh. "Yes, well. I believe we both had a lot to learn back then, didn't we? You about magic. And I about humanity. Heart. What it means to be a true friend." He came to stand beside the bed, placing a hand on Darius's arm. "What you're doing for him, Gray… He's quite blessed to have someone like you in his life."

"You say that as if you *don't*. Liam, you've got me, too. I know we're not perfect, but that doesn't make it any less real."

After a beat, Liam finally nodded, still struggling to accept that I cared for him. Still struggling, I sensed, under the very heavy, very human weight of his guilt.

"There's… something else I wanted to discuss with you," he said softly. The sparkle in his eyes dimmed, and I felt the energy in the room shift. "I have been called to hear the final sentencing. Tonight, at exactly midnight, I'm to travel out over the ocean in my raven form. One of the servants of the Old One will collect me, and I'll be brought before the tribunal one last time to hear their decision."

"Tonight? Already?" My eyes widened, my heart thumping with a mix of anticipation and fear. "Maybe that's a good thing, though. Right? If they've made a decision that quickly, maybe there's a chance they'll overturn everything and restore your powers! What if I went with you? I could testify for you, tell them about Emilio and what's coming and the prophecy and—"

"It doesn't work that way, Gray." Liam smiled, but it didn't match the new sadness in his eyes. "Though I do appreciate the show of support."

I rose from the chair and met his gaze. "Don't give up, Liam. You never know what might happen."

"In the long and spiraled history of time, a cosmic tribunal has never overturned its decision, nor have they issued a lesser sentence for such a crime. But if there's one lesson I've learned from you," he said with a wink, "it's that impossible odds are no reason not to try."

"Liam." I lowered my eyes, my lashes wet with tears. There was so much to say, and once again, no time to say it. I slid my arms around his waist and pressed my cheek to his chest, breathing him in. His heart beat strong and steady, human, the press of his chin on the top of my head simultaneously comforting and heartbreaking. "Why does it feel like we're always saying goodbye?"

"No, not goodbye. I promised myself I would stop saying goodbye to you, Gray Desario. So let me say this instead." He took a step back, then tilted my chin up toward his, forcing me to meet his infinite blue gaze once again. Stars collapsed and were born again in those eyes as I awaited his words. Galaxies. Universes. "Be well, little witch. I shall keep you in my heart, and I ask—though I don't deserve the kindness—for you to do the same." He bent down and kissed me, soft and gentle, pressing something cool and smooth into my palm.

There was a final spark across my lips, and then our kiss was broken.

Once again, Liam Colebrook was gone from my life.

I opened my fingers to find a heart-shaped piece of granite, worn smooth by the constant tumble of the ocean. Carved onto its face was a tiny raven's feather.

THIRTY-FIVE

GRAY

I was starting to become an expert at bedside vigils—a skill I hoped I wouldn't have to call on too often. Finally alone with him, I sat by my vampire's side, holding his hand, reliving every one of our shared memories. I didn't want to risk interfering with Haley's spellwork, so I didn't add any additional magic to the mix, but it felt like the right thing to do, letting those moments replay in my mind. Letting them fill me with happiness and hope, with the love I'd felt for him, the connection we'd shared from the first moment he'd tasted my blood that night in Black Ruby.

Exquisite, he'd said then, and I smiled now, seeing the moment with new eyes. We'd already had a connection by then; our blood promise had only solidified it. But neither of us could've predicted where that promise would lead, or how much deeper that bond would become.

"You'll remember," I whispered, pressing a kiss to his palm. A tear slipped down my cheek, but it wasn't from sadness or worry. It was hope. Faith. It might not happen overnight, but Darius would regain his memories. I knew it in the way that I'd known Emilio was still alive. In the way I knew Asher would survive the prison. In the way I knew Ronan and I would find a way to break Sebastian's curse.

"You just take your time, D. All the time you need. And when you're ready, you find your way back to me, and I'll be here waiting for you. I promise."

Darius didn't stir. He didn't toss and turn, seeking the coolest part of the pillow. Didn't twitch or fidget. He didn't even breathe. Just lay perfectly still, one hand over his heart, the other in mine. He was utterly at peace.

I shifted in my chair, trying to get comfortable. I'd just started to get feeling back in my butt when I heard a soft knock at the door.

Emilio. I sensed him before he announced himself, and wasn't the least bit surprised when I opened the door to see him standing there with a triumphant look on his face, his now-shaggy hair sticking up all over the place, hands hiding behind his back, a chocolate smudge on the side of his mouth.

"I've got something for you," he said with a grin.

"Hmm. I bet." I leaned up against the doorframe, my arms crossed over my chest. "Does this something start with a 'b' and rhyme with 'rownies?'"

"Is it that obvious?"

"You're wearing the evidence, Detective." I stretched up on my toes and kissed the edge of his mouth, licking the smudge of chocolate.

"Damn," he whispered when I pulled back, his eyes darkening with desire. "I should've been more strategic in my chocolate smudging. Wait—be right back."

"Oh no you don't." I was about to smack him on the shoulder—I still wasn't quite used to his flirty innuendos—but he saved himself by pulling his arms out from behind his back and revealing a plate of still-steaming brownies.

I nodded for him to come inside, then shut the door behind him. "Only *you* would think to bake brownies in the middle of a multi-pronged crisis."

"Trust me, *querida*. There's no better time. Baking calms me, and the scents of chocolate, cinnamon, and vanilla make others feel at home. But hey, if you've got some kind of moral opposition to them, I'm sure I can find another taker."

"And another girlfriend, while you're at it." I grabbed the plate from his hands and took the brownie from the top of the stack, shoving in a bite. "Defaulting on the gift of chocolate?" I mumbled, not even caring that I was talking with my mouth full. God, his brownies were incredible. Sweet and decadent, with that deliciously spicy kick at the end. "Definitely grounds for a breakup."

"Girlfriend?" He arched a teasing eyebrow and grabbed a brownie for himself. "Is that what you are?"

"Pretty sure we've established that." I set the plate on the bedside table next to the candle still burning for Darius, then pulled Emilio in for another kiss.

He tasted like the richest, darkest, most velvety chocolate ever, and as he deepened the kiss, a flame of red-hot desire flickered inside my core. My libido went from zero-to-sixty in a single heartbeat.

Emilio must've scented the change in me. He let out a quiet moan against my lips, his kiss becoming more insistent, his hands sliding inside my shirt, huge and warm on my back.

I leaned into his touch. I'd missed it *way* more than I'd missed his brownies, and it'd been entirely too long since I'd felt him against my bare skin.

We weren't alone, exactly. But here in my bedroom with only a passed-out vampire for company, it was the closest we'd gotten to actual privacy since the night before the warehouse liberation, and I wasn't about to let the opportunity pass.

"Come here." I dragged him across the room to the closet on the other side. It wasn't a walk-in, but it was large enough for two people to get into just the kind of trouble we were looking for. I pulled him inside and closed the door partway behind us, leaving it open just a crack so we could keep an eye on Darius.

"But Darius—"

I pressed a finger to his lips. "Haley said he'll sleep for at least six hours."

"Are you sure?" he asked, but he was already slipping out of his shoulder holster, setting the weapon on the top closet shelf. His shirt and jeans were next, along with everything else, until he was standing naked before me, fully erect.

I slid my hands over his shoulders, taking in the feel of

his smooth, golden skin, marred only by the faint residual scarring from the silver blade. "I haven't even unzipped my jeans yet, Detective Alvarez, and you're already naked. So much for your noble protests."

"If there's one thing my trip to the other side taught me, it's not to take anything for granted, and not to wait around for a better moment when the present one is perfectly damn good."

His mouth was on mine in a heartbeat, claiming me, marking me, making up for all the time we'd lost. Without breaking the kiss, he unbuttoned my cardigan, sliding it off my shoulders, his hands roaming every inch of exposed skin. I kicked off my jeans and underwear, and Emilio lifted my arms up, guiding my hands to the bar that ran the length of the closet.

I curled my fingers around it, holding tight as he kissed me senseless, devouring my mouth, my neck, my breasts, his massive hands and lush lips everywhere at once, heating my blood from a simmer to a boil.

"I can't get enough of you," he breathed, kissing my stomach, licking a path from one hipbone to the other. His fingers fluttered between my thighs, teasing me open, his hot breath swirling over my clit. Emilio inhaled my scent, burying his face against my flesh, moaning as he tasted me.

He felt incredible, and part of me wanted to close my eyes and sink into his kiss, let him claim me with his mouth, again and again, teasing and sucking and licking me until my legs trembled.

But I needed him inside me. All of him. And I couldn't wait another second.

"Emilio," I begged, sliding a hand into his hair and fisting it. "Kiss me."

He grabbed my ass and pulled me closer, his tongue sliding inside me, deeper, pure ecstasy, but it wasn't enough.

"Not there," I panted. I tugged on his hair, guiding him upward, losing myself again in the pleasure of his mouth as he kissed a path up my stomach, through the valley between my breasts, alongside my neck, my jaw, finally claiming my mouth in another breathless kiss.

As always, Emilio seemed to know exactly what I needed in that moment, what I craved, and as I wrapped my fingers around the bar again, he lifted me up, his hands cradling my ass, guiding me onto the tip of his massive cock. I sank onto him, feeling every inch as he plunged inside me.

"I missed you," I breathed, my thighs clamping tight around his hips. I held him there, and he buried his face in my neck and breathed me in, slowly rolling his hips as I braced myself on the bar. Despite his earlier hunger, my wolf's frenetic energy shifted, and once again, he was the slow, tender lover he'd been the first time we'd shared a bed together. With one arm holding me up, he cupped my face with his free hand, kissing me softly, sensuously, tasting me as if every time was the first. His hand trailed down my throat, grazing my collarbone, my nipple, my ribs, slowly sliding between us. With a soft, gentle pressure, he traced slow circles over my clit, drawing me closer to the edge as he shifted inside me, slow and steady, deliberate.

It snuck up on me, that heat. That deep, dark pulse of pure pleasure, bursting inside me like a dam. As my thighs trembled around him, I held on tightly to the bar and turned my head, biting my upper arm, muffling my cries of ecstasy. Emilio gripped my ass, pushing in deeper and holding me steady, his breath coming out in a sudden rush as he bit my shoulder and finally let go, shuddering against me until he was finally spent.

I let go of the bar and looped my arms around his neck, slowly sliding down his body, kissing him as I went.

My feet had just hit the floor when the closet door swung open, and we both turned with a start to see a smirking, bed-headed vampire looming in the doorway.

"You've dragged the wolf into the closet." Darius glanced around the dark space, his eyes glinting. "Is this some kind of metaphor? Perhaps your subconscious is telling you he's not the man for you."

Emilio let out a hearty laugh, his hands still firmly gripping my ass. "Judging from the sounds she was making, bloodsucker, I'm guessing that's not the case."

"Yes, I did wonder about that." Darius stepped fully into the closet, looking around again as if he were considering moving in. "Does she always do that?"

"You tell me."

"You guys." I rolled my eyes. "I'm right here."

"Mmm." Darius's gaze drank us in, head to toe and back up again. "Indeed, you are."

"How are you feeling?" I asked, reaching forward to sweep the hair from his eyes. I didn't care that I was naked. In fact, standing there in that closet with a still-erect wolf shifter by my side and a mischievous-looking vampire in front of me, I was pretty damned turned on.

"Haley said there might be some initial confusion," I said. It was hard to keep the hope from my voice. She'd also said he'd sleep a few more hours, yet here he was, wide awake and already teasing me. Was that a good sign?

Do you remember? Did it work?

"I seem to recall something about that," Darius said, offering no further explanation.

"So…?" I gave him an encouraging smile, but my insides were tying themselves into knots. His thoughts were hidden from me, his face a mask. Only his eyes held a glint of their former mischief—the only hint that a bit of the old vampire might have resurfaced.

"I'm feeling," he said, stroking an elegant finger along my cheek, "in the mood for a story. The one where a devilishly handsome vampire spends an evening with an entrancing young witch in his Astin Martin Spitfire in the parking lot of Luna's café. Are you familiar with that one, love? Because I'd *really* like to know how it ends."

THIRTY-SIX

DARIUS

"Cookies!" she shouted, unexpectedly throwing herself into my arms. I couldn't help but embrace her, despite the fact that her luscious scent was currently being overpowered by the wolf's. Her skin was warm and soft, her body curving against mine as if it'd been created to do just that.

"Cookies, huh?" Emilio laughed. "And here I thought she only had eyes for my brownies."

"No, the story." Gray pulled back from my embrace and beamed at me with tears in her eyes, her gorgeous smile nearly as bright as the sun. "After the… the car stuff… We ended up inside the café, and you bought me a latte and chocolate macadamia cookies and told me how you loved cheeseburgers and sweet potato fries."

I nodded, the once-familiar flavors rolling over my tongue again, unleashing flashes of other memories. Black Ruby—the club I owned. Late nights balancing the books, eating the leftover fries.

"Now that you mention it," I said, "I do love those things. I remember… pieces. It's just… I'm not sure the spell has taken hold. I'm afraid there are still so many gaps."

"I know, but don't you see? It's just the beginning!" Gray's enthusiasm refused to be tempered, and I couldn't help but return her smile. It was absolutely infectious. Regardless of what I'd remembered, I'd spent many hours since our return from the Shadowrealm gazing into the haunted depths of her eyes, wishing I could erase every last worry, every last fear.

This was the closest I'd come to bringing her pure happiness in a long, long time.

"Tonight was just our first attempt," she continued, her skin glowing. "Haley and I are daughters of Silversbane. With our combined power, her blood magic expertise, and a little more practice, we'll figure this out, D. I promise you that."

D. The nickname floated into my consciousness, settling into my chest. That, too, I was remembering.

"Wait, can we go back to that part about the parking lot sex?" Emilio asked, sliding a hand over the curve of her hip. The man was rock hard, and had made no effort to control or cover himself on my account. "As an officer of the law, I feel it's imperative to gather all the evidence for detailed analysis."

Gray laughed, then turned to me again, her eyes shining with fresh hope. "What else do you remember about that night at Luna's? Any other details, conversations, anything?"

I closed my eyes, traveling back in time to that night, back to the butter-soft leather seats of the car. I was in the driver's seat, Gray sitting beside me, whispering my name as I kissed the pale skin of her inner arm.

"I've tasted you," I said now, opening my eyes, and I could tell from the surprise in hers that she knew the *exact* moment I'd just recalled. I'd whispered the words in response to her own breathless utterance: *I don't know how you do that… It's like you know exactly how to touch me…*

"I can smell the blood running through your veins," I continued now, the words echoing strong and clear in my memory. "Hear the tempo of your heartbeat."

Then, just like I had that night, I leaned in close, inhaling her sweet scent, my body burning with desire. "I can feel where you *ache*."

Gray gasped, and without hesitation, I claimed her mouth. Emilio steadied her hips, kissing the back of her neck, her ear, his soft black hair brushing against my cheek as we both tasted her.

Gray's hands dipped inside the waistband of my jeans, fumbling with the button and zipper. I was already in such a state of intense arousal, one brush of her fingertips had me gasping with pleasure.

"Are you absolutely sure, love?" I asked her. "Both of you?"

All teasing aside, I didn't want to make any assumptions—not about either of them. I was fairly certain I'd never shared her with the wolf, and though he and the others had assured me time and again that we were brothers, bonded by our deep love for and loyalty to this woman, that didn't mean I could invite myself into their most intimate moments like this. Especially when my memory was still so spotty, with no guarantees it would ever return.

"There's nothing I want more," Gray whispered, her hands coming up to cup my face. "I love you, Darius. And I know you love me, even if you're still trying to remember how we got here."

"There's no need to stand on ceremony with me, Beaumont," Emilio said, still nuzzling her neck. "You could come back from all this convinced you're a damned toy poodle, for all I care. You're still one of us. Still my brother."

Not wanting to waste another precious second, I kissed her again, giving myself over to her touch. She slid inside my jeans again and gripped me, stroking me with absolutely perfect pressure.

Without warning, she and Emilio knelt down before me, Gray sucking me between her lips, slowly guiding me into her hot, velvet-smooth mouth as Emilio took her from behind, her soft moans of pleasure vibrating across my skin.

Everything inside me came undone. Gray had me at an absolute disadvantage, her mouth on my flesh, licking and teasing with such perfect, knowing strokes I could only assume she'd done this before.

I slid my hands into her hair, fisting her silky curls, my gaze trailing down the graceful arch of her back to the place where Emilio plunged inside her, the muscles of his abdomen rippling with the movement. Everything about the moment was perfect, beautiful, and as he brought her to her second epic orgasm of the night, I lost the very last shred of my own control, exploding in a white-hot burst of intensity, my body shuddering as she brought me back from the dead.

She leaned back against Emilio, breathless and breathtaking, her cheeks dark, her eyes glassy. I sat down on the floor beside them and leaned back against the wall, waiting for my heartbeat to steady.

None of us spoke.

Moments later, the closet door swung open, and a swath of light fell on Gray's face.

"What the hell?" she gasped, her cheeks darkening further as she scrambled for her clothing. It took her a moment to recognize the figure looming in the doorway, grinning at her like a dammed idiot.

"Who has an orgy and forgets to invite the fucking incubus?" Asher demanded.

"Did it occur to you, hellspawn," I began, "that the oversight was intentional?"

"Then you should've gotten a hotel across state lines, because the energy you three are giving off is like a nuclear sex bomb calling out across the miles."

"And you felt you had to answer that call because…"

"Because I'm *super* into sex bombs, bloodsucker." He stepped into the closet, crowding us. There'd been very little room to begin with. Now, I couldn't move without feeling the warm brush of someone's breath on my neck. "Besides, I couldn't sleep."

"There are lots of ways to pass the time, demon," I said. "Perhaps you could play a game of hide-and-seek on the other side of the city. Or better yet, the country."

"Don't be rude," Gray teased, nudging me with her foot. "There's plenty of room in here for everyone."

"In *where*, precisely?" I slid my hand across her thigh, spreading her legs and slipping two fingers across her clit. She gasped, no doubt still sensitive, but her hips rocked into my touch.

That was apparently all the invitation he needed.

With a speed and grace that would impress any vampire, the incubus was out of his clothes and kneeling before Gray, claiming her mouth in a savage kiss.

I took the gentlemanly route and removed my hand from between her thighs, allowing him a turn. He pulled her into his lap, wrapping her legs around his midsection, burying his length inside her. Gray whispered his name, then Emilio's, then mine, and though we'd only just finished devouring her, she reached for us both again, stroking, teasing, taking. I was instantly hard again at her touch, ready to give her anything she wanted, to take anything she had to offer.

As before, she touched me like she truly knew me.

And for the first time since those damned memory eaters stole my history, I allowed myself the faintest flicker of hope that maybe I'd remember how she liked to be touched, too. That I'd remember not just flashes of stolen moments in the car or in the Shadowrealm cabin, but every precious moment we'd shared together.

On my knees at her side, I leaned in close, kissing my way up the curve of her neck, sucking her earlobe between my teeth, grazing her flesh with my fangs. She arched her back like a feline, rising up on her knees until Asher was nearly completely exposed, then sliding down on him once again, driving the incubus wild. The scent of her desire pulsed from her body, in her blood, in the air, mingling with ours into a divine perfume that had my head spinning, my cock throbbing, my entire body aching for more.

Asher was the first to lose control, setting off a chain reaction that, in a matter of mere minutes, had us all trembling and weak.

Again, we sat in silence, heartbeats and breath and heat cresting, then receding, slowly bringing us back down.

The wave of shared pleasure had only just begun to fade when a hard and most unwelcome rap on the bedroom door had us all scrambling for our clothes.

"Shite," I mumbled under my breath at the same time Asher shouted, "Fuck off!"

"Emilio?" Elena called. "Sorry for the interruption, but we've got something."

"Better be something good," the wolf snapped, but he was already on his feet, awkwardly stuffing his considerable bulk into his jeans and reaching for his weapon on the top shelf.

The rest of us followed suit, spilling forth from the closet and stumbling into our various undergarments and bits of clothing. It was a terrible end to an otherwise magnificent evening, but it was an end none of us would fight.

We all knew the deal. Elena wasn't banging on the door like a woman offering a round of coffee or even one telling us to keep it down in here.

She was banging on the door like a cop.

"Just got a call from Seattle PD," she said from the other side, all business. "Two women were just detained after an altercation at Sea-Tac, boarding a flight bound for Toronto. They're being transferred to Raven's Cape PD as we speak."

"We got IDs?" Emilio asked, opening the door.

Elena handed him a folder, her face severe. "Norah Hanson and Delilah Pannette."

THIRTY-SEVEN

GRAY

"Multiple counts of kidnapping. Human trafficking. Assault. Abuse of a minor by a person in a position of trust. Aiding and abetting a fugitive. Murder one. Forgery. Fraud. And this is just off the top of my head." Emilio dropped a thick folder onto the table, and the woman cuffed to the chair behind it flinched.

The woman. Staring through the one-way glass into the RCPD interrogation room, I couldn't bring myself to call the prisoner Norah Hanson. She looked nothing like the leader of Bay Coven. Where Norah had been tall and elegant, with steely gray hair and intelligent eyes, this woman was easily fifteen years younger, with cropped, jet-black hair, violet eyes, and a scowl that would make most people cross the street just to avoid her.

"My name is Donna Calabrese," the woman insisted, her voice flat and exhausted. Rehearsed. "I'm traveling to Canada with my daughter. You've got the wrong—"

"Save it, Hanson. Your fingerprints don't lie. And once that protection spell wears off, your face will corroborate the evidence."

She tried to feign ignorance again, but I'd seen the twitch of her jaw at the mention of the word spell.

Verona had told us that Delilah had come into her shop a while back, using Norah's credit card to buy a combination of magical ingredients that would only ever be used for a particular spell. According to Verona, that kind of magic was intended to erase a person's existence by altering the way they looked, their identity, their public records, other people's memories of them, everything.

We'd gotten lucky that Norah had done the spell in haste. She'd missed a few crucial steps, and while it'd changed her appearance, everything else had remained the same—including her fingerprints and public records. The fake IDs she'd procured for herself and Delilah might've helped her slip beneath the radar, but apparently, she and Delilah had gotten into a heated argument on the jet bridge during boarding. An airline employee tried to calm things down, but Norah hit her, and everything escalated from there.

I turned to look over my shoulder. Delilah sat on a bench between Elena and Haley, wrapped in a blanket, sipping hot chocolate that Detective Hobb had brought her. Norah had been magically coercing her for months, manipulating her into doing her bidding. But like Norah's identity spell, the magic she'd been using on Delilah required precision and clear intent, and Norah, in her haste to escape, had gotten lax. Delilah had begun to remember her true self. And just before they'd stepped onto the plane that was supposed to ferry them out of the country, Delilah pushed back.

"Let me be *real* honest here, Hanson," Emilio said. "You're facing multiple life sentences. I'm not here to play good cop or offer you any favors in exchange for your coop-eration. No matter what happens in this room, or in any lawyer's office or courtroom hereafter, you're going to die in a cell. You're going to die alone. And you're going to die with the knowledge that you were responsible for the slaughter of your own people, and possibly the downfall of humanity."

I didn't expect Emilio's dire speech to have any effect on the woman, but in the heavy silence that followed, her head slumped forward and her shoulders began to tremble. Tears slid down her cheeks and plopped onto the folder in front of her.

It was a long time before she spoke again, but Emilio waited her out, his hip cocked against the table, arms crossed over his chest, his breathing steady and even as if he had all the time in the world.

The strategy worked.

"You're right," she finally said, and I heard the break in her voice. The moment when she'd finally realized there was nothing left to do. No tricks, no spells, no lies. Just the truth. "The walls are closing in on me, and I've got nowhere left to turn. No hope for a future. No hope for freedom. So what, Detective, could you possibly do for me?"

"You tell me," he said.

"Shoot me. Right now. Tell them I became violent and belligerent. That I attacked you and left you with no choice."

"Not gonna happen. But I *can* offer you one thing, Norah."

It was the first time he'd used her given name, and she looked up at him, a flicker of hope flashing through her eyes despite the reality of the situation.

"You give me the information I need—information that leads to the capture or death of the dark fae and hunters behind this, the rescue of additional supernatural prisoners, and the liberation of the city of Blackmoon Bay—and I might be able to offer you a few nights' sleep, knowing that at the end of all your scheming and machinations and plotting, you were offered one last chance to do the right thing, and you took it."

He picked up the folder and tapped the papers into place, then left her alone with her thoughts, joining the rest of us behind the glass.

"She's not going to crack," Emilio said. "I've got nothing to offer her. No leniency, no community service, nothing. She's broken too many human laws for that, and she knows it." He crossed the room and crouched down in front of Delilah, offering her a compassionate smile. It reminded me of the first time I'd met him officially, the night of Sophie's murder, when he'd come to our house to investigate. His kindness was one of the few bright spots I remembered from that night, along with Ronan's rock-steady support.

"How are you holding up?" he asked her.

Delilah blew out a breath. "I'm… okay. I just wish I could remember more. I was with her this whole time, and I've got nothing to show for it."

"Be gentle with yourself," he said, squeezing her knee, and Haley grabbed her hand, holding it tight. "You've been under her spell for months—no one blames you for anything that happened."

"I know. I just wish…"

Emilio nodded. "We all wish we had more to go on here. But we'll get there. Together, we'll figure it out, piece by piece, just like we've been doing. Okay?"

She smiled, faint but true, and Emilio rose, heading out with Hobb to get hot chocolate and coffee refills.

When they returned, I downed the coffee Emilio offered me, then said, "I need to see her. Face-to-face."

"Gray, that's not the best idea," Elena said. "She's unstable, and as we already know, a master manipulator. We've got her cuffed and warded, but that doesn't mean she couldn't call up some spell, something we haven't thought to protect against."

"She won't," I said.

"How can you be sure?"

I glanced through the glass again, taking in her dead eyes, the dejected bend of her head. She looked nothing like the Norah I remembered, but there in her eyes, I saw a piece of her broken soul, and I knew. Her guilt ran bone-deep, and it was eating away at her like a poison.

"Because she's already given up," I said. "She didn't

lose control and slip up at Sea-Tac today. She wanted to get caught. She's ready to end this."

"Then why didn't she turn herself in to the authorities?" Emilio asked.

"And tell them what? That she's a rogue witch who betrayed her coven by aligning with witch hunters and dark fae in a magical plot to destroy supernatural and humankind?" I shook my head, biting back a sarcastic laugh. It all sounded so ridiculous, I couldn't believe this was my life. "She knew if she got booked, Seattle PD would get in touch with you and Elena right away. She's been a fugitive for months, and she's known since Sophie's death that you've been investigating her. Then she risks Delilah using her credit card at The Phoenix's Flame? I'm not buying it. She's not dumb, Emilio. She's just... She's just done."

Emilio closed his eyes and sighed, and I knew I'd finally gotten through to him.

"Let me talk to her," I said, reaching for his hand. "The minute anything starts to feel wonky, I'll back off. You can be in there with me the whole time."

"You bet your witchy little ass I can be." He wrapped his hand around my fingers, his touch warm and protective, like always. Then, pressing a kiss to my palm, he said, "Alright, *mi brujita*. Let's see what kind of interrogation skills you've got."

THIRTY-EIGHT

GRAY

"Why?" I asked, knowing I didn't need to elaborate.

It was the same question I'd asked Fiona the night Darius had brought her back from New York. The same I'd asked Jonathan. The same I'd asked anyone who'd ever gotten to such a dark place in their lives that they truly believed bringing harm and death to witches—to anyone who was different from them, for that matter—was the only way out.

But unlike Jonathan, who'd always treated his mission as if it were God's work entrusted to him by an army of holy messengers, or Fiona, who'd been temporarily blinded by love and devotion to a despot, Norah had no such convictions. And when she finally glanced up and met my gaze, I saw the echo of a thousand regrets in her eyes.

Her shoulders trembled again, her face crumpling like wet paper.

Like Emilio, I crossed my arms over my chest, prepared to wait her out. It didn't take long; it seemed she was almost out of tears.

"I had two... two... d-daughters once," she said, suddenly and softly, the words barely finding their way out of her mouth. I got the sense she hadn't said them in a long time.

"Did you know that?" she asked.

I shook my head, shocked. I'd always assumed Norah was a self-contained, self-sufficient superwitch. The idea of her raising children was almost impossible to reconcile, even knowing she'd taken Reva in. Of all the words I'd thought to describe Norah over the last few months, motherly hadn't even been a contender.

"No, I suppose you wouldn't," she said, a small, faraway smile touching her lips. "It was a long time ago. They were around Reva's age back then—fourteen and seventeen. Their father lost his battle with cancer when they were just out of diapers. I'd raised them up by myself."

"I... I'm sorry," I said, hating the flicker of sympathy in my chest. Hating that Norah was getting under my skin, but letting her do it anyway. "That must've been difficult."

Norah nodded. "Oh, but it was worth it. They were beautiful. My greatest challenge, yes, but also my greatest joys. There's nothing I wouldn't have done for them, nothing I wouldn't have given them." She took a deep, shuddering breath, and my skin erupted in goosebumps. Whether it was more manipulative bullshit or the purest truth Norah had ever spoken, there was no way this story had a happy ending.

"I will spare you the gruesome details," she said, "because they are irrelevant. Suffice it to say my daughters died at the hands of witches. Witches who sold them out to the highest bidder, leaving me to linger, to try to make some semblance of a life when all I wanted to do was evaporate clean out of existence."

I glanced at Emilio and shook my head. It wasn't that I didn't believe her; I knew what it was to crawl through the endless hellfire of grief searching for a loved one who would never return, no matter what bargains you whispered into the darkest hours of the night. The pain in Norah's voice rang true.

I just couldn't believe what I was hearing. Could anyone really be so blind? So willfully ignorant?

"You've done the same thing, Norah," I said. "Can't you see that?"

Norah shook her head, willful till the end. "I know you think I'm a coward. I can see it in your eyes—all of you. Delilah, too. Even after she'd been under my enchantment, I'd still catch her looking at me that way. Judging. Pitying." At this, her face twisted into a scowl, and she turned a fiery, wild gaze on me. "But *you're* the one who turned your back on who you really are, Gray. It was so easy for you, wasn't it? Walking away. Pretending that the witch inside you— that sick, flawed part of you—had never even existed, when all along it was festering, rotting you from the inside—"

"Alright, we're done here." Emilio reached for my hand again and nodded toward the door, but I held firm. I appreciated the backup, but I *wasn't* done here. Not by a long shot.

"What you call sick and flawed?" I leaned across the table, getting right in her face. "That has *nothing* to do with witchcraft, Norah. It's called being human, and it exists in all of us. Even you, and yes, even me. *Especially* me. I've made a lot of mistakes in my life—hell, I'm probably making a few right this minute. But I have *never* sold out my own kind. Never turned a sister over to the hunters. Never bought into their bullshit about witches being evil and wrong. That's on the witches who murdered your daughters. That's on *you*."

But Norah only laughed, bitter and manic, the sound of it making my skin crawl. "Do you know what it's like to hate yourself so completely, to look in the mirror every single day and force yourself to find another reason not to carve out your own eyes? Not to slice open your veins and spill your own blood down the drain?"

I exchanged another glance with Emilio, then shook my head, fighting off a shiver.

Even at my lowest points, even when I'd cocooned myself up in blame and guilt over the deaths of the people I loved and all the pain and suffering they'd endured, I still couldn't imagine such self-loathing. Such emptiness. Such a desperate need for the final escape.

"You are blessed, then," she said with a defeated sigh.

"Truly blessed. Perhaps you should take that blessing, turn your back on all of this once again, and walk out that door. Because trust me, Gray. This is not a road you want to go down."

I turned toward the glass and closed my eyes, trying to gather my thoughts.

All the time I'd been thinking about Norah, going over every detail of our conversation at her house the day she'd banned me from the coven, poring over Sophie's book of shadows for more clues, looking for something that would tie her to Sophie's death or to the disappearance and murder of the other witches... In all that time, it'd never once occurred to me that she might be suffering so deeply. That something—someone—had broken her, just like someone had broken Jonathan. Just like someone had tried to break me.

Again, I was reminded of this lesson, this simple truism that we as people—as witches, as supernaturals, as gods and goddesses, as cosmic forces and elemental energies and unfathomable beings as old as time—just couldn't seem to grasp:

Hatred was made, not born.

And unless someone did something to stop the cycle, it continued. I could rally a hundred witches, a thousand, a million. Unite all the covens on the planet, kick that prophecy up into high gear, wipe out the hunters and dark fae, and establish a new world order where everyone wore yoga pants to work and spent our free time playing with puppies and having amazing sex and coloring mandalas in adult coloring books. But even with all of that, hatred would always be the biggest threat, the poison that could seep in undetected and rot us from the inside out.

If we didn't find a way to end it, it would surely end us.

THIRTY-NINE

GRAY

"You can still honor your daughters, Norah," I said softly, compassion sneaking into my voice against my better judgment. I turned to face her once again. "It's not too late."

Another bitter laugh. "They're dead. It doesn't get any later than that."

"So honor their memory and do the right thing here. Help us." I leaned across the table again, close as I dared. The violet in her fake eyes was starting to fade, the natural slate gray peeking through underneath. "Who is Orendiel of Darkwinter working for?"

"I was not involved with the dark fae specifically," she said, breaking our gaze. Her whole body had gone rigid with fear. "My arrangement was with the hunters."

"Jonathan Reese?" I asked.

Norah shook her head. "Phillip Reese. Jonathan was just a pawn."

"Our understanding," Emilio broke in, "was that Phillip didn't become involved until shortly before Jonathan's disappearance."

"Your understanding—or, rather, your lack thereof—is the reason this was able to escalate so quickly."

"Explain," he demanded. And this time, whether she truly was ready to cooperate, or just wanted to make us suffer at the telling, she obeyed.

"This has been an operation years in the making, detective. Phillip has never lost track of his son's whereabouts, nor his aspirations. And while Jonathan has always been unstable, Phillip recognized the genius in many of his ideas, if not the execution."

She went on to tell us that Phillip allowed Jonathan to develop his weapons and run his experiments under the misguided belief that he'd rid himself of his father's influence. But Phillip had a hand in things all along, sending rogue supers to infiltrate Jonathan's operations under guise of joining the cause, tracking Jonathan's every move and discovery. He'd been aware of the experiments with vampire blood, of Fiona Brentwood's involvement. Even the hunters in Raven's Cape that we'd assumed were loyal to Jonathan had been moles planted by Phillip.

"What about the witches in other states?" I asked. "Countries? Washington wasn't the only state affected by this. Sophie told me that she and Haley had found communications from other covens, asking you for help."

Norah closed her eyes, her lips pressed into a thin line.

When she looked up at me again, her eyes were fully back to their natural color.

And fully engulfed in regret.

"Jonathan had already begun experimenting in other locales long before they reached the Bay, making a lot of mistakes and risking exposure at every turn. But through those mistakes, he also revealed much about the inner workings of his mind, about his plans, about the hybrid technology he'd been working on. Phillip saw the seeds of true brilliance there, but knew Jonathan could never pull it off himself. That's when Phillip took a more active role, sending in his spies and surreptitiously nudging Jonathan toward the Bay. From that point forward, things began to coalesce quickly."

"So you knew all along," I said, unable to keep the venom from my voice. "The witches from the other covens that'd reached out to you for help—you turned them down. Not because you wanted to keep your head down and protect the Bay Coven witches, but because you wanted to protect Phillip. You wanted to protect yourself."

Norah didn't bother denying it. "Phillip and I have known each other a long time, crossing paths many, many times over the years. For most of that time, we kept an uneasy truce and stayed out of each other's business. It'd been a few years since we'd even communicated, when he suddenly reached out for a meeting. There, he shared with me a glimpse of his plans, and offered me a deal. Protection, survival. All I had to do was give him a little bit of information now and then, and turn a blind eye to his and Jonathan's activities."

"You are unbelievable," I said.

Norah merely shrugged. "At the time, I thought he was my best shot at survival. This war was coming whether I helped Phillip or not. The hunters had come out of the woodwork, developing an international underground network that, unlike the witches, was united in a single purpose. There would be no stopping the coming storm. Who are witches to stand up to this kind of power, Gray? Who am I? We can't even agree on the best way to cast a banishing spell."

Rage boiled in my gut at her words. How could she doubt us so much? How could she take such an easy way out?

I took a deep breath, reeling in my anger. Hadn't I doubted us, too? Wasn't I *still* doubting us? How many witches had gathered in the lodge, all of them willing to come together against a threat with a thousand faces, all because they knew fellow witches were in trouble? That our community was in grave danger? And I'd yet to trust them. To fully join them. I was there, sharing the space with them, helping with odds and ends, sitting in on some of the trainings. But I was still separate. Still holding myself apart. Still not claiming my magic or my blood.

"How does Orendiel fit into all this?" Emilio asked, and I turned my attention back to the interrogation. "You claim you don't know who's pulling his strings, but Phillip must've mentioned something about the fae involvement."

"Orendiel has his own agenda," she said. "But according to Phillip, when he heard about Phillip's work—presumably through a rogue fae that had been working with Jonathan to capture supernaturals for experimentation—he approached Phillip with a deal: the dark fae and Phillip's hunters would join forces, working together to hybridize supernaturals for their armies, then eradicate both the witches and other problematic supernatural races. Phillip would have access to elite Darkwinter Knights as well as fae technology to meld with Jonathan's research, Darkwinter would have access to the hybrids they created, and once the war was over and the only groups left standing in power were the dark fae and the human hunters, they would divide the spoils. The fae would become the ruling class, and in return, the magic of the witches would be returned to its rightful keepers—the hunters."

"Back to this again," I said, throwing my hands up. It was always the same story. Power and magic. Magic and power. "Do the fae even have the capability to do such a thing? Magic can be manipulated, even channeled. But it can't be extracted and transferred. The hunters have been trying it for centuries, and it's never worked."

Norah frowned. "Greed blinds us all to logic and reason, Gray. I'm sure Orendiel knew exactly how to play on Phillip's base desire for the eradication of witches and the reclaiming of their magic—the hunters have never made their manifesto a secret. I imagine Orendiel spun quite a tale, and Phillip heard exactly what he wanted to hear, and here we are. Darkwinter doesn't *need* to have the capability to extract witch magic, because they have no intention of keeping up their end of the bargain. My guess? Darkwinter will turn on the hunters the moment their usefulness has run its course."

"So in the end, it's only Darkwinter that's left standing," I said with a shudder.

"And their hybrid army," Emilio said. "One way or another, we need to get to Blackmoon Bay and end this."

"You're too late, detective," Norah said. "Blackmoon Bay and the experimentation in Raven's Cape were just testing grounds. For years, they've been quietly installing magical infrastructure and soldiers in other cities across the globe. Those soldiers—dark fae and hunter alike—are simply awaiting orders. Once those orders are issued..." She trailed off, blowing out a breath and closing her eyes. Her face was even paler than before, with deep grooves lining her forehead.

"Is there anything else you can tell us?" Emilio asked. "Any other details, names, locations, anything you may have seen or overheard?"

"What's the point? There is nothing you can do to stop this, Detective. The wheels were set in motion long ago, and now they're spinning, full speed ahead. Your only chance is to gather up the ones you love and find a safe place to weather the storm."

"This isn't a storm," I said. "It's a war. One that you helped facilitate. And if we don't do something to end it, there won't *be* a safe place to weather the storm."

She nodded, resignation heavy on her shoulders.

"There's an outpost," she said. "About sixty miles southwest of Blackmoon Bay, hidden away inside the Olympic National Forest. I can show you on a map. I've been there twice, both times to deliver... to deliver prisoners."

"Witches," I clarified. "Women and girls that you kidnapped and sold."

"Witches," she confirmed. "It's fae-spelled to look like an abandoned cemetery, but there's a modern facility beneath it, with a high-tech lab, prison cells, and bunkers. That's where witches and other supernaturals are evaluated and processed for Phillip's higher-level experimentation. Phillip has since relocated to the Bay with Orendiel, but I'm sure the outpost is still operational. If any of the prisoners are still alive, that's where they'll be."

"How can we trust you're not sending us into a trap?" Emilio asked.

"Oh, but it *is* a trap, Detective. Just because Phillip isn't there doesn't mean he's left it unprotected. It's likely still under heavy guard, magical and physical. Enter at your own risk."

"You'd like that, wouldn't you?" I asked. "Send us right to the slaughterhouse, then collect your reward from your masters for being such a good little witch-slave. Right?"

Another bitter laugh escaped her lips. "There's nothing left they can offer me, Gray. I've got nothing more to give them, and nothing more to bargain with. Everyone I've ever cared about is dead. And I've sent dozens—maybe even hundreds—of innocent people to their deaths."

Her shoulders began to tremble again, and she squeezed her eyes shut tight, as if she were trying to force her tears back inside.

"That feeling?" I said. "That jackhammer in your head, the acid eating through your gut, the fire licking up your spine? That's guilt, Norah. And you deserve every ounce of pain it brings you. I hope you—"

"Gray." The touch of Emilio's hand on my shoulder silenced me, and I closed my eyes, breathing in his scent, letting his presence steady me once again. He was right. Ranting against Norah wouldn't do us any good. For all her lethal mistakes, she *had* given us good intel. At least we had the big-picture view of their plans now, whatever that was worth. And what she'd said about the outpost could prove useful, even if it *was* a trap. We'd find a way to get in there, just like we always did.

"Oh, Gray," Norah whispered. "You can't even begin to imagine the guilt I'm carrying."

"You made your own bed, Norah. You—"

She held up her hand, cutting me off. "Sophie... I need to tell you about Sophie."

I gasped, the pain of hearing my best friend's name passing through this woman's lips almost unbearable. Not because I couldn't handle hearing the sound of Sophie's name, or because I felt like I had some claim on her memory.

But because in that moment I just *knew*. Right here, right

now, handcuffed to a chair and facing down the very end of a life she'd squandered, Norah would only have one reason to bring up Sophie in that way.

Tell me about her? No. She wanted to confess.

A shiver rolled through me, starting between my shoulder blades and working its way down, making my knees weak, my stomach roil, my mouth go dry.

"What... what did you do?" My voice was no more than a whisper, no more than a breath. Again, I felt the calming touch of Emilio's hand on my shoulder, but he knew, too. I could feel it, the change in his body, the tension tightening his muscles.

"I visited her in your home in South Bay that night," she began. "Before our coven meeting. We had a pleasant enough conversation."

"Did you...?" I let the question hang there between us. *Kill her? Did you kill her? Did you fucking murder my best friend...*

"Did I inject her with vampire blood? No, I did not," she said firmly, and I blew out a breath. But then, "I merely unlocked her bedroom windows, setting the rest of the evening in motion."

The room spun, the walls closing in on me even as bits of conversation flashed through my memory of the night of Sophie's murder.

No sign of forced entry...

The front door was unlocked... her bedroom windows were wide open...

Maybe she knew him...

Maybe they came in through the windows...

The pieces clicked into place in a flash. Norah was already working with Phillip at that point. They'd known Jonathan was searching for me—that he'd been searching for me his whole life. Under Phillip's orders, Norah aided and abetted Jonathan in murdering her. She *knew* Sophie was going to die that night. She made it happen.

I couldn't breathe. I felt myself being dragged back into that hellfire of grief, the weight of Sophie's death pressing on my lungs, squeezing out my air. Sophie was never far from my thoughts, from my heart, but hearing Norah's confession now was like being set on fire all over again.

Something inside me snapped, and I lunged across the table, my hands wrapping around her throat. Magic sparked across my skin, electric currents that pulsed into Norah's pathetic body, calling forth her broken soul. I felt its pull, its resistance, and I shattered it, willing it out of her body. The first gray-black wisps of it emanated from her mouth as she watched in resignation.

"Do it," she choked out.

As if I needed her permission. Her pathetic encouragement.

You are going to die, bitch...

I tightened my grip. Her eyes bulged, her soul slithering out. All I had to do was reach out and grab it...

"Come back to me. Come back to me, *querida*. This isn't a road you want to go down." Emilio's hand was on my back, warm and steady, his words reaching across the void of pain and anger, filling me with his love. His patience. His support.

"This isn't going to bring her back, Gray," he said softly. "Nor will it bring you even a moment's peace."

My hands were still locked around Norah's neck, but my magic pulled back, releasing its thrall on her soul. The gray-black wisp sunk back into her mouth, then vanished completely.

"Come back to me," Emilio whispered, and that was it.

I let her go, allowing Emilio to guide me to my feet again. He led me out of the interrogation room, through the back room where the others had been watching through the glass. He took me down the hall, out the back door of the precinct, out into the freezer-burned Raven's Cape night, where the snow swirled before our eyes in feather-sized flakes and the cold air filled my lungs, washing away the fires once again.

Emilio held me close, his heart hammering against my ear, his hand on my back, the other caressing the back of my head, his breath warm in my hair.

"I'm... I'm okay," I finally whispered, pulling back to look up into his eyes. In their beautiful depths, I found my center, my heart. "I'm sorry I lost it in there."

"There's nothing to apologize for, *querida*. I'm just glad you're back. You were..." He blew out a misty-white breath. "You were in another realm."

I fought off a shiver, snuggling into his embrace once again.

Emilio had been right to stop me. Killing Norah, stealing

her soul… It wouldn't have done a damn thing to bring Sophie back. There was *nothing* I could do to bring her back —her soul had already moved on.

I closed my eyes, reaching out for her now, remembering her passion, her drive, her love of life.

For Sophie, solving the mystery of the other rumored witch murders and visions she'd had about uniting the covens had never been an obligation or a burden. For her, it wasn't about some ancient prophecy or magical blood curse or an inexplicable power she spent half her time losing control of, and the other half recoiling from.

No. For her, it had been about something else entirely: love and friendship, sisterhood, the things that truly made life worth living.

More than anything, I wish she were still with me. Right here, right now. She would know what to do.

Oh, Sophie. What am I supposed to do now? Go to this cemetery outpost? What will we even find there?

Immediately, an image appeared in my mind—two Tarot cards from Sophie's favorite deck. I recognized the cards and their placements from the reading I'd found in her book of shadows.

She'd drawn the Six of Wands, featuring a winged creature with a face shaped like a moon, rising from the center of a flower bud. Five hands raised wooden staffs in her honor, ready to follow her leadership. Then, crossing the Six of Wands, she'd drawn the Four of Swords. In that card, the moon-faced creature was buried in the ground, surrounded by dirt and roses. One sword was buried next to her, with three others piercing the earth above.

There are four of you, Sophie had said. *The swords represent four witches. Three standing their ground, waiting for the fourth to rise, to find them and give them purpose.*

And then, when I'd pressed for more details, *You have to find the others, Gray. The four of you must unite the covens…*

Back then, I'd had no idea who the four witches could be. But it was clear to me now. They weren't just any witches. They were me and my sisters.

I blinked back tears, gulping in a fresh blast of cold air as the implications of those cards—of Sophie's message—hit.

Yes, we would go to that cemetery. And whatever else might've been waiting for us there, we'd find my sisters. We'd find the power to unite the covens and take down the hunters for good. I knew it with utter certainty—more than I'd ever felt about anything in my life, with the exception of the love I felt for my rebels.

My best friend died wanting to help her fellow sisters. She died wanting to help me and every other woman who'd ever called herself a witch, whether that witch was ready to claim her power or not.

So no, maybe I couldn't save her from Norah's treachery or the hunters' twisted plans. I couldn't even bring her back from the dead, despite my powers—her soul had already moved on.

But I could honor her memory. I could carry on *her*

legacy… by finally accepting the responsibilities inherent in mine.

I could pick up my sword, find my sisters, and rise the fuck up.

"Let's get back to the lodge," I said suddenly, my voice steady and resolute as I blinked the snowflakes from my eyes. "We've got some troops to rally."

FORTY

GRAY

The fireplace crackled to life at the back of the common room, around which every occupant of the lodge had gathered. Some were sharing couches, others had brought in chairs from the dining room. Some were sitting cross-legged on the floor, shawls wrapped around their shoulders, coffee mugs in hand.

All eyes were fixed on me.

Tucked into my shirt pocket, close to my heart, three small objects gave me an infusion of strength: the Page of Cups card, in honor of Sophie. The High Priestess, for Calla, the only mother I'd ever known. And the granite heart Liam had given me, carved with the feather I would forever associate with him, no matter how long we might be apart.

I pictured the three of them standing by the fireplace now, their eyes shining with love. With encouragement. And with unshakeable faith in me—faith that I was finally starting to find for myself.

I looked out over the sea of faces gathered before me. Some of them—Haley, Darius, Ronan, Emilio, Asher—I'd come to know, to love. Others were quickly becoming like family, too—Elena, Detective Lansky, Reva, Sunshine, Sparkle. And a few were virtual strangers I'd seen only in passing, women whose names I hadn't even fully learned.

But all of them were part of this. And all of them deserved my gratitude. My trust. My authentic self, flaws and fears and all.

"Thank you all for being here," I said, my voice steady despite the jumble of nerves inside. "For those of you who don't know me, my name is Gray Desario."

Haley let out a whoop, and everyone laughed. Leave it to my sister to turn this moment into a pep rally.

Grinning at her, I continued.

"I am a Shadowborn witch. My birth name is Morgan Susanna Sil—" I hesitated on the last word, knowing that this moment would change my life in so many ways. It felt big and important, all-encompassing, and I took another steadying breath, letting the feelings wash over me. Inside, my magic simmered, sending tendrils of heat and electricity crackling through my veins.

"Silversbane," I finally said. "I am the third daughter of a third daughter of a third daughter, all of us descended from the first witches—those chosen by the Elemental Source to be the guardians of earth's magic."

A murmur rippled through the group, and I felt the energy in the room rise and warm in response, but no one laughed at me. No one called me a heretic or rolled their eyes or pelted me with crystals. No one stormed out or tried to talk over me. No one called me insane.

Letting out a breath, I caught Ronan's eye, and he winked at me, flashing that crooked grin I'd always loved. Next to him, Asher gave me the thumbs up. Darius was next, offering a supportive and seductive smile—I was pretty sure he couldn't differentiate between the two. Then Emilio, his hand on his heart, his eyes locked on mine, sending me his love. Haley was at the end, smiling brightly, a beam of light I felt down to my very soul.

I touched the cards in my pocket and continued.

"My sister Haley and I, along with two other sisters we haven't yet found—Georgina and Adele—are part of a prophecy that dates back millennia. It states, among other things, that under my leadership, we're to unite the covens against all who seek to oppress us, and bring our global sisterhood—witchcraft, in all its many forms and practices —back into the light."

I told them everything I knew. Everything I'd learned from Deirdre, all the details she'd shared about the original prophecy and the scholarly interpretations that'd followed. I told them the little bit I knew about our birthmother, about what had happened to us as children. And I told them about my belief that we'd find the remaining Silversbane heirs—my sisters—at the cemetery outpost Norah had told us about.

"Whether you're a believer in all of this prophecy talk or not—and most days, I'm not even sure where *I* fall on that scale—one thing is certain," I continued. "We *are* under attack. A threat is upon us, not just here in Raven's Cape and Blackmoon Bay, but in cities and states throughout our country and beyond. Witches have been kidnapped, tortured, experimented on, murdered. And this threat, this looming black cloud of death and destruction... It's no longer just about witches. Every living being is at risk now, supernatural and human alike."

At this, Emilio and Elena joined me at the front of the room, sharing all the details they could about the ongoing investigations, about the information Norah had provided, and about the Fae Council's betrayal, putting every last one of our theories on full display.

No stone was left unturned, no puzzle piece unexamined. Some of the witches asked questions. Others shared their own observations from their time in the cave prisons or from rumors and whispers they'd picked up in their covens. Reva told us about things she'd witnessed as she'd traveled the shadows of Norah's house, back when she'd been living there, corroborating a lot of what I'd discovered in Sophie's book of shadows. And others remained quiet, simply taking it all in.

But again, no one laughed, or shouted, or turned their backs on us. They were with us. One hundred percent.

I took center stage again, knowing that the next part had to come from me. Knowing that every moment in my life had led me here, to this one.

Liam and I had spent countless hours debating destiny versus free will, fate versus choice. He'd always insisted I had some grand destiny, a special path that had been mapped out in the stars long before I was even born. I'd always believed I made my own choices—that no universal forces, no bloodlines, no supernatural conspiracies, no magic could conspire to bend my will, no matter what the prophecy or Death himself said.

But choice and destiny weren't mutually exclusive. They could both exist, they could both be honored. Perhaps destiny merely nudged us in certain directions, placing opportunities in our path at every step. The rest? That would *always* be up to us.

I smiled, knowing I wouldn't have wanted it any other way.

"We all took a different road to get here," I said, looking out again at the witches and loved ones that'd gathered. "Some of you were imprisoned, and you ended up here because by the time you were liberated, it was too dangerous for you to return home. Some of you had no homes to return to. Others came because there's safety in numbers. Some of you just wanted to be part of something bigger than yourselves. But one thing we have in common is our sisterhood. Our magic. And our desire to live and love and practice in peace."

"Give peace a chance, y'all," Haley said, again making everyone chuckle. She had a knack for shining a light on the dark places, that was for certain.

"Unfortunately," I continued, "that peace now comes at a price." I took a deep breath, again drawing on the love and support of my rebels, my sister, my friends. "In three days, we'll be leading a team to the cemetery outpost in the

Olympic National Forest to liberate any remaining prisoners and gather additional intelligence about the siege in
Blackmoon Bay and the enemy's larger plans. We'll need
protective magic, offensive and defensive spellcasters, heal-
ers, fighters. What we're facing there… It's likely going to
be brutal. We'll fight monsters that used to be men, and
men that made monsters out of their brothers. We'll fight
dark magic the likes of which we've never encountered
before. And worse—we'll fight the ideologies that allowed
that magic to manifest in the first place."

Fighting off a shiver, I pressed on. "Some of us may die.
And those of us who do make it out alive will come back
here, only to regroup for a bigger, deadlier mission:
reclaiming the city of Blackmoon Bay—the place that many
of us in this room once called home. Make no mistake—this
is just the beginning of a much longer, much more difficult
battle, and none of you signed up for it. So, if any witch,
shifter, demon, or other ally wants out, now is your chance.
There are *no* judgments here. You will still be protected, still
have a home here, still be welcomed. Understood?"

Everyone nodded. I had no idea which way this was
going to go, who would be left standing at the end of it all. I
was running on those two magic words again—hope and
faith.

Taking a deep breath, I made my final declaration. "I ask
that we all close our eyes now. Those who wish to remove
themselves from consideration for the upcoming operation
can quietly leave the room. For those who remain in this
room after a count of one hundred, we'll break up into

groups, assess everyone's skills and abilities, and make our plan of attack."

I watched as everyone closed their eyes, then closed mine and began the count out loud. Over the sound of my voice, I heard the soft rustling of people rising from their chairs, shoes scuffing against the hardwood, footsteps bearing witches to the perceived safety of some other place.

I tried not to let my disappointment show. I'd made my choices, after all. It was only fair to give them the same opportunity, and to stand by my promise not to judge.

"Ninety-nine… one hundred." I opened my eyes.

And my heart nearly stopped.

Every chair and couch was empty.

Because every person in the room was now on their feet, standing before me. Not a soul remained seated, and not a soul had left. They'd merely risen, closing the spaces between them, drawing together.

From the center of the group rose a sparkling mist of the palest pink light, pulsing warm and bright, and their faces turned toward it, smiling. It was their magic. Their hope. Their solidarity. Their promise.

Haley looked up at me with tears in her eyes, her own smile bold and beautiful as ever.

"We're with you, Gray," she said. "All the fucking way."

FORTY-ONE

RONAN

Fucking hell, I hated the cold. Hated the waiting. Hated standing around in balls-deep snow with my thumb up my ass, counting down for the signal from the witches on the other side of the hill.

But once that signal came—the night sky lighting up with a fireball of bright orange attack magic—you bet your ass I wanted nothing more than to go back to that waiting. Back to the part before all hell broke loose.

But going back wasn't an option. Not tonight.

"Ronan!" Ash shouted. "On your left!"

Heeding the warning, I spun around fast, swinging my sword for all it was worth. The Darkwinter soldier bearing down on me caught it in the face, dropping like a bag of wet sand. I had no idea whether he was dead or just wounded, and no time to check. I was already on the move.

Seven days to the hour after Gray's meeting, after some of the most grueling magical, combat, and strategic training we'd ever endured, here we were, converging on a cemetery in the middle of the damn forest like a virus attacking its host.

Ten witches had comprised the first wave, slipping through the snow-covered forest from our makeshift base camp on light feet, getting into position to launch the spell that would alert the whole forest to our presence. For the rest of us, there would be no sneak attacks, no quiet infiltration. Our best chance, we'd decided, was a full-on blitzkrieg.

Motion on my right, and Beaumont blurred into view, tearing out the throat of a hunter who'd had his sights set on Haley. She and Gray stood back to back a few feet ahead of me, channeling each other's magic to fight through a cluster of Darkwinter guards who looked like they'd just been caught with their dicks in their hands. Hell, for all I knew, they *had* been standing out here pulling off a big old circle-jerk, no idea what was coming for them. It wasn't every day your secret cemetery hideout got invaded by a bunch of pissed off, kickass, magic-toting broomstick riders.

One of them opened his mouth to shout something, but he didn't get the chance. Gray lit 'em all up like firecrackers.

That's my girl.

"Lansky!" I shouted, spotting three more hunters ahead, charging toward two more witches fighting on the east side of the cemetery. "Twelve o'clock! Take those motherfuckers out!"

Lansky, who'd remained in his human form for just this purpose, raised his weapon and took aim, squeezing off three rounds. The hunters dropped out of sight, off the fucking planet.

Elena and Emilio were in full-on wolf mode, and now they charged ahead, barreling into a group of hunters and taking them down like bowling pins.

The snowmelt ran red with their blood.

I crept up behind an unsuspecting hunter trying to get the drop on Lansky, carving a fresh path from his shoulder to his kidney. Ahead of me, Jael lit up one of the dark fae with his own brand of fae magic—a golden orb that surrounded his prey and squeezed the life right out of him. Apparently, that particular spell only worked on other fae, but it was a neat trick, and way more effective for him than swinging a sword.

On the other side of the cemetery, Sunshine and Sparkle had staked out their own live buffet, devouring any hunter or Darkwinter snack in their path.

I never thought I'd be so grateful to roll with a pair of hellhounds.

"Heads up, hellspawn!" Beaumont blurred past me again, and I followed his path, teaming up with him on two more dark fae. One of them got a good jab in, slicing my forearm down to the fucking bone, but I repaid him in kind.

"Nothing says thanks like a sword to the throat, dick-hole." I watched him gurgle and choke on his last breath, then I spit on his corpse.

"Alright?" Beaumont asked, glancing at the blood soaking through my jacket sleeve. Looked like he was wearing the same amount, but the blood spilled down the front of his clothing wasn't his.

"I'll live." I took a deep breath, shaking off the pain. That was one good thing about the cold—shit went numb a whole lot faster.

Fae-glamoured or not, everything about the cemetery was absolutely real: headstones jutting out of the ground at odd angles, just waiting to catch someone in the shins. Short, wrought-iron gating buried in the snow like caltrops, eager to tear through the soles of our feet. Crypts looming up out of the frosty mist, providing the perfect cover for a hunter damn near pissing himself at the chance to jump out and knife one of us.

Despite the odds, we persisted.

Side-by-side, with a combination of magic, speed, bloodlust, and brute force, my crew and I—no, fuck that. My *family* and I—we fought our way through three dozen guards, a combination of Darkwinter Knights and hunter pricks just like the ones we'd taken down in the warehouse back at the Cape. The brutal cold, slippery conditions, and fake-cemetery obstacle course made tonight's assault a hell of a lot more challenging, and I was pretty sure we'd all be getting stitched, bandaged, and dosed up later.

But somehow, we survived it. We always fucking survived it. Gray, Darius, Emilio, Asher, and I—hell, even Liam, wherever his spooky ass was at the moment—we made sure of it. After everything we'd already been through, there was no way we were letting anyone on *this* frozen wasteland take us down.

"We clear?" I asked Ash, catching up with him after icing one last fae guard.

"Looks like." He waved to Beaumont across the cemetery, and the vampire gave a thumbs-up. After doing a final sweep to ensure we'd obliterated every last guard spotted aboveground, we plundered the bodies for whatever useful weapons we could find, then regrouped in the middle of the cemetery to catch our breaths. So far, everything had gone according to plan. Norah's intel had proved solid.

At least the traitorous bitch had been good for something.

She'd told us about a crypt at the end of a flagstone pathway in the southwest corner of the cemetery that would lead us underground, down into the facility proper. The location itself was easy to find—a large stone mausoleum, an archway carved with pentacles and moon symbols, an iron gate marking the entrance. Problem was, we had no idea what to expect beyond the gate. Because of the weather and the remote location of the cemetery, we weren't able to do a full surveillance. We'd hiked a mile in from our makeshift base camp, doing our best to stick to the paths with the most tree cover and the least amount of snow, but the first wave of witches had to move in fast. Once we'd gotten a visual on the place, we knew it was only a matter of time before they'd get a visual on us.

Now, we stood before the gate, wondering how many guards were down below. Did they have surveillance? Had they set a trap? Or had they all rushed out during our initial attack, leaving the rest of the place unguarded, free for the taking?

What, exactly, was worth taking down there?

"Alright, guys," Gray said, wrapping her hand around the gate. "Let's see what fresh hell awaits us next, shall we?"

She turned and caught my eyes for just a second, and I mouthed the only words I knew in that moment. The only ones I wanted her to know.

I fucking love you, Desario.

Without another word, Gray turned back toward the gate and wrenched it open.

But not before I'd caught that smile.

FORTY-TWO

GRAY

Blood. It was all around me, filling my nostrils, filling the air, coating my tongue with its acrid tang. It made *my* head spin, and I wasn't a vampire. I could only imagine how Darius was dealing with it.

But dealing with it he was, never leaving my side, not for an instant. His hand on my shoulder kept me steady as I waited for the initial shock to recede.

"Breathe through your mouth, love," he whispered, his lips brushing the shell of my ear. "It will be less unpleasant that way."

After descending the dark and twisted staircase to the lower level, we'd assumed the lack of guards meant a trap, some mindfuck designed by the fae to lure us deeper into their maze of chaos.

But now, standing in the center of the large chamber that held the facility's prison cells, I realized the truth.

At the first sign of our attack, any guards that might've

been stationed down here had probably abandoned their posts, grateful for any excuse to get out into the fresh air, even if they had to risk death to do it.

The room was nearly identical to the one we'd found on the top floor of the warehouse back at the Cape—brightly illuminated, with morgue-like steel tables and shelves surrounded on three sides by glass-fronted prison cells. But where the warehouse room had been surgically spotless, this one was filthy. Each cell was smeared with blood, inside and out. The tables were slick with it. Walking across the floor was like walking across a viscous shallow river, each step more treacherous than the last. There were drains at the center of the room, but they'd overflowed long ago.

The worst part, though, wasn't the blood.

It was the prisoners.

A dozen witches, two or three to a cell, all of them so weak and drained they hadn't even flinched when we'd hit the lights. Eight shifters—a mix of wolf, panther, mountain lion, fox, most of them in their animal form, all of them trembling with fear. There were two deceased human males —vessels, Ronan and Asher determined. Demons that had likely been injected with Jonathan's infamous devil's trap venom, left to die. Three female vampires lay near death in another cell, chained to the wall, surrounded by blood yet prevented from drinking any of it.

One of them was Fiona Brentwood, so far gone she didn't recognize any of us. Not even Darius.

I felt my mind trying to shut down inside, to block out the horrifying scene. But I forced myself to stay present, to take in every gruesome detail. I needed to see this. To feel it. All of us did.

If anyone had come here tonight with even a shred of doubt about the importance of our mission, the sight before us surely eradicated it.

"I'll get to work on the security," Jael said. The cells were locked by the same type of magical weave he'd found in the warehouse, and he needed a few minutes to untangle its complicated threads.

As he worked in silence, and the others spread out to guard the entrances, I grabbed Haley's hand, holding it tight. Her face was as pale as mine must've been, and with good reason.

Somewhere in these cells were our sisters. I'd felt the connection as soon as we'd entered the chamber—a tug on my magic, on my heart. It was the same feeling I'd gotten when Haley and I clasped hands during the ice storm behind Elena's house—when we'd transferred magic through our blood.

Like attracted like. Silversbane blood ran through my veins. It ran through Haley's. And it ran through Adele's and Georgie's.

And right now, that blood was singing a siren song.

I only hoped we weren't too late.

"Got it," Jael announced, and the glass doors slid open.

Still, the prisoners didn't move.

"They're all in really bad shape," McKenna said. She and Yvonne, another witch gifted with healing magic, tried to assess the situation. I didn't know much about healing, but it was obvious that these beings had been imprisoned for much longer than the ones we'd found in the warehouse.

I didn't even want to *think* about what kinds of torments they'd been subjected to.

"Gray," Haley whispered, tugging on my hand. "Over here."

I followed her to a cell in the far right corner, where three witches huddled close, their eyes glazed. They were no more than skeletons with a thin layer of skin, barely breathing, unblinking.

"Adele?" she whispered. "Georgina?"

"They might not go by those names," I reminded her.

"No, but hearing them might bring something back. A memory, a flash, anything."

"Adele?" she tried again. "Georgie?"

My heart hammered in my throat, my stomach twisting. It was all I could do not to vomit, not to scream, not to break.

Please say something. Anything. Please.

"Adele?" she said once more.

And then, it happened.

One of the witches twitched. Slowly, agonizingly, her head turned toward us.

And I knew. I just knew.

The realization crashed over me, hard and fast. I'd seen her before. Blonde hair like mine, expressive brown eyes. Long limbs that held the ghost of muscles. And though she'd been brutalized to within an inch of her life, nearly unrecognizable, I knew in that instant she was our sister.

"It's her," I said to Haley. "I saw her in a vision. You and Georgie were there, too." It was the dream I'd had in the Shadowrealm, when they'd tried to warn me not to follow the man chasing the deer. They'd appeared again on the boat with Liam, floating on one of Hell's lakes. They'd told me it was time to seek my own sword.

The one with the shorn head had been Haley. This one was Adele.

"Do… do I know you?" the blonde croaked out, her lips barely moving.

Haley burst out laughing, and I cried silent tears, both of us falling to our knees in relief.

"We're your sisters, Adele," Haley said. "And we're here to liberate you from this one-star shithole."

FORTY-THREE

GRAY

It took all of us the better part of three hours to transport everyone from the underground cells. They had to be triaged and temporarily healed as best as McKenna and Yvonne could manage, bundled into warm gear, and slowly brought up to the mausoleum, where Lansky, two more RCPD wolf shifters, Sunshine, and four more of our witches would stand guard, waiting for the rest of us to do a full sweep of the underground facility.

After that, we would begin the long trudge back to base camp, and then to the lodge. We had about eight hours until sunrise to get all the vampires to safety, and something told me we'd be using every last second to finish this job.

It had been a long and brutal night, and the end was nowhere on the horizon. But fatigue and soreness were no match for the joy that Haley and I felt at finding Adele, and as we watched Ronan carry her up to the top, my heart was instantly lighter. I wanted nothing more than to stay with her, to keep her in my sights, but I had to believe we'd have plenty of time for that later.

Right now, we had a lot of work ahead of us.

Including locating Georgie, who—much to our frustration and concern—had not been among the imprisoned witches.

"Okay, the prison is clear," Ronan said when the last vampire prisoner had been taken upstairs. "Time to move."

After securing everyone in the mausoleum, there were only a dozen of us left down here—Haley, me, and two other witches named Bex and Sasha from Verona's group; Ronan and Ash; Darius; Jael: Sparkle; Elena and Detective Hobb in their wolf forms; and Emilio, who'd shifted back into human form. We fanned out down a long corridor that branched off from the prison chamber, creeping past dozens of abandoned offices, unoccupied cells with barred entries, and bare-bones sleeping chambers without them. Asher managed to find a couple of dead tablets and a cell phone, and Darius tracked down a file box containing four thumb drives, a few maps of Washington, two hand-written note-books, unused shipping labels to an address in Blackmoon Bay, and a bunch of receipts, all of which we'd sort through later.

Other than that, we'd come up pretty empty on the intel front.

"Seems like they started clearing out days ago," Emilio said. "The food wrappers in the trash cans are at least that old."

"You're right." Darius sniffed the air. "No human or fae

has been down in this section in at *least* that long, maybe longer. They've probably moved on to Blackmoon Bay."

"And left their prisoners behind?" I shook my head. "No way. There has to be more to it than this."

"The prisoners we've just liberated couldn't possibly be of use to them anymore, Gray," Darius said. "To the hunters and fae, transporting them probably seemed like a liability —look how long it took us just to get them aboveground. Perhaps they decided to cut their losses."

"I might agree with that," Emilio said, "but something isn't adding up. Why leave so many guards behind just to deal with a couple dozen prisoners who don't even have the strength to stand, let alone mount an escape or attack?"

"We need to keep looking," I said, and Haley nodded. Our other sister was here somewhere, or, at the very least, she *had* been—recently, too. My instincts were screaming at me loud and clear. I wouldn't leave until we found her, or found some clue that would indicate her whereabouts.

We continued down the corridor, checking every single room, until we finally reached the T at the end. There was a large, locked door in the center of the T, made of heavy oak and carved with runes, bigger and stronger than any of the others. From there, the corridor branched out again in both directions.

We cleared the corridor first—just more of the same abandoned office spaces with a few rooms in between that looked like doctors' exam rooms.

I tried not to linger too long in those—the dried blood

smeared on the floor and exam tables was enough to make the bile rise in my throat.

The only additional pieces of intel we'd come up with were a couple of folders containing some kind of medical records, presumably for the prisoners.

None of them bore my sister's name, or anything that sparked even a glimmer of recognition.

We finally converged again at the large door in the center of the T. Those of us who'd brought weapons drew them, Haley and I readying our magic as Emilio kicked in the door.

For such an imposing piece of wood, it splintered and swung open easily, the runes remaining as dead as every-thing else. Motion sensors triggered the lights, bathing the space before us in a warm, pleasant glow.

Leaving Elena, Sasha, and Detective Hobb to patrol the corridors, the rest of us headed into the office. Instead of the same basic setup we'd expected to find, this one was massive and ornate, with gleaming hardwood floors, floor-to-ceiling mahogany bookshelves stuffed with dusty old tomes and lore books, a wall of high-tech computer periph-erals, a small conference table with six leather chairs, and a huge mahogany desk situated square in the middle—some-thing you'd expect to find an in an executive suite in Manhattan rather than in an underground outpost.

"Whoever worked here was pretty high up the ladder," Bex said, running her hand along the conference table. Like Sophie, Bex was able to pick up on the psychic imprints people left behind on objects, and now she let out a deep sigh. "A lot of people got fired in this room. Some of them were killed."

Suppressing another shiver, I glanced at Haley, who had the same wide-eyed look on her face as I felt on my own.

"I've been here before," I whispered, images of the place flickering through my mind's eye.

"Me too," Haley said. "It was the place we saw in our vision during the blood spell for Darius."

She was right. I could almost see the woman again now, paging through the books spread out across her desk.

"She's a vampire," Darius said, his voice holding a note of surprise. He scented the air again, then slid open a recessed panel on the far wall between two bookcases. The space he'd revealed lit up immediately.

"It's a refrigerator," he said, and I peered over his shoulder to peek inside.

Every shelf was lined with neat, unbroken rows of the same thing.

Blood. Bottles and bottles of blood.

"This is the expensive stuff," he said, opening one up and sniffing it. I waited for him to take a sip, but he didn't.

"From the blood bank?" I asked, though I had my doubts. In all my time delivering blood orders for Waldrich's Imports, I'd never seen anything like that.

"I'm afraid not." Darius capped it without drinking it and set it back on the shelf. "This collection was bottled at the source, so to speak."

My stomach churned. Humans. She'd been draining humans, bottling their blood for her own personal collection. Who knew whether she'd kept them alive? Perhaps they were the people whom Bex had thought died here.

After making my way back to the center of the room, I looked through the books on the desk, finding nothing of particular interest, then moved on to the drawers. There wasn't much—just a few random office supplies, a phone charger, a chocolate bar.

And then the pin. Shaped like a crown, with two swords crossing beneath it, it shone like liquid silver, catching the light and reflecting it in tiny prisms that scattered rainbows across the ceiling.

"It's definitely her office," I said, passing the pin to Haley. "She was wearing this on her jacket lapel in the vision."

Emilio caught sight of it, his face ashen. "Are you sure, *querida?*"

"Positive. I saw a silvery crown with two swords underneath, exactly like this. Do you recognize it?"

"It's the council's insignia." He met my gaze, the space between his eyebrows pinched with new concern. "As far as I know, there is only one pin—*this* one. I'd heard the custom had fallen out of favor decades ago, but back then, they used to give it to the ultimate ranking member."

"So the woman we saw in the vision was Talia?" I asked.

Emilio shook his head. "Talia is powerful, but the title of ultimate ranking member is typically reserved for fae royalty. One who has the last word in all council matters, but who seldom visits our realm. He or she typically sends emissaries. I wasn't even aware the council had someone in the position right now."

"Emilio, why would Gray and I get a vision from some random royal fae?" Haley asked. "And if she's so important, why would she have an office at the bottom of this outpost? Wouldn't she have more important things to focus on?"

"Like plotting the downfall of the entire human race?" Ronan asked. He and Asher had been quietly searching the bookshelves up until that point, and now they joined us at the desk, a large leather attaché case in hand.

Inside, they'd found a half-charged tablet containing all kinds of unencrypted notes and plans. There were digital and paper maps, travel itineraries for an entire staff that appeared to have been regularly moving into and out of the Bay from other international destinations for at least a year. There was a leather calendar, also full of notes and details about meetings and missions.

"Darkwinter isn't interested in eradicating all supers and humans," Jael said, scrolling through the tablet. "They're planning to enslave them. Once the witches are out of the picture and the hybrids have done their work ushering in the destruction of most of the world's communities, those left standing against the dark fae will be captured and enslaved."

"Bloody hell," Darius said.

"There are a bunch of passports, too," Ash said, fishing them out of one of the attaché pockets. They were all from different countries, issued in different names, but the photo inside every single one was identical.

"It's her," I said, and Haley confirmed with a nod. "The woman we saw."

"Employee ID badges," Ash said, pulling them out of the bag as well. "Same chick. Looks like her actual name is… Trinity O'Leary. Same name on three badges, plus some of the paperwork and notes we found."

"Trinity," I whispered, my heart pounding. "She's… she's not a random fae royal, Haley. She's not fae at all. She's a witch. And apparently a vampire. And I believe she's our birthmother."

"Holy shit," Haley whispered. Her face was sheet-white.

"Looks like there's an assistant, too," Ash said, flipping through more of the paperwork.

My chest constricted, all the air whooshing out of my lungs. I knew what he was going to say before he'd uttered another sound.

"Georgina Mertz."

The last name didn't matter. No witch in her right mind would use the name Silversbane.

Just like with Trinity, the first name was all the confirmation I needed.

Our mother had infiltrated the fae council, using them to spearhead a plan of mass destruction—to what end, I had no idea. And my sister, *our* sister, the one who—along with Adele—was prophesied to help us unite the covens…

She was our mother's right-hand woman.

Haley's mouth rounded into a pale pink O. But before

she could formulate a single question, Asher dropped the case, his eyes wide with panic.

"Uh, guys?" Asher said, and Sparkle issued a low, warning growl behind him. "We've got a serious fucking problem, and it ain't your family tree."

FORTY-FOUR

GRAY

Shadows came to life, peeling themselves from the walls, morphing into the brutal monsters of nightmares. In the span of three heartbeats, we were completely surrounded.

No, not shadows, I realized. Hybrids. Part shifter, part vampire, part wild creature I couldn't even identify, they'd emerged from a passageway that'd been spelled to look like a bookcase, baring sharp teeth and wielding razor-sharp claws that glinted in the light. By the time we realized what was happening, they'd already divided our group in half, six of us on the inside, six near the outer door we'd entered through.

They outnumbered us four to one.

All that was left to do now was fight.

Instinct took over as the office erupted in pure chaos, a blur of gore and flashing blades and gnashing teeth. Deep underground, my connection to the earth was strong, and I called on its magic to infuse my own, drawing it deep within, then sending it out through my palms in white-blue electric arcs.

All of this happened in an instant. My first attempt crashed into one of the bookshelves and fizzled out, but my next hit was true, igniting one of the hybrids in flames. I didn't have time to watch him burn; I was already charging up for another hit, shooting it at one of the beasts just before he swiped at Bex.

In the blur of my peripheral vision, Darius was in perpetual motion, grappling with one vamp-monster after another, fighting off their attacks. They seemed nearly evenly matched in speed and strength, and for every one he managed to take down, another took its place. Two wolves charged in through the door—Elena and Hobb—trailed by Sasha, wielding her own magic, yellow-green flames bursting from her palms.

"Asher, duck!" Ronan shouted, and Ash dropped to the floor just as Ronan threw a silver dagger into one of the beasts' chest. Part vampire, part shifter, the thing dropped to the ground instantly, the silver poison already wreaking havoc on its bloodstream.

I had no vampire superstrength or speed, no shifter instincts, no weapons but my own magic. It took every ounce of strength and focus to control it, but somehow, I managed to take out three more monsters, burning each one to a crisp.

Unfortunately, the office was now burning too. If we didn't get to the exit soon, we'd all be engulfed.

"Jael, behind you!" Darius shouted, then put up his

arms to fend off another attack. Jael was near the doorway, but it wasn't an escape route. Hybrids had surrounded him on all sides, closing in fast. He swung his fae blade, decapitating one of them, but another took a chunk out of Jael's arm. The sword clattered to the floor.

"Ronan, help him!" I shouted, firing another bolt of magic at a monster charging Emilio, who was back in his wolf form, his powerful jaws descending over a hybrid's throat. Sparkle took down two more, all of us desperately trying to reach Jael.

I'd nearly broken through when I saw Ronan's eyes go wide with fear, clear on the other side of the room. He opened his mouth to shout at me, but it was too late. In an instant, I was slammed into a bookcase, the wind knocked out of me, my skull cracking against the wood. I hadn't even seen my assailant, but he was on me now, one impossibly strong hand around my neck as he lifted me a foot off the ground.

I felt the insistent push of his vampire influence on my mind, paralyzing my body as he flooded me with images of all the things he wanted to do to me.

Fangs shone inside a wicked grin, his chin already stained with blood.

The room was darkening around me, acrid smoke and the monster's tight grip choking off the last of my air supply. I couldn't call on my magic, couldn't even swing a fist.

I was fading.

The beast hauled me close to his mouth, inhaling my

scent. His tongue darted out to lick my cheek, the rotten funk of his breath and the low, desirous growl in his chest my final warning. My final goodbye.

I'd never felt so weak. So powerless.

I am going to die...

I closed my eyes, waiting for the bite of those teeth.

And then he dropped me.

My ass hit the floor hard, my shoulders crashing into the bookshelf behind me. I had just enough time to cover my head before an avalanche of books cascaded down on top of me.

When the room finally swam back into view and I could actually breathe again, I saw the monster at my feet, his head cleanly separated from his body, blood pooling beneath him. I looked up to see an outstretched hand reaching for mine. Grabbing it, I got to my feet and came face-to-face with the man who'd just saved my life.

The ancient blue light of his eyes called me home.

"Liam," I breathed.

"No time," he said, a fae sword held firmly in his other hand, dripping with blood. "We need to move, Gray. Now."

"Jael!" I shouted. "Go help Jael!" But Liam shook his head, his grip on my hand tightening. He wouldn't leave my side, not when we were still surrounded by deadly hybrids, with more emerging from the walls with every passing heartbeat. Smoke billowed around us, thickening, blotting out the light.

At a painfully slow pace, Liam and I fought our way to the doorway where I'd last seen Jael, but it was too late. In the intermittent flashes of my magic attacks and the fire eating up the walls behind us, we watched in horror as the beasts dragged our fae prince down the left corridor, descending on him like a pack of rabid dogs. Seconds later, a wall of flames cut him off from us for good.

"Jael!" I screamed, my throat raw, my legs propelling me forward, even as a strong arm looped around my waist and hauled me backward. Eventually, I stopped fighting it, and I collapsed against Liam's chest. Tears streaked my face, my insides burning with shame and grief. None of us could reach Jael. None of us were even close enough to hear his final cries.

"Move, Gray! Now!" Liam's panicked voice shook me out of my stupor, and I slipped out of his hold just in time to avoid a strike. I dropped to the ground as Liam swung his blade, taking our attacker's head clean off.

He hauled me to my feet again and we spun around, looking for another exit, some way to lead everyone to safety, but every corridor was rapidly filling with hybrids. With nowhere else to go, we ran back into Trinity's office, trying to discern friend from foe amidst the chaos.

With the notable exception of Jael, I spotted everyone in our group. They were all still on their feet, still fighting hard.

And then Haley went down.

I charged back into the melee, shooting an electric bolt at a hybrid who'd jumped into my path. When I got to my sister, she was on her knees, her head bent back at a severe angle, her eyes half-lidded. She seemed to be in a deep trance.

In one hand, she gripped a bloody dagger. Her other hand was clenched in a fist, dripping with blood.

I knew at once she was doing a spell.

Calling up another surge of earth magic, I channeled everything I had into protecting her, drawing up an iridescent shield around her as Liam continued to swing his blade at any beast in our periphery.

Temporarily safe inside the shield, Haley used her blood to draw a pentacle on the floor, then pressed her palm against it. The symbol glowed at her touch.

All around us, the team continued to fight. And the beasts continued to emerge from the darkness.

And then the chanting began.

It started soft—so soft I almost wasn't sure it was Haley. But then her voice grew stronger, louder, more powerful, the tenor of it reverberating inside my chest.

The words felt sinister, dark, so unlike anything I'd ever heard come out of my sister's mouth, I had to check again to make sure it was her.

Slowly she got to her feet, her eyes closed, her head bowed, her words rising above the sounds of our battle, raising the hairs on the back of my neck.

> *Blood of hell, blood of night*
> *I call on the darkness to show us the light*
> *May evil and malice and violence intended*
> *Return to its hosts uprooted, upended*

Dark Goddess I bend, Dark Goddess I bow
Hear my petition, and thusly I vow
My service is yours, by blood and by blade
Until my last breath shall deem it unmade.

Nine times she spoke the spell, her words growing more impassioned with each repetition. My shield was dimming, revealing Haley in her full, terrifying glory. Blood shone on her lips, her eyes wild, her face stark white. A deep and chilling darkness seemed to emanate from within her, but still, I held onto that shield for as long as I could, pouring all of my magic into it, all of my power, all of my love.

I had no idea who she'd petitioned or what, precisely, she'd promised, but I didn't dare disturb the spell.

Haley's magic was working.

Slowly at first, and then all at once, the tide changed. There was a single heartbeat of silence, as if someone had hit the reset button.

The smoke began to clear.

All of us looked on with awe and wonder.

And one by one, the hybrids turned their attention away from our group and onto each other.

I'd never seen such brutality, such gruesome violence. Such single-minded determination. They tore into each other, shredding flesh and bone, destroying, devouring.

I was mesmerized.

Strong hands suddenly gripped my arm—Asher's? Emilio's? I had no way of knowing. Snapping out of my near-trance, I grabbed my sister's hand, and all of us charged for the door.

Just like the monsters in the office, the hybrids in the corridors seemed bent on self-destruction, their bone-chilling screams of agony providing the gory soundtrack to our escape. After a quick head count, we rushed down the main corridor, back through the prison chamber, up the winding staircase to the mausoleum.

I didn't dare let go of Haley. Didn't dare open my eyes. Not until the pounding of my heart subsided, and I finally felt the sweet relief of snowflakes melting on my cheeks.

FORTY-FIVE

LIAM

Sitting on a bench on the outer perimeter of the cemetery, I cupped my palm, mesmerized by the snowflakes melting against my skin.

Snow felt different now. The warmth of Gray's presence beside me felt different. My heartbeat felt different.

Everything felt different.

"I'd all but forgotten what it meant to be human," I said softly. "I used to think humanity was destined to fail, and that my responsibility in escorting your souls out of these vessels and into the Shadowrealm was a kindness as much as a duty. What, after all, was the point of all this so-called living?" I shook my head, my very human breath condensing before me. "What a fool I've been."

Gray leaned her head on my shoulder, and I turned to press a kiss to her crown.

"And now?" she asked. "Do you still wonder what the point is?"

I left her question hanging in the cool air between us, where it lingered a moment longer before drifting away in the breeze.

The tribunal had ended. I'd been permanently banished here, all remaining powers stripped. I'd no longer be able to shift into my avian forms, no longer see a thousand upon a thousand upon a thousand possible outcomes. I was vulnerable now, just as any other man. Powerless but for that which I drew from within.

I'd been condemned to the fate of humanity, possibly condemning humanity in the process.

For with my banishment and the permanent dissolution of my duties, there would be no Death. No transformation, as I'd warned them before. Winter had already begun its deadly dance, but soon it would spread. Soon the restless souls would gather. Soon the hauntings would begin.

The Old One had offered only one alternative, only one service for which they'd grant a full reversal of this curse: I must sacrifice another Shadowborn witch, forcing upon her the mantle I'd once so proudly carried.

The refusal was on my lips before they'd even finished the proclamation.

Their only concession, their only grace, was in allowing me to serve out my remaining days as a mortal man in the company of the woman I loved, for as long as she would have me.

I'd explained all of this to her as we sat on our bench, watching the others make arrangements for the return to base camp. They'd managed to salvage some of the intelligence they'd found inside, and were organizing that now, along with treating injuries.

Jael's body had not been recovered. When the wolves returned to the corridor to investigate, they found only ashes.

"I would do anything to fix this, Gray," I said now. "Anything."

She didn't say anything for a long moment. And then, just when I thought my human heart would arrest, she tilted her head to meet my gaze, and a soft smile touched her lips. "You and I are a lot alike, you know."

"Rule-breakers and seekers of trouble. Defiers of cosmic law." I laughed softly, but Gray's eyes had turned serious.

"People who'd do anything to protect the ones we love," she said. "People who've learned, deep down, the most important lesson." She slipped her hand into mine, melting the last of the snow between our palms. "No matter what the risk, love will *always* be worth it."

She leaned forward, brushing her lips across my mouth in a kiss I felt all the way to my toes. There were no magical sparks this time. Only the ones I felt inside.

I returned her kiss, slowly deepening it, tasting her with a new appreciation for all of life's richness. For all of its blessings.

I kissed her as I'd loved her—without hesitation, without regret, without fear.

When we finally broke apart, I cupped her face, gazing into the depths of her twilight blue eyes.

"I'm in love with you, little witch. So much it makes my

heart feel like it's going to go supernova every time you're near me. Is that… Is that normal?"

Gray laughed, her eyes lighting up despite the heaviness of tonight's battles. She pressed a hand to my chest, and I covered it with my own, feeling the frantic pounding of my heart through both.

"It's normal," she said. "I'd say you get used to it, but you don't. And that's a good thing."

"I shall take your word for it."

Silence drifted between us once again, and in the calm, I spoke the words in my heart.

"I cannot say I've come to this banishment unwillingly," I said. "For I've longed to return to my human form, to live out the remainder of my days as a mortal. But I would not have wished this upon you. Upon any of you. My one regret, Gray, is that when I am gone from this realm, you and those who carry on your legacy will still be dealing with this fallout. Yes, I will die, and without another to carry on the sacred duties, my soul will be as cursed as all the rest. But in so many ways, I am getting the easy way out."

"No, Liam. You're not." She shook her head, staring at me as if I'd just spoken the most ridiculous words known to man. "You gave up your life for me. For Emilio. For us to have another chance at life and love. You gave up your eternal soul. And you did it all over again when they gave you a chance at redemption, and you turned them down."

"I will not sacrifice another."

"I know. And in that refusal, you gave up absolutely everything."

I took her face in my hands, pressing another kiss to her lips. "And I will do so again," I whispered. "For as long as I have something left to give, for as long as I am here to give it."

"Okay," she said firmly, rising from the bench and brushing the snow from her legs. "Here's the deal, Colebrook. I love you, too. Don't ask me how it happened, because there are too many little moments, too many conversations, too much anger, too much laughter, too many sparks. But it *did* happen. You're as much a part of this family as the rest of us. And that means you're bound to us, and we're bound to you, and mortal or not, you're not going *anywhere* without us. We won't give you up without a fight. We won't give *any* of this up without a fight."

She turned to head back down the path.

"Where are you going?" I asked.

"To make damn sure we win this fight, and the next one, and every single one we're facing after that. Because guess what? This little witch still has something left to give, too."

FORTY-SIX

GRAY

I trudged through the snow, back the way Liam and I had come, back to the mausoleum. The injuries had all been treated, and now the group huddled together, checking over the liberated prisoners one last time. Haley had her arm around Adele, their heads bent together, both of them sitting on the mausoleum steps. Adele's eyes were closed, but some of the color had returned to her cheeks.

Haley's eyes were haunted. She hadn't wanted to talk about the blood spell she'd done, about what dark energies she'd called upon, about what it would mean for her later.

About what it would mean for any of us.

But I knew she'd sacrificed something important.

Just like Liam had done. Just like Jael had done. Just like the prisoners had done. Just like everyone from our group had done—all the brave witches and allies and my strong, beautiful rebels standing before me. Every single one of them had put their lives on the line, making their own personal and private sacrifices, all because I'd asked them to follow me into the darkness, and they'd come without question.

I hadn't guaranteed them a victory. Hadn't even guaranteed their survival. Yet they'd put their trust and faith in me, and they'd come anyway.

Now it was my turn to step out over that endless void, to leap with no guarantee of a net below. To be bold and brave. To trust that I was making the right decision—not just for me, but for all the witches I'd led here. The ones I'd yet to meet. To unite. For the men who would give their lives for me. The men who'd already given me their hearts.

We'd lost a friend tonight. A man who died protecting us, honoring the memory of the woman he loved—my best friend.

We'd fought a ravenous army of vampire-shifter hybrids, terrifying and brutal, yet no more than a fraction of the size and skill of the armies that likely awaited us in the Bay. That may also be waiting in the shadows of other cities, in other countries, their masters counting down to Armageddon.

We'd discovered that my mother was the mastermind behind a worldwide supernatural conspiracy that left the fate of humankind hanging in the balance, and my sister—a sister whose existence I'd only just discovered—was doing her bidding.

We'd liberated another sister, who—along with other witches and supernaturals—was fighting her way back from the edge of death, and would heal from her physical wounds only to unleash the horror of all the emotional torments she'd endured at the hands and direction of our mother. And Haley… I had no idea what was in store for her, but from the haunted look in her eyes, I knew it wasn't going to be pleasant or easy.

Despite all we'd lost, all we'd endured, there were still so many battles to face. Still so many nasty surprises on the horizon.

I closed my eyes, recalling the moment of utter powerlessness I'd felt at the hands of that hybrid. I'd felt his thoughts, seen the glint of blood on his fangs. His breath had misted on my cheeks, and in that moment, I'd known it was the breath of death.

If not for Liam, I wouldn't be standing here.

I didn't know what awaited us around the next corner. But I did know this: I would *not* be made to feel that way again.

It was in our blood, I realized. The key to everything.

Darius's blood had healed me in the Shadowrealm, and my blood had begun to restore his memories. With help from my magic, Asher's blood had built up an immunity to Jonathan's devil's trap nanotech. Haley's blood had saved us tonight, causing our enemies to turn on each other. Silversbane blood had brought us together, had led us to our other sisters, had carried the legacy of our magic from one generation to the next.

Silversbane blood had allowed my mother—a witch—to survive the change and become a vampire. And it would do the same for me.

GRAY

"Out of the question." Darius folded his arms over his chest, his mouth pressed into a grim line.

Lined up inside the mausoleum, Asher, Ronan, and Emilio stood at his side, the fire in their eyes smoldering, the stiffness in their muscles telling me exactly where they stood on the matter.

Only Liam stood at my back. Only Liam understood.

"I'm asking you to give me the strength to protect myself," I said. "The power. The freedom of choice."

"You're asking me to condemn you to a life of blood and death," he snarled. "You will lose your soul, Gray. I cannot —I *will* not facilitate that."

"I won't lose my soul." I placed my hand over his heart, offering a tender smile. "My soul is here. With you. All of you. As long as we're together in this world, it—"

"No, Gray." He grabbed my wrist, his grip almost painful. Anger coursed through his blood, making his skin hot. "That's not enough. As far as I'm concerned, this world doesn't even exist without you. *You* are the beating heart of it, love. *Our* beating heart. If we lose you, none of it is worth it. There's no more fight. No more reason."

"My soul is promised to Sebastian!" I shouted.

How many more times would we have to go over this? Why couldn't they understand?

"There are two outcomes here, guys," I continued. "Only two. Either we lose this war, and I die fighting, because I'm not immortal like Darius and Ronan and Ash. Or by some miracle, we win, and after all the dust settles, Sebastian shows up to collect on my contract. I'll never see any of you again. Don't you get that?"

"You don't need immortality," Darius said. "You've got magic, and—"

"My magic isn't enough. You saw what happened in there tonight. If it wasn't for Liam, I'd already be gone. I need strength. Speed. Predatory instincts. There's a full-on war coming to our doorstep, Darius—"

"One you don't have to fight alone." He gestured beyond the flagstone path to the spot where the rest of the group had gathered, waiting for us to take them back to camp. "All those witches out there—"

"They're depending on me to lead them! To rise up and claim my legacy!"

"And you *will*. You'll rise up like the witch you are. That power is already inside you, Gray."

"It sounds nice, doesn't it?" I asked. "Like something you could print on a T-shirt or make into an internet meme, right? But the reality is… We don't stand a chance. Not a real one, not for the long haul. How many more nights like this can we take? Jael is dead. Everyone else is beat up and exhausted. And we haven't even scratched the surface of what's coming. We're lucky we survived the night. How do you think Blackmoon Bay is going to roll out? And that's assuming we can even get there in time."

I clutched my head in my hands, drawing a deep breath, trying to dial down the anger. I didn't want to fight them on this. I just wanted to make them understand. To feel the rightness of this. To grant me my choice.

"I know what I'm asking you to do," I said. "I know the risks. But for the first time since I was a little kid, I have real faith in my magic. In my intuition. And most importantly, in my blood. My mother survived the change because she's Silversbane, just like me."

"You don't know that's what allowed her to survive," Darius said. "There could be any number of reasons—"

"There *could* be, but there aren't." I pressed my hands to my chest, the magic rising to the surface, pulsing against my palms. "I can *feel* the rightness in this. *This* is my path. Please, Darius. I want this, but I won't do it without your support." I turned to look at each of them, imploring them. "That goes for all of you. I'm asking you to back me up on this. I'm asking you to trust that I know what's right for myself, for my body. I'm asking you to trust *me*."

"You *will* lose your soul," Darius said again, but his resolve was finally weakening, and I smiled, shining a light through the tiny crack he'd left behind.

"Actually, my soul might have another option." I looked at Liam as a new idea dawned and rose inside me like the sun, fresh hope filling my chest, bolstering my plan.

Liam understood my intention immediately, but his eyes dimmed, and he shook his head. "I would do anything for you, Gray. But I'm fully human now. I no longer possess the power to create moonglass or to guide your soul into its orb."

"Perhaps not," a voice echoed from beyond the shadows of the mausoleum, and we all turned toward the sound. Weak and bloodied, burned and weary, but alive, Jael stepped through the doorway at the top of the stairs, his yellow eyes glittering in the darkness. "But I do."

FORTY-EIGHT

GRAY

We'd been blessed with a full moon, and now Jael stood in the center of the cemetery, snow falling on his shoulders, an opalescent orb glowing in his hands. "It is time, Gray."

Asher. Emilio. Liam. Ronan. Darius. Each one stood before me, their eyes filled with secrets and emotions and all the things they hadn't said. There hadn't been time.

But we didn't need words. The love and trust we shared transcended every last one.

What they'd given me tonight was a precious gift: their trust and support. Their unconditional love. I wouldn't squander it.

I stood before Asher, claiming his mouth in a kiss that burned all the way to my toes, giving in to the familiar call of his incubus hunger, offering him one more dose of my magic.

I moved on to Emilio, who blinked back tears, enveloping me in a bear hug that infused me with strength.

Liam was next, a shy smile that turned into a passionate kiss the moment our lips met.

When I got to Ronan, the demon held my gaze, unwavering, his eyes saying a million things. He didn't want this for me. None of them did. But he would stand by my decision no matter what. He was my first love, my best friend. And no curse or transformation or war would ever change that.

Swallowing the tightness in my throat, I took a chance and pressed my lips to his, both of us ignoring the burn, just for a moment.

And then there was Darius. My vampire. We'd shared so much already, come through so much. And there was so much more to do, to see, to reclaim.

I smiled at him, and stood up on my toes, my lips brushing his ear.

"You're still taking me to New York after all this," I teased. And then I kissed him, deep and delicious, his whiskey-and-leather scent enveloping me once again.

We broke our kiss, and Darius pierced the skin on his wrist, pressing it to my mouth, gently holding my head against it. I closed my eyes and drank, letting the richness fill me, warm me.

Too soon, he pulled away.

And then he spun me around, my back against his chest, and swept the curls off my nape.

In front of us, Ronan gave a single nod.

The vampire's mouth descended on my flesh.

I cried out as his fangs pierced my skin, deep and

deadly, their purpose singular. The pain was fierce, delicious, intense, my head spinning as he began to suck.

I don't know how much time passed, how long he drank from me, because for me, time stopped. There was no yesterday, no tomorrow. Nothing but the heat of his lips, the pure pleasure of the bite.

I tried to stay conscious, tried to hold on to everything about the moment, to follow the pleasure to its logical end. But a numbness spread throughout my body, and from my mouth, a cloud of gossamer smoke emerged, a deep and velvet gray, shot through with bright silver threads and indigo points of light.

My soul.

The iridescent pulse of the moonglass loomed large before my eyes, and I finally gave in to the numbness, letting it sweep me out of the snow-blanketed night, far and away to another world where pain no longer existed and everything was blissfully, unapologetically black.

When darkness descends, who will survive the Battle for Blackmoon Bay? *Rebel Reborn*, the sixth and final book in the Witch's Rebels series, is waiting for you! **Get Rebel Reborn now!**

Are you a member of our private Facebook group, <u>Sarah</u>

Piper's Sassy Witches? Pop in for sneak peeks, cover reveals, exclusive giveaways, book chats, group therapy to deal with these killer cliffhangers, and plenty of complete randomness! We've got a great community of readers and fans, and we'd love to see you there!

XOXO
Sarah

ORIGINS OF THE WITCH'S REBELS

I was primarily inspired to write this series by three things: my fascination with Tarot, my love of all things witchy, and my desire to see more kickass women telling stories for and about other kickass women.

I've always enjoyed books, movies, and TV shows about witches, monsters, and magic, but I never found exactly the right mix. I wanted a darker, grittier Charmed, an older Buffy, and most of all—as much as I love the brothers Winchester (who doesn't?)—I *really* wanted a Supernatural with badass bitches at the helm, hunting monsters, battling their inner demons, and of course, sexytimes. Lots and lots of sexytimes.

(Side note: there's not enough romance on Supernatural. Why is that? Give me five minutes in that writers' studio…)

Anyway, back to The Witch's Rebels. We were talking about badass bitches getting the sexytimes they deserve.

Right.

So I started plotting my own story and fleshing out the character who would eventually become our girl Gray, thinking I had it all figured out. But as I dove deeper into the writing, and I really got to know Gray, Darius, Ronan, Asher, Emilio, and Liam, I discovered a problem. A big one.

With so many strong, sexy guys in the mix, I couldn't decide which one would be the hero to win Gray's heart. I loved them all as much as she did!

I agonized over this.

It felt like the worst kind of love triangle. Er, love rhombus? Love—wait. What's the word for five of them? Pentagon! Yes, a love pentagon.

Pure torture!

But then I had my lightbulb moment. In the face of so much tragedy and danger, Gray fights hard to open herself up to love, to trust people, to earn those hard-won friendships. Her capacity for giving and receiving love expands infinitely throughout the story, so why the hell *shouldn't* she be able to share that with more than one man?

There was no reason to force her to choose.

So, she doesn't. And her story will continue!

You, dear reader, don't have to choose either—that's part of the fun of reverse harem stories like this. But if you happen to have a soft spot for a particular guy, I'd love to hear about it!

Drop me a line anytime at sarah@sarahpiperbooks.com and tell me who's winning your heart so far! I'll tell you mine if you tell me yours! *wink wink*

Paranormal romance fans, I've got even more sexy books ready to heat up your bookshelf!

VAMPIRE ROYALS OF NEW YORK is a scorching paranormal romance series featuring a commanding, dirty-talking vampire king and the seductive thief who might just bring him to ruin… or become his eternal salvation. Sizzling romance, dark secrets, and hot vampires with British accents abound!

TAROT ACADEMY is a paranormal, university-aged reverse harem academy romance starring four seriously hot mages and one badass witch. Dark prophecies, unique mythology, steamy romance, strong female friendships, and plenty of supernatural thrills make this series a must-read!

ABOUT SARAH PIPER

Sarah Piper is a witchy, Tarot-card-slinging paranormal romance and urban fantasy author. Through her signature brew of dark magic, heart-pounding suspense, and steamy romance, Sarah promises a sexy, supernatural escape into a world where the magic is real, the monsters are sinfully hot, and the witches always get their magically-ever-afters.

Readers have dubbed her work "super sexy," "imaginative and original," "off-the-walls good," and "delightfully wicked in the best ways," a quote Sarah hopes will appear on her tombstone.

Originally from New York, Sarah now makes her home in northern Colorado with her husband (though that changes frequently) (the location, not the husband), where she spends her days sleeping like a vampire and her nights writing books, casting spells, gazing at the moon, playing with her ever-expanding collection of Tarot cards, binge-watching Supernatural (Team Dean!), and obsessing over the best way to brew a cup of tea.

You can find her online at SarahPiperBooks.com, on TikTok at @sarahpiperbooks, and in her Facebook readers group at Sarah Piper's Sassy Witches! If you're sassy, or if you need a little *more* sass in your life, or if you need more Dean Winchester gifs in your life (who doesn't?), come hang out!